PRAISE FOR YUKITO AYATSUJI'S BIZARRE HOUSE MYSTERIES

'Fiendish foul play... This is a homage to Golden Age detective fiction, but it's also unabashed entertainment'
SARAH WEINMAN, *NEW YORK TIMES*

'Highly ingenious'
GUARDIAN, BEST CRIME AND THRILLERS

'Very clever indeed'
ANTHONY HOROWITZ

'From the first page you know you're in the hands of a master. The atmosphere, the setting, the characters... it is flawless'
IAN MOORE, AUTHOR OF *DEATH AND CROISSANTS*

'A terrific mystery, a classic... Very much in the manner of Agatha Christie or John Dickson Carr'
MICHAEL DIRDA, *WASHINGTON POST*

'A brilliant and richly atmospheric puzzle... Every word counts, leading up to a jawdropping but logical reveal'
PUBLISHERS WEEKLY, STARRED REVIEW

'One of the most enjoyable classic crime novels I've ever read. It'll keep you guessing until the very end'
ALEX PAVESI, AUTHOR OF *EIGHT DETECTIVES*

'Another ingenious puzzle... John Dickson Carr would be proud to come up with as clever a locked room mystery as this... exceptional fun and superbly plotted'
PAUL BURKE, *CRIME TIME FM*

'Behold, the perfect escapist drug! If I could crush this book into a powder and snort it, I would'
VULTURE

'A stunner of a plot, with an ending which I simply could not believe when it was first revealed'
AT THE SCENE OF THE CRIME

'Exceptional... Superbly plotted and wickedly entertaining'
NB MAGAZINE

'A captivating read, culminating in an ending as satisfying as it is shocking... Can stand shoulder to shoulder with the very best mystery novels'
THE JAPAN SOCIETY REVIEW

T0322939

YUKITO AYATSUJI (born 1960) is a Japanese writer of mystery and horror novels and one of the founding members of the Honkaku Mystery Writers Club of Japan, dedicated to the writing of fair-play mysteries inspired by the Golden Age greats. He started writing as a member of the Kyoto University Mystery Club, which has nurtured many of Japan's greatest crime writers. *The Decagon House Murders* and *The Mill House Murders* are also available from Pushkin Vertigo.

HO-LING WONG is a translator currently living in the Netherlands. He is also both a member of the Honkaku Mystery Writers Club of Japan and former member of the Kyoto University Mystery Club. He did not commit any murders on Mystery Club excursions.

THE LABYRINTH HOUSE MURDERS

YUKITO AYATSUJI

TRANSLATED FROM THE
JAPANESE BY HO-LING WONG

PUSHKIN VERTIGO

Pushkin Press
Somerset House, Strand
London WC2R 1LA

First published in 1988 in Japan by Kodansha Ltd., Tokyo.

Publication rights for this English edition arranged through Kodansha Ltd.

English translation © Ho-Ling Wong 2024
First published by Pushkin Press in 2024

1 3 5 7 9 8 6 4 2

ISBN 13: 978-1-80533-527-6

Designed and typeset by Tetragon, London
Printed and bound in the United Kingdom by Clays Ltd, Elcograf S.p.A.

www.pushkinpress.com

For Y.U. and Y.T.

CONTENTS

PROLOGUE

It was on Friday, the 2nd of September 1988, that a book was delivered to Shimada, who had been sleeping off a summer cold at home.

Was the colour of the cover lavender, lilac or orchid? He wasn't sure, but it was a light purple shade.

The book was a common size for paperbacks. In the centre of the cover was a frame in the same colour, tilted at a forty-five degree angle, and inside of it was a picture. Against a scarlet backdrop, reminiscent of a sea of blood, was the dark head of a bull…

The title was printed in relief to the upper right of the frame, on the light purple background, and to the upper left, the name of the author was also printed in relief.

Shishiya Kadomi

THE LABYRINTH HOUSE MURDERS

A green strip of paper was wrapped around the cover, a so-called *obi*, a common practice in Japanese publishing. "Kitansha Novels—September Release" it read, with a tagline printed in Gothic typeface and a white outline around the letters.

AN ORIGINAL
HONKAKU MURDER MYSTERY!

The Truth Behind the Labyrinth House Murder Case Finally Revealed!

Shimada thought to himself: "Hmph, the marketing slogans for these kinds of books are getting sillier and sillier lately."

He had heard books weren't selling much nowadays, but apparently there was still a market for mystery fiction. The number of whodunits on bookshop shelves had been increasing over recent years…

To be honest, there were so many of them now, it was difficult to tell them apart. While it was none of his business, he was starting to worry that readers would eventually just drop murder mysteries entirely because the market was being flooded with mass-produced books of questionable quality.

Shimada looked at the back cover. There was a blurb, a short biography of the author and his photograph. Shimada didn't think the picture was very flattering.

The Labyrinth House is famous for its complex underground maze. One day, four mystery writers gather at the house, each planning to write a story set inside the bizarre building. But little do they know that they will be caught up in a whodunit themselves! Soon, the writers find themselves cut off from the outside world, and then a series of murders strikes the Labyrinth House… Readers of this superlative mystery must prepare themselves for the most baffling of puzzles, the most shocking of twists! An unrivalled sensation!

Shimada couldn't help but grin, as he imagined how the author must have felt when his editor came up with this overly dramatic copy.

This was the kind of novel he might pick up in a bookstore, but never buy. He certainly didn't dislike murder mysteries, but he tended to prefer the translated ones. And while he occasionally did read Japanese mysteries, he was always disappointed by them.

But of course, this book was different, as he knew the author very well. It had been sent to Shimada as a gift, so he felt obligated to read it. Especially since it was about the Labyrinth House Murder Case.

Shimada took the book back to his futon, where he lay on his stomach.

He had got over the worst of his fever the previous night. His muscles were still aching slightly, but he was on the mend and beginning to feel eager for stimulation. He could get through a novel this size in a few hours.

He rested his chin on his pillow, and flicked through the book. He had a look at the table of contents. When he saw there was an afterword, he quickly paged to it, as he had a habit of reading afterwords before the main story.

AFTERWORD

These words should really have come at the beginning of the book, but because so few readers are disciplined enough to actually read an "Afterword" after the main story anyway, I thought I might as well put it at the end instead. Please consider the following as a kind of introduction for people who have yet to read the book.

*

Even now, I still feel somewhat uneasy about publishing this story as a novel. As I assume many of you will have gathered when you saw the title, *The Labyrinth House Murders* is directly based on a real-life murder case.

It occurred in April 1987, over the same days as in the book. The media made a sensation out of the incident at the time, since it was such a baffling case, and because it occurred at the curious residence of a well-known mystery writer.

However, it is safe to say the press have not managed to provide a proper analysis of the whole affair.

That is only to be expected, of course. The incident occurred under highly singular circumstances and all those who knew the truth declined to speak to the press. Even the police were perplexed by this extraordinary case, and while they ostensibly accepted the "truth" that had been revealed, they did not make any definitive announcement about it. The press were therefore restricted to writing vague articles based on non-committal police statements.

If the truth about the case was never made public, what gives me the right to write about it, you might wonder. Perhaps it seems arrogant, or presumptuous of me to do so.

Allow me to make a confession, therefore. I was present when it all happened. I, Shishiya Kadomi, was one of the people in the Labyrinth House in April 1987, when that series of murders occurred there.

I have decided to publish an account of my experience in this format for two main reasons.

The first is that a certain editor very strongly urged me to do so. As for the other reason, perhaps I could say this is my memorial to those who passed away during the tragedy.

That might sound somewhat tasteless, but I know at least some of the victims were great lovers of the unique genre

12

that is the murder mystery. That is why I truly believe that a reconstruction of what happened in the form of a book is the best way to honour those who perished.

However, I doubt many readers will care much about these personal circumstances.

No matter what inspired me to write it, after all, this is nothing more than a murder mystery, a piece of entertainment that allows the reader to escape the boredom of daily life. Of course, that is perfectly fine. No, in fact, that is precisely what this book should be.

Finally, I want to make clear that after careful consideration, I have changed the names of most of the people and places in this novel. I appear in the story myself, but not under my pen-name of Shishiya Kadomi.

So which of the characters is Shishiya Kadomi?

Some readers might be interested in that mystery. But some things are best left a secret.

Summer of 1988
Shishiya Kadomi

Shimada was already familiar with the details of the murders that had occurred in April last year at the Labyrinth House. It had been a truly bizarre affair, but he knew that the matter had, in a certain way, been resolved.

"Recreating a real-life case as a murder mystery, huh?"

Shimada opened to the beginning. The face of the author, whom he had not seen for some time now, appeared in his mind.

"Well, let's see what you came up with."

Shimada started reading.

THE LABYRINTH HOUSE MURDERS

BY
SHISHIYA KADOMI

KITANSHA NOVELS

AUTHOR: SHISHIYA KADOMI
© 1988 SHISHIYA KADOMI. Printed in Japan.

Publisher: Uchida Naoyuki
Publishing House: KITANSHA Ltd.

Tokyo, Bunkyō-ku, Otowa *-* *-* *
Postal Code: ***
Telephone: Tokyo (03)-***-**** (main number)

Printing House: Takagi Printing Ltd.
Bindery: Nakatsu Book Bindery Ltd.

CONTENTS

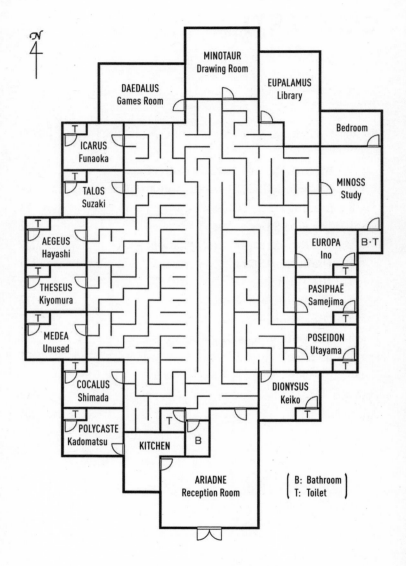

Fig. 1 Floor Plan of the Labyrinth House

LIST OF CHARACTERS
(WITH AGES IN APRIL 1987)

All names are given in Japanese order, family name preceding given name.

Miyagaki Yōtarō (60)   A veteran in the world of Japanese mystery fiction; owner of the Labyrinth House

Kiyomura Junichi (30)   Mystery writer

Suzaki Shōsuke (41)   Mystery writer

Funaoka Madoka (30)   Mystery writer

Hayashi Hiroya (27)   Mystery writer

Samejima Tomoo (38)   A critic

Utayama Hideyuki (40)   An editor

Utayama Keiko (33)   Hideyuki's wife

Ino Mitsuo (36)   Miyagaki's secretary

Kadomatsu Fumie (63)   A housekeeper

Shimada Kiyoshi (37)   A mystery novel aficionado

For them

PROLOGUE

"It is nice to see you again after such a long time," Utayama Hideyuki said once more, taking a seat on the sofa that was offered to him. "I am glad you are in good health."

"In good health?" The frowning man sitting opposite Utayama pouted his dry lips. The small eyes behind his lightly tinted, gold-rimmed spectacles blinked slowly. "Healthy is the last thing I am. You of all people should know very well that I've been cooped up here ever since I sold off my place in Tokyo."

"Oh, well, yes…"

The man's splendidly white hair was brushed back above a square forehead; he had thin cheeks, a sharp chin and a large, slightly crooked nose. Miyagaki Yōtarō, the elderly gentleman as reflected in Utayama's eyes, hadn't changed much since they had last met the previous spring.

The man's pallor did indeed look unhealthy. His cheeks were sunken and the spark had disappeared from his hollow eyes.

Miyagaki had developed the habit of complaining about his health over the last few years. Each time they'd meet, Utayama was subjected to a litany of woes about the old man's physical condition. And yet Miyagaki detested doctors, and no matter how much the people around him urged him to have a check-up at the hospital, he refused to do so.

"Has your condition really worsened that much?" Utayama asked seriously, to which Miyagaki shrugged, before replying with a smirk:

"It's the worst. I've already given up. Nothing I can do about it any more. Nothing more natural than to grow old and die. When I was young, I always said I wouldn't grow old. That a short life is a grander thing than a long one. I'm not going to go back on those words now. I've got no intention of becoming the world's oldest living person."

"Oh…"

Utayama nodded and forced an understanding smile onto his face, but deep down he felt uneasy. Miyagaki sounded more defeatist than ever.

Utayama, an editor in the literary department of the major publisher Kitansha, had known the detective murder writer Miyagaki Yōtarō for a long time, both as his editor and as a fan. Miyagaki's first mystery had been published when he was just twenty-one, in 1948, in the period after the Second World War when detective novels were enjoying a revival in popularity. His debut *The House of the Meditating Poet* had been praised at the time by a big name in the industry: "An impressive, riveting masterpiece. I almost can't believe it's written by a young newcomer. Hats off to him!"

Since then, Miyagaki Yōtarō had remained a slow writer, generally publishing a full-length novel only every year or so. His father had been a very wealthy man, so he didn't need to write to make a living, which was one reason for his slow pace. However, this also made it possible for the quality to remain consistently high. Even when the wave of social detective novels took over the world of Japanese mystery fiction, shoving traditional puzzle mysteries aside, Miyagaki persevered and carved out a place for himself on the crime scene.

In particular, his novel *For a Magnificent Downfall*, published ten years earlier when he was fifty, was seen as his magnum opus, the ultimate "Miyagaki Mystery", and garnered much praise. *For a Magnificent Downfall* went on to be considered one of the great classics of Japanese mystery, alongside the three giants: *The Black Death Murder Case* by Oguri Mushitarō, *Dogra Magra* by Yumeno Kyūsaku and *Offerings to the Void* by Nakai Hideo.

Utayama had always considered Miyagaki the shadow master of contemporary mystery fiction. He had never been a big hit with the wider reading public, never what one would call a best-selling author. But there were very few mystery writers who could boast such a large number of long-standing, dedicated fans.

His books brimmed with his unique philosophy and were a showcase for his vast knowledge of matters both academic and trivial. Along with his refined writing style and deep characterization, this won the approval of even those critics who were usually only concerned with "pure" literature, although they would always add the caveat "for a mystery novel" to any words of praise they offered. What Utayama loved most about Miyagaki, was the innocent, childlike conviction that led him to stick to his signature style.

"*For* a mystery novel? But they are mystery novels!" he'd say.

The stubbornness with which Miyagaki continued to pour his heart and soul into his beloved mystery genre was even in a way reminiscent of the grand master Edogawa Rampo. After the publication of *For a Magnificent Downfall*, Miyagaki mainly focused on editing his mystery fiction magazine *Reverie*, looking for new blood to carry the genre forward.

But then, last April, Miyagaki had suddenly dropped all of his work, sold off his house in Seijō, Tokyo, and moved to Tango, where his father's family came from.

"This metropolis is too busy for an old man like me," he had told Utayama. "Too many people, too much information flying

25

around. I'm going to retreat to the peaceful countryside. It's time to say farewell."

Miyagaki had also declared he would leave all of his work on *Reverie* to other people, that he had no intention of writing any more books—or indeed anything at all.

For Utayama, this news came as a bolt from the blue. He had been posted to the magazine editorial department for some time and had only recently returned to his old home on the literary editorial team. He had been hoping to work on a new novel with the master, so the retirement announcement was a big shock to him.

When discussing today's meeting on the phone a few days earlier, Miyagaki had made one thing very clear:

"You can come to visit, but don't bring up work. I'm not interested in even doing short pieces. You'll remember I told you that in no uncertain terms when I moved here last year."

Like many authors, Miyagaki could be very stubborn when it came to protecting his personal life especially the last few years, since he had stopped writing. He had always been very difficult to handle, and now would not even talk to editors who had worked with him for a long time. Utayama thought this behaviour was a reflection of Miyagaki's frustration at the decline of his creative capabilities.

Thus Utayama had chosen his words very carefully on the phone, making sure not to offend the great author.

"Of course, I understand. This has nothing to do with work, I just wanted to see you again after such a long time. I'm going back to my home town for New Year anyway, so I thought I could visit you too."

"Oh, yes, I remember you're from Miyazu, aren't you?"

Utayama's family ran a *ryokan*, a traditional Japanese inn, in Miyazu in Kyōto Prefecture, near Amanohashidate, famous as one of the country's great scenic views. Utayama tried to return home every year for New Year and the O-Bon festival. Miyagaki's house was nearby, at the end of the Tango Peninsula, just outside T— Hamlet.

Utayama had borrowed a car from his older brother, who had taken over the family business. Although his wife had come to Miyazu, she wasn't making the trip with him. He didn't have the confidence for the mountain road in the winter, so he took the long route, via the coastal National Highway. From Miyazu, the drive wouldn't even take two hours. The landscape was carpeted with snow, but fortunately, the roads were safe.

The Labyrinth House had been built over ten years ago by Miyagaki Yōtarō as his second home. At first, he had only stayed in the house during the summer, and Utayama had visited him then. As the name suggests, the building was designed in a very peculiar manner, with complex hallways that made a maze. On his first visit, Utayama had been absolutely baffled by it to Miyagaki's delight. He always took a mischievous, childlike pleasure from the looks of surprise on his guests' faces.

"Sir, do you really have no intention of picking up your pen again?" Utayama now finally dared to ask, as he spooned some sugar into the tea that the elderly, but not particularly friendly housekeeper had brought him. He had promised Miyagaki on the phone not to bring up work, but as an editor he still hoped he could get the "Shadow Master" working on a new book again.

"Hmm… I knew it."

Utayama was prepared for an angry outburst. But despite his fears, Miyagaki didn't seem too offended by his question. He wrinkled his nose as he took out a cigarette from the case on the table.

"You're still far too young to set aside the pen completely," Utayama went on. "Mystery writers have become lazy recently, complacent, but you could spark the genre into life again."

Miyagaki lit his cigarette. "That's a fantasy. I can't write any more."

"No, sir, you still have so much…"

"Don't expect too much from me. Van Dine was right: no one can write more than six good detective novels during their lifetime. How many do you think I have written these last forty years? Even if you only count the full-length books, I have easily written more than double that limit."

Miyagaki closed his eyes, and suddenly began to cough heavily. When he finally stopped, his hollow eyes stared at the tip of the cigarette between his fingers.

"I had been thinking things over until last spring, when I finally decided to put an end to my career myself. I don't have what it takes to write a murder mystery I can be happy with any more. Almost a year later, my feelings have not changed."

"Sir, with all due respect, it sounds to me to like you are going through a episode of self-doubt."

"Do I have to say it again? I have always been a coward. Would you like to know the desire I've harboured ever since I was young? I have always wanted to kill someone with my own hands. Just once. But of course, I never was able to do it. Writing stories about murder for all these decades: that was little more than a surrogate for this wish."

Miyagaki glared at Utayama as he roughly stubbed out his cigarette. Actually, the old man seldom smoked. Utayama opened his mouth to speak, but was forestalled by a short chuckle.

"I'm just joking, of course. But… hmm, I do fear failure. Detective novels are in a way my *raison d'être*. If I could, I would very much like to continue writing them. But the last thing I want is to write a bad novel, a work that would blemish the reputation of Miyagaki Yōtarō. That fear is stronger than my wish to write. That is why I decided it'd be better to give up on writing altogether."

Utayama was conflicted. If he could convince Miyagaki to write a new book, it would be a coup for him as an editor. But what if, as Miyagaki himself claimed, he truly didn't have the ability any more to produce a novel worthy of his reputation? As a true Miyagaki Mystery fan, to publish a book like that would feel like a betrayal.

"No need to look so upset," Miyagaki said, as the scowl on his face relaxed slightly. "You know me, I might change my mind again. Actually, I am playing around with an idea now. When the time comes, I will be sure to let you know."

"Do you mean an idea for a new book?" Utayama's voice jumped an octave higher. Miyagaki grinned, reaching out for his teacup.

"You just can't help it, can you? No, forget about it for now. Don't make me remind you what you promised me on the phone."

Utayama felt a bit embarrassed at that. He evaded Miyagaki's piercing gaze and glanced around the room.

It was square with an ivory carpet and walls of a calming terracotta colour. In the centre of the carpet was an antique sofa set, on which Utayama and Miyagaki were sitting. This was the drawing room, to which Miyagaki had given the name Minotaur.

A low sideboard was placed against the wall behind them, and on top of it stood the stuffed head of a bull with two splendid horns, a decoration no doubt inspired by the room's name. The Minotaur was a monster from Greek mythology with the head of a bull and the body of a man. The monster was said to live in the labyrinth of King Minos on the island of Crete. This room named after it was located in the deepest part of the Labyrinth House.

The lights were reflected in the glass beads embedded in the black bull's eye sockets, making the head look almost alive. Utayama shuddered. It felt almost as if the bull's head was glaring disapprovingly at him, impolite guest that he was.

"Oh, yes, there's something I should tell you, even though it's not set in stone yet," Miyagaki said.

"Uh… Huh?"

"You don't have to look so surprised."

Utayama shook his head, a little embarrassed. He didn't want to explain to Miyagaki he had been distracted by the bull's eerie eyes.

"I was thinking of having a little party here at this house, for my birthday, the first of April," Miyagaki said. "It's my sixtieth. I would like for you to come. You can bring your wife along too."

"Oh, of course, we'd love to!"

Up until two or three years ago, Miyagaki, who was single, had hosted gatherings at his home from time to time. In fact, he would often invite young writers and editors around for drinks.

"I will have an invitation sent to you, so keep your schedule open," Miyagaki said. Utayama looked at the pale face and asked who else would be invited.

"I haven't decided yet. But it won't be a big thing. Just people I know well, like yourself."

A few faces flashed through Utayama's mind.

"There is one interesting guest I might invite, actually."

"Yes?"

"I only became acquainted with him recently. He's from Kyūshū, the son of a priest who's in charge of a temple… I think you'll find him an interesting man too once you meet him."

"I can't wait."

"Anyway, how about having dinner here before you return? My housekeeper is actually a very good cook."

Utayama looked at his wristwatch. "Oh, no, thank you, but my wife is waiting for me back home. She's pregnant… so, you know, I'd like to get back."

"Oh, I didn't know."

Miyagaki's white eyebrows furrowed deeply. Utayama knew the old man hated children, but also knew he could only refuse the dinner invitation by being honest.

"I'm sorry," said Utayama, bowing deeply. Miyagaki nonchalantly assured him that he wasn't offended and took a fresh cigarette from his case. After a few drags, he started coughing again, so put it out.

They chatted for another half an hour or so, then Utayama announced he had to leave.

He couldn't quite tell whether the writer for whom he still had high hopes was doing well or not. But he could see Miyagaki's creative flame was not extinguished yet. That alone made the day's long trip worth it.

Of course, Utayama could not have known then that this was the last time he would ever speak with Miyagaki Yōtarō in this life.

CHAPTER ONE

AN INVITATION TO THE LABYRINTH HOUSE

1

"It's really spring now. Everything looks completely changed from when we were here over the New Year. Even the sea looks different," said Keiko from the passenger seat, in a carefree, almost childlike tone. Utayama grinned. Keiko was seven years younger than him, though that still made her thirty-three this year.

His eyes followed Keiko's gaze to the Wakasa Bay on their right. Indeed, the sea looked completely different from when he was here about three months earlier. The sunlight was different. The blueness of the calmly lapping water was different. The whiteness of the splashing waves was different.

"But I like the Sea of Japan in the winter better actually, when it looks so intensely deep," she said.

They had been married for four years now, and their first child would be born this summer. Utayama had to reflect for a second before replying:

"I think I'm more inclined to be afraid of the sea in the winter. When I was in primary school, my older cousin drowned in the winter sea. He went out fishing and was swept away by the waves."

"Oh… did you tell me about him before?"

"I think so…"

It was a Wednesday afternoon, the 1st of April, and Utayama Hideyuki and his wife Keiko were on their way to the Labyrinth House. They were driving along the coast on National Highway 178, the same road Utayama had taken last time. Once again, he had borrowed his brother's car.

Utayama had received a letter from Ino Mitsuo, Miyagaki's secretary, exactly two weeks earlier, that explained there would indeed be a party to celebrate Miyagaki's sixtieth birthday. It was to start at four o'clock on the 1st of April. Location: Labyrinth House. Guests were expected to spend the night there. Ino would answer any further questions.

Utayama had made sure to keep the date free after he had heard about the party during his visit in the winter. He was also happy to bring his wife along. Miyagaki and Keiko had already met, when he was still living in Tokyo, and she was now in her second trimester and could safely travel.

Utayama had been a bit worried about the number of guests at first, even though Miyagaki had told him there wouldn't be many. He didn't feel like taking Keiko anywhere crowded. She might not be truly introverted, but she was still a bit shy. Considering she was pregnant, he didn't want to burden her with meeting too many new people.

However, Utayama had been reassured after a telephone call to Ino, at his home in Tokyo where he usually stayed these days. Eight guests had been invited, including the Utayamas, and most of them Keiko had already met.

"How much longer is it?" she asked after a short yawn. She had grown bored with the view.

"Less than an hour. We're almost at Kyōgamisaki, the northern tip of the Tango Peninsula."

"Mr Miyagaki really moved to the sticks, didn't he? I can't believe he's gone this far away from Tokyo, even at his age. I could never do it."

"I believe his father came from this area."

Keiko cocked her head. "Still, it must be very lonely here."

"He's always said he loves being alone."

"And he's stayed single all this time, right? And he doesn't like children either… He's a bit of a strange guy, isn't he?"

"You could say that. But, he's not a bad person."

"Yes, that I know. He's always seemed happy to chat with me whenever we visited him in Seijō."

"I think he likes you."

"Really?"

A shy smile appeared on Keiko's face. She mumbled to herself once more about how lonely it must be around here.

"But I heard he used to be rather the ladies' man?"

"Yeah, I think so."

Utayama had heard more than a few rumours about Miyagaki's relations with women. Apparently, Miyagaki had been a very attractive young man. Even in middle age, he wouldn't have had any trouble finding a partner if he wanted one. But naturally, over recent years the romantic rumours had dried up.

"Has there never been someone in his life he wanted to marry?"

"Hmmm…"

Utayama gave a long sigh as he remembered Miyagaki's face when they had met three months before. A lonely old man. Those words perfectly described how Miyagaki appeared to him then. Miyagaki had never looked like that when they met in Tokyo.

"I bet he must feel a bit lonely now though, having retired and moved away. I mean, he's having a party and has invited us. And all the guests are people he likes, are they?"

"Yeah."

Utayama looked at his wife. He then recalled the names Ino had told him over the phone:

"Suzaki Shōsuke. Kiyomura Junichi. Hayashi Hiroya. Funaoka Madoka. And Samejima Tomoo. You've met them all before, haven't you?"

"Yes. They're all writers, I think?"

"Samejima's a critic."

"Close enough. Hmm... What were their pen-names again?..."

Keiko closed her eyes, and put her index finger to her fair forehead. She tried to recall the noms de plume of the four writers and the critic.

Utayama had just said their real names. All five had won the Newcomer Award handed out by Miyagaki's magazine *Reverie*, and all of them published their work under pen-names.

However, Miyagaki Yōtarō, who was in a way their mentor, did not like pseudonyms. He could barely accept them on paper, but the idea of calling each other by pen-names in real life, he thought to be completely tasteless.

Utayama on the other hand liked them. He was of the opinion that people whose profession involved coming up with fantastical dreams (or nightmares) removed from reality, needed to wear a mask appropriate for that task. It was perhaps only a matter of opinion, but that was why Utayama found it odd Miyagaki was so against pen-names. Miyagaki had held on to the name his parents had given him throughout his career, so perhaps that was why he would have liked these five to do the same.

Because of his disapproval, Miyagaki's "disciples" never used their professional pseudonyms when they were in his presence. Everyone close to Miyagaki, from the disciples to his editor, was aware of this unwritten rule.

"One, two, three..." Keiko was counting on her fingers, when she turned to her husband at the driving wheel. "I thought you said there'd be eight guests, including us. Who's the last one?"

Utayama searched for a cigarette in his shirt pocket.

"Oh, I don't really know actually. He's not a writer or critic. A priest from some temple, I believe?"

"A priest?" Keiko now looked at her husband in surprise.

"I think Mr Miyagaki mentioned something like that when I visited him over New Year. Said I'd find him interesting once I'd met him myself."

"Huh."

"You can handle one new face, can't you?"

"I guess so... Hey, what are you doing?"

Utayama's hand, holding a cigarette lighter, stopped in mid-air. "Oh, I'm sorry, force of habit..."

Naturally, Utayama wasn't allowed to smoke in the car with Keiko while she was carrying their child.

"Let's stop for a break if you're desperate, then. Oh, is that Kyōgamisaki?"

In front of them, to their right, a headland protruded into the sea. At the end of it they could occasionally make out a lighthouse. Utayama nodded, and parked the car on the shoulder.

2

The road was bordered by a white guard rail on the coast side. The sound of the waves relentlessly breaking against the rocks below was pleasant. The wind was still a bit chilly, but the peacefully shining sun warmed Utayama.

The weather made him realize once again that it was truly spring. How long had it been since he last visited this part of the country during this season?

As he replenished the nicotine levels in his blood, Utayama looked out at the sea and yawned loudly. He was beginning to feel at one with the serene scenery, and to understand why the elderly writer had wanted to escape the hustle and bustle of the capital and take refuge here.

Footsteps approached him from behind. At first he thought Keiko had got out of the car too.

"Err, excuse me," a low voice said.

Utayama turned around, surprised.

"I'm sorry to bother you, but I'm having a bit of car trouble…"

The stranger appeared to be slightly younger than Utayama, probably around thirty-six or -seven. He was wearing a loose black sweater and black jeans. He had a swarthy, bony face and a rather large nose. Two drooping, deep-set eyes squinted beneath his thick eyebrows.

"Sorry to have startled you."

The man suddenly bowed. He was too lean and tall, so as he bowed, his eyes came down to the level of those of the shorter Utayama.

"What's the matter?" Utayama asked politely, while carefully observing the man for any suspicious signs. The stranger softly ran a hand through his hair.

"I'm having some trouble with my car," he said again, and with an embarrassed look, pointed up the road.

It curved to the left up ahead. A jutting cliff blocked most of the view to that side, but further up the road, Utayama could indeed make out the back of a red car.

"A flat tyre?"

"No, I think it's something to do with the regulator," the man explained.

"Oh, that is quite a predicament."

"I wanted to call a mechanic, but I can't find a telephone box around here. So I am really at my wit's end. I don't suppose you could give me a lift to the nearest telephone?"

"Aha," Utayama mumbled as he took another good look at the man. While his appearance was a bit suspicious, his manner was quite normal. In fact, Utayama found him quite friendly.

"Of course. My car is over there."

Utayama led the way, glancing at his wristwatch. It was ten to three. There was still time before the party.

"What's the matter?" Keiko asked with a puzzled look. She had got out of the car.

"This gentleman's car broke down."

"Hello. I'm terribly sorry for bothering you."

The man, now at Utayama's side, raised his right hand to Keiko, and then looked at his wristwatch.

"Hmm, I guess I won't make it," he mumbled.

"Is there somewhere you need to be?" Utayama asked.

"Yes. At four o'clock."

"At four?" Utayama repeated. That was the same time as they were to be at the party.

"Where exactly are you headed?"

"Somewhere just outside T— Hamlet, up ahead…"

Surprised, Utayama took another good look at him.

"Are you perhaps… going to visit the mystery writer Miyagaki Yōtarō?"

"Huh?" The man looked back at Utayama, baffled.

"Oh, sorry, my misunderstanding," Utayama quickly said, but the other smiled back at him.

"No, you are completely right. Aha, I guess you are a fellow guest."

"It seems so." Now Utayama bowed to the man. "My name is Utayama. I am an editor at the publisher Kitansha. This is my wife Keiko."

"What a coincidence. I am—"

Among the guests invited to the Miyagaki home, there was only one person Utayama hadn't ever met, so he could guess this man's identity.

"Don't tell me. You must be the priest. You don't look like one though," he said in a jovial manner.

The man showed his white teeth as he smiled.

"I suppose Mr Miyagaki told you about me then? My name is Shimada Kiyoshi. Very nice to meet you."

*

Utayama knew that further down the National Highway there was a small rest area. After some discussion, they decided they'd tow the disabled car there and leave it for now. Shimada would then get a lift with the Utayamas, so they could all make it in time for the party at the Labyrinth House.

By the time Shimada had arranged things with the person in charge of the rest area and got in the back seat of Utayama's car, it was half-past three. Utayama drove off, estimating they'd arrive just around four.

"You really saved me there. What would Mr Miyagaki have thought of me if I'd arrived hours late after his kind invitation?" Shimada said, clearly relieved. "You said you were an editor at Kitansha, didn't you? Have you been Mr Miyagaki's editor for long?"

"Yes, I think I've worked with him close to twenty years now."

"Oh, so did you also work on *MagDown*?"

"*MagDown*?" Utayama cocked his head upon hearing the unfamiliar word.

Shimada gave an embarrassed chuckle. "Excuse me, I meant Mr Miyagaki's magnum opus. *For a Magnificent Downfall.*"

Keiko giggled. "Aha, I get it. *MagDown*, right? Do people call the book that?"

"General readers probably don't, but it seems students with a love for the genre do. I have a friend who's in his university's mystery club, you see."

"I guess you must be quite the mystery buff yourself too, then?"

"Oh, no, I wouldn't dare call myself that. But of course, I do find mystery stories more interesting than chanting Buddhist sutras whenever I have to help out at my home temple…"

While one wouldn't have guessed from his appearance, it seemed Shimada Kiyoshi was indeed a temple priest.

"How did you and Mr Miyagaki become acquainted?" Keiko asked.

"I'm just one of his readers, a simple fan," Shimada mumbled. "I have read all of his work, including his short stories and essays. Oh, now I think about it, I recall having seen your name mentioned in his acknowledgements a few times, Mr Utayama."

"I am honoured."

Utayama stole a glance at Shimada in the rear-view mirror. He looked like he was having a good time, and quite innocent.

"I was told Mr Miyagaki met you late last year by chance. Mind if I ask how?"

Shimada seemed at a loss for words for a moment.

"Oh, how should I explain this? I truly was already a fan of his work, but the reason I met him a few months ago was… Hmm, I guess I could say it was the building that brought us together."

"The building? You mean Labyrinth House?"

"Yes."

In the mirror, Utayama could see the grave expression that came across Shimada's face.

"Have you ever heard the name Nakamura Seiji?" Shimada asked.

"Nakamura…" Utayama knew he had heard it before, but couldn't remember right away where. Shimada watched him silently in the mirror.

"I know the name," Keiko said, as she unfolded the hands resting on her stomach. "I think I saw it in some magazine. Yeah, he was some kind of strange architect."

That finally rang a bell. Utayama recalled he had seen the name in a newspaper or magazine. Nakamura Seiji was an eccentric architect, who had passed away some time ago. He had built a few curious buildings and…

"Aha, Nakamura Seiji, of course…" Then it suddenly struck Utayama why Shimada had mentioned the name. "Oh, you don't mean…"

"So you didn't know…"

Utayama could not tell whether Shimada did it consciously, but suddenly he was speaking in a weighty, ominous tone:

"The Labyrinth House was built by that very same Nakamura Seiji."

3

From T— Hamlet they drove through the hills, before turning onto an unpaved road. They followed it through a dark wood until, eventually, they found the open steel gate to Miyagaki's residence on their right.

Inside was a large parking area to the left. Two cars were already there. Utayama recognized the black Mercedes-Benz owned by Miyagaki. The other car was an old white Corolla. The other invitees to the party weren't coming by car as far as Utayama knew. Did that mean there was another person here besides the eight scheduled guests?

The three got out of the car, and walked down a dark, narrow path flanked by pine trees until they saw a building in front of them. It looked like a massive crag of rock.

"Is that the house?" Keiko asked, amazed. "It looks... really creepy."

"Precisely how he likes it," said Utayama.

"Isn't it a bit small? Is the labyrinth in the back?"

It did look like a small building at first sight. It was about four metres wide, and at three metres high appeared to be only a single storey. The structure resembled a little shrine carved out of a rock formation. Low stone walls extended from both sides. From where they stood, it appeared there was only a dreary-looking expanse of grass on the other side of those walls. No wonder Keiko was so astounded by the sight.

"Oh, have you never been here before?" Shimada asked.

"No, this is my first time..."

"That building is just the entrance," Utayama explained to his wife.

"Huh? What do you mean?" Keiko ran her fingers through her short hair as she looked at him.

"The actual Labyrinth House is beneath this building. It's underground."

"Huh, you mean the whole house?"

The first time Utayama visited this place must have been about ten years ago. He was told beforehand that the Labyrinth House had been built underground. When he first saw the "entrance", he was reminded of the Venus Grotto of the Linderhof Palace, which he had visited on a trip to Germany.

The three walked down the path and approached the building. As they came closer, they got a better look at the field behind the "shrine".

The stone walls enclosed an area of well over 650 square metres. Buried in the ground were low pyramids, each side about a metre long. They were constructed from steel frames and thick glass, and looked almost like dark waves rising from the ground. The pyramids actually formed the rooftop of the underground residence.

The square entryway was set into a mass of granite that protruded from the earth. Beyond was a sturdy-looking bronze lattice gate before a pair of gigantic doors seemingly hewn from rock—but in reality probably made of concrete and treated to look like stone.

In front of the gate, on the right side, stood a marble statue that came up to an adult's chest height. It had the lower body of a beast, with four legs, while the upper body was that of a man. This was not a creature with the head of a bull and the body of a human, but the head and torso of a human and the body of a bull. It, too, was a minotaur, as apparently, many writers, including Dante, had mistakenly interpreted the nature of the monster from Greek mythology, leading to this grotesque variation.

Standing in front of the statue, Utayama pointed at its face and said to Keiko:

"Put your hand in its mouth."

"What!?" she cried. "Why?"

"Just try it. Put your hand in its mouth and try feeling for something."

The monster had the face of a handsome young man, but its mouth was wide open, as if it were screaming. Keiko timidly started to place her right hand inside, looking back at her husband in shock.

"You mean… like this?"

"Yep, that's it."

"Should I just pull it?"

"Yep."

Shimada, who had been standing behind them, suddenly let out an approving groan. "I see, that's the doorbell."

This was the kind of playful game Miyagaki was good at. The doorbell was hidden inside the Minotaur's mouth.

After a few moments, the double stone doors beyond the gate opened. Out came the old woman whom Utayama had met during his previous visit.

"We're Utayama Hideyuki and Keiko. And this is Shimada Kiyoshi."

There was a slight pause before the woman's reply came. "Understood." She seemed to recognize Utayama. She then opened the lattice gate.

"Follow me," the old woman said in a cold, raspy voice, as she led the three guests inside. Actually, although she was getting on a bit, she didn't seem quite old enough to be called an "old woman". She was plump, and rather short. Keiko was quite petite herself, but this woman was even smaller. As she wobbled deeper into the cavern-like building ahead of them, Utayama couldn't help, despite knowing how rude it was, but be reminded of the Hunchback of Notre-Dame.

The stone doors led into a small hall. Bare, dark rock walls enclosed the space. A doughnut-shaped stained glass window, about two metres wide, was set in the ceiling. The chandelier light at the centre of the ceiling was not switched on, but the room was lit by the afternoon daylight shining in through the coloured glass.

"Have the others arrived already?" Utayama asked. It was a bit past four o'clock.

"Follow me," the housekeeper repeated, and continued towards two doors set in the opposite wall. Before them, in the middle of the wall was another bronze lattice door, similar to the gate outside and it led to the main building. To the right was a wooden door, which Utayama knew opened to a storeroom.

The three guests followed the housekeeper through the lattice door. Beyond was a wide staircase leading down. They began to descend in silence, the sound of their footsteps muffled by a thick carpet.

"It's like a passageway to another dimension," Keiko whispered from behind her husband.

"Indeed," said Shimada from the rear. "When I first visited here some months ago… Well, let's say I was very impressed. This was a home fit for the author of *MagDown*, a building worthy of the name of Nakamura Seiji…"

Once more, Shimada's voice sounded ominous as he pronounced the architect's name. Utayama began to feel a sense of foreboding.

He thought of the other bizarre buildings he knew Nakamura Seiji had designed: The Decagon House, The Mill House… And then he thought of the incidents that had occurred in those houses.

Shimada had mentioned something about the building bringing him and Miyagaki together. What did he mean by that? Did Shimada simply have an interest in Nakamura's architectural creations, and one of them just happened to be Miyagaki Yōtarō's home? Was that really all there was to it? Or was there some deeper meaning behind their meeting?

At the bottom of the staircase was another small hall, with a navy carpet and grey stone walls. The weak light hanging from the high ceiling only strengthened the feeling they had entered a deep cavern.

In front of them stood two large double doors of black wood, set with faded stained glass in primary colours.

The housekeeper turned the doorknobs and opened the double doors, which led directly into the reception room.

"Come in," she said, moving to one side. The three guests stepped out of the dimly lit hall and into the room, with Utayama leading the way. All of a sudden, they heard a voice groaning in pain.

"Help…"

Just then, a shadowy figure appeared from Utayama's right and collapsed on his shoulder.

Utayama cried out and jumped back. Keiko let out a short scream. The falling figure, having lost its support, dropped to its knees, before sprawling on the floor.

"It's Kiyomura!" gasped Utayama.

The man's face was turned towards them, with one side buried in the carpet. Utayama was utterly baffled.

"What…"

"What's happening?" Keiko asked, pulling at her husband's sleeve.

"He–help…" Kiyomura Junichi moaned once more, his tanned face contorted in a grimace.

Utayama was so stunned that he just dropped his bag on the floor. Shimada slipped past him and squatted at Kiyomura's side.

"Sir, hello? Are you all right? Can you hear me?"

Shimada shook the prostrate man's shoulders, and Kiyomura's eyes slowly flickered open. His empty gaze took in the sight of

47

the stranger crouching over him, then settled on Utayama, who was still in shock.

"Mr... Utayama..."

Kiyomura's lips trembled. Utayama noticed a dribble of red liquid coming from the corner of his mouth and felt a wave of nausea sweep through him.

"Blood..." he muttered. "No, it can't be..."

The Decagon House and the Mill House: both creations of Nakamura Seiji, both sites of terrible tragedies. Would the Labyrinth House be next?

"It can't be!!" Utayama cried again, as he stumbled past Kiyomura's body into the room. "What's going on here!?"

4

The other guests were sitting spread out across the L-shaped room. All eyes were fixed on the pale, panicked Utayama.

There was Samejima Tomoo, as well as Funaoka Madoka and Suzaki Shōsuke. The last guest, Hayashi Hiroya, wasn't there, but Utayama didn't have the presence of mind to notice that.

"Hello, it's been a while," said Samejima Tomoo from a sofa on the left of the room, waving a hand holding a cigarette at Utayama. "And I see congratulations are in order. When is the baby due?"

Utayama turned away dumbly, baffled by the completely non-chalant tone in which he had been addressed. Near the door, Kiyomura Junichi was still lying on the floor. Shimada looked up at Utayama in puzzlement from where he was crouched next to the body.

Utayama spun back around to face the room.

"I don't... What the hell's going on?"

Still no answer to his question came. Suzaki Shōsuke was seated on the right side, in an armchair set before a large full-length mirror on the wall. He was leaning forward, looking down at an open book in his lap, as if all this was none of his business.

Funaoka Madoka was sitting at the table in front of Suzaki, her elbows resting on the tabletop and her pretty face cupped in her hands. She got to her feet now.

"Hello, Mr Utayama." She smiled as she came towards him, her lips bright with lipstick. The contrast between her calm demeanour and what had just happened behind him only added to his bewilderment.

"Enough of your games now," Madoka said to the back of the man lying on the floor. "You're being rude. There's someone here you haven't met yet."

Only after Madoka had spoken did Utayama finally realize what had been going on. He blushed as he turned back towards the doorway.

"So, that's it…"

As Utayama muttered those words, Kiyomura got up from the floor. Shimada stared at him in amazement.

"Excuse me. But you have to admit, I played the role pretty well." Kiyomura chuckled, wiping away the "blood" around his mouth with a handkerchief.

"I told him to not do it, but he can be so childish…" Madoka said.

"No harm done, right?" Kiyomura said.

"It wasn't funny. It's just this kind of thing that I can't stand about—"

"Oh, please, don't be so strict with me, dear Ms Funaoka."

Shimada rose to his feet and put his hands behind his head as he looked at the bickering pair.

"Ha, I guess you got us there. An April Fool's prank!"

*

"So you're the third son of a family of priests? Meaning you're not a priest yourself?"

"No, but during the busier periods like the O-Bon Festival and O-Higan, I do help my father out a little at the temple."

"So besides that, what do you usually do?"

"Oh, you know, this and that."

Kiyomura Junichi had been extremely pleased with his successful April Fool's joke. Shimada also appeared amused by it, and didn't seem to mind having been utterly tricked. It didn't take long for the pair to get a lively conversation going once they got seated around the big table in the middle of the room.

"Will your oldest brother take over the temple one day?" Kiyomura asked.

"Well, that's a bit complicated actually…"

"How so?"

"I guess I'm revealing a family secret here, but my oldest brother is missing. His name is Tsutomu and he went abroad fifteen years ago, but never returned."

Shimada had revealed this information in a rather light-hearted manner, even though it must have been a very grave matter to his family.

"That sounds serious."

"And as for my second brother, he has no intention whatsoever of taking over the temple. His current work is as far as removed from Buddhist teachings as it is possible to be."

"What does he do?"

"His work actually has something to do with all of you gathered here today. Every day he's busy with robberies and killings and things like that…"

"Haha. So he's a…"

"Police Inspector of the First Investigation Division of the Ōita Prefectural Police."

"Aha, I see what you mean."

Kiyomura Junichi was thirty years old and had made his debut four years earlier with *Bloodsucking Forest*, which won the *Reverie* Newcomer Award. His work was well received: it combined atmospheric occult elements with a dry, ironic tone. Kiyomura was a tall, handsome man, who was wearing a green cardigan, and seemed pleasant at first sight, but Utayama knew there was more to him than met the eye.

The Utayamas were sitting on a sofa, with Samejima opposite them.

"He really got you there," Samejima said. "I don't think I've ever seen you so startled."

"Haha…"

Utayama gave an embarrassed smile.

"Can you believe he thought of getting the ketchup from the kitchen? You can tell he's an actor, the way he played his role."

"Oh, is he an actor?" Keiko asked her husband.

"He was in a small theatre company called the Dark Tent. I think he quit though," he explained.

"Wow. He gave me a shock too, you know," his wife said.

"Yeah, suddenly appearing out of nowhere like that."

"And don't you think that housekeeper was amazing too?" Keiko glanced over at the door to the left of the entrance doors, leading to the kitchen, through which the housekeeper had disappeared. "She never even blinked. Perhaps she's already gone a bit senile…"

Samejima grinned. "That's just the type of person she is. Does everything she's paid for, but isn't interested in anything else. In fact that's exactly what Mr Miyagaki likes about her, I think. And add to that, it was the second time that prank had been played."

51

Utayama leant back in his seat, a smirk on his face. "Ah, so he got you too?"

"No, I was the first one here. Kiyomura was here third, after Madoka."

"So it was Suzaki who got pranked?"

Suzaki Shōsuke was forty-one years old, the oldest of the "disciples" of Miyagaki Yōtarō gathered there that day. He specialized in thick *honkaku* novels set in medieval Europe, but he wrote very slowly, so editors often tried to avoid working with him.

"Yes, but Kiyomura should've picked his victim more carefully," said Samejima in a low voice. "Suzaki was very upset and hasn't spoken a word since."

"I can understand that."

Utayama looked over at Suzaki, who was still in the armchair, reading his book. A pair of black-rimmed glasses were perched on his nervous-looking face. He had a skinny frame and a stoop, and wore a brown sweater. Utayama tried to imagine how Suzaki would've reacted to Kiyomura's acting, but he just couldn't visualize it.

"And Hayashi hasn't arrived yet?" Utayama asked. It was almost half-past four. Samejima nodded, taking out a cigarette box. Keiko frowned.

"Oh, excuse me."

The critic noticed Keiko's disapproval just as Utayama was about to say something and hurriedly put the cigarette away. Utayama bowed in thanks.

"Second-hand smoke isn't great when you're pregnant, is it?" said Samejima, smiling at Keiko, who was wearing a blue maternity dress. "What is it, six months now?"

"I'm due in August," Keiko replied.

"How wonderful. Do you know if it's a boy or a girl? They can check for that with ultrasound these days, I think?"

"Oh, no, we decided to let it be a surprise."

"How is Yōji doing, by the way?" Utayama asked in turn.

"Oh, he… he's doing fine, thanks," said the critic, looking slightly troubled. Yōji was Samejima's only son and had turned nine this year. Utayama had met him once. Yōji had been born with a severe intellectual disability and other physical problems. He was taken care of at a nursing home.

"Physically, he has grown a lot stronger. But I've been raising him all by myself, so of course, I'm always worried about his emotional growth…"

"Oh, it must be difficult for you…" Utayama, realizing he was touching upon a sensitive subject, quickly tried to change the topic. "Have you not seen Mr Miyagaki yet?"

"No," Samejima replied, carefully putting the cigarette box away in a blazer pocket. "I arrived at three, but he hasn't shown up yet."

"Oh, that's odd," said Utayama. Then recalling the second car parked inside the gate, "How did you travel here from Tokyo?"

"I took the Shinkansen train to Kyōto yesterday, where I stayed for the night. And then I travelled here this morning."

"By local train?"

"Of course… why?" Samejima raised a quizzical eyebrow.

"Did someone else arrive here by car?"

"I don't think so. I'm sure Suzaki doesn't have a licence, and Kiyomura and Madoka mentioned they came by taxi."

"I thought so." Utayama crossed his arms, and then considered the last possibility. "Does that housekeeper live here too?"

"I don't think so. I think Mr Miyagaki told me she lives in the village."

"So she comes by car?"

"By car… Oh!" Samejima finally seemed to realize what had been bothering Utayama. "You're thinking of that Corolla outside."

"Yes. I was wondering whose car that was."

"I've been wondering about that myself, but Kadomatsu Fumie—the housekeeper—normally comes here on foot."

"She walks here?" put in Keiko. "Isn't it quite far?"

"I believe she sometimes stays here if it's raining or snowing, or Mr Miyagaki will drive her back home."

"Yes, that'd make sense."

"I see," muttered Utayama. "So that means—"

Just then Funaoka Madoka cut in:

"What are you three talking about?"

Funaoka Madoka was thirty years old, the same age as Kiyomura. She was small, but her very voluptuous proportions were set off by her black dress. Her long black hair hung down to her breasts. When she had made her debut five years ago, she had attracted a lot of attention as a young, attractive female author, but her career had stalled somewhat since.

"We were just wondering who owns that Corolla parked outside," Utayama explained.

"Isn't it the secretary's car?"

"I think Ino drives a Prelude," Samejima said.

Madoka shrugged. "What then? Is there someone else here besides us?"

"It seems so."

The kitchen door opened, and in came the housekeeper, Kadomatsu Fumie, carrying a tray set with cups of tea. She placed it on the table where Shimada and Kiyomura were seated before heading back to the kitchen without a word. Utayama had wanted to ask her about the other guest, but was put off by her cold, aloof demeanour.

At that moment, the sound of a bell rang in the reception room. Someone was at the main door. Fumie had almost reached the kitchen door, but upon hearing the bell she headed towards the double doors of the reception room.

"It must be Hayashi," Madoka said, looking over at Kiyomura.

Kiyomura of course got up from his seat with a grin, and quickly slipped into the kitchen. He needed to "borrow" some blood-ketchup.

Hayashi Hiroya was the youngest of the invited writers, at twenty-seven. He was a small, quiet young man, with a timid demeanour: the perfect victim for Kiyomura's prank.

Madoka sighed. "Are you really going to do it again? What a child you are!"

5

Hayashi Hiroya, plump, moustachioed and curly haired, wearing a shabby coat, naturally became the third victim. Then, with all the guests now present, they enjoyed the tea Kadomatsu Fumie had prepared for them, while they were awaiting the master of the Labyrinth House.

However, by five o'clock there was still no sign of Miyagaki, or of his secretary, Ino Mitsuo.

"I find it hard to believe not even Ino has come to welcome us..." Utayama said, somewhat worried, but Samejima quickly corrected him.

"He did put his head in once, soon after I arrived."

"Oh. What did he say?"

"Nothing in particular. But now I think about it, he seemed somewhat flustered."

"Did something happen perhaps?" Utayama wondered out loud.

"Like what?"

"What if Mr Miyagaki's suddenly fallen ill?"

Utayama suddenly recalled the self-mocking smile on the author's face when he had spoken about the state of his health three months ago. "The worst," he'd called it.

"That's possible," agreed Samejima gloomily. "Early last month, Mr Miyagaki invited me over and I visited him here. He seemed to be in pain."

Samejima Tomoo was a writer with a consistent output of intelligent literary criticism and reviews. Of all the guests, Utayama thought Miyagaki probably trusted the critic the most. Utayama had heard stories of how the two had once spent a whole summer together here in the Labyrinth House, having heated discussions about the murder mystery genre that lasted through the night. Samejima was three years younger than Suzaki, at thirty-eight, but had actually become acquainted with Miyagaki before any of his other disciples. Miyagaki had heaped praise on one of the critic's pieces in *Reverie*, which had then gone on to win the magazine's first Newcomer Award in the literary criticism category ten years previously. Since then Samejima had left a high-school teaching job in the capital and embarked on this new career.

Samejima was slender and of average build, with a fine-boned, intellectual-looking face and neatly parted hair. Some years ago, the critic might have been taken for a very handsome young man indeed, if only Samejima had made a little more effort to dress fancier.

"When I saw him over New Year, he did seem very tired and defeatist," Utayama said.

"He was the same last month," Samejima said. "He's not getting any younger and was even talking about what would happen after his death."

"What was he saying exactly?"

"Just how he wanted to establish the Miyagaki Prize again. He wanted to bequeath his entire fortune to fund the award."

Utayama had heard about the Miyagaki Prize before too. The great Edogawa Rampo had himself set up a literary prize bearing his own name, which was run by the Mystery Writers of Japan. Miyagaki wanted to have his name immortalized in the form of an award too.

"His entire fortune? That must be quite the sum…"

"Indeed. He owns land in Tokyo as well as everything else, so it should be at least a billion yen…"

"Wow!" broke in Keiko, an astonished look on her face. "Doesn't he have any family?"

"Don't think so," Utayama said.

Keiko smiled mischievously. "Over a billion yen… Imagine if there was a struggle over his inheritance, leading to murder…"

"Haha, that's a good one."

It was already long past five when the secretary, Ino Mitsuo, finally appeared, emerging from the door in the right side of the back wall of the reception room.

"I am terribly sorry for the long wait."

Ino's stiff, but clearly articulated voice echoed through the large room. The somewhat chubby secretary was wearing a grey suit and his thin hair was neatly side-parted. The first impression he gave was that of a very businesslike, serious person.

"Something unexpected has occurred… I have been considering what to do until now. I am very sorry."

"Something unexpected?" Suzaki Shōsuke repeated. He was

seated closest to the door Ino had come through. This was the first time Utayama had heard him speak since his arrival.

"What happened?"

Ino nodded deeply, and slowly looked at the faces of all eight guests in the reception room with his small, elephantine eyes, before his gaze dropped to his feet. Then, very slowly, he began to speak: "This morning, Mr Miyagaki ended his own life."

CHAPTER TWO

A CONTEST: THE LABYRINTH HOUSE MURDERS

1

The murmuring in the reception room was suddenly replaced by a deathly silence.

In the armchair, Suzaki Shōsuke had looked up from the book in his lap. His eyes behind the rimmed glasses could only blink in shock. Hayashi Hiroya, hunched over the table, gawped, open-mouthed. Kiyomura Junichi rose halfway out of his seat. Shimada Kiyoshi, sitting next to Kiyomura, stopped fiddling with his fingers and stared at Ino Mitsuo.

The guests next to the Utayamas on the sofa reacted similarly. Samejima Tomoo and Funaoka Madoka were both leaning forward in their seats, their eyes fixed on the secretary. The announcement had taken Keiko's breath away, while Utayama, stunned, was staring at Ino. The next moment, he felt both his hands searching inside his jacket pockets as he unconsciously started looking for a cigarette.

"Hahaha…" Kiyomura was the first to speak. He was looking straight at Ino as he pushed himself up from the table. "Ino, too bad, but I am not going to fall for that one."

The secretary raised an eyebrow.

"What do you mean?"

"You can drop the act." Kiyomura showed his white teeth as he smiled at Ino. "We've all had our share of April Fool's jokes today already."

His words instantly lightened the atmosphere in the room. Madoka leant back on the sofa, mumbling about how Kiyomura was the one to talk.

Kiyomura continued: "But it's a bit rude to just ignore this special event thought up by Mr Miyagaki, so let's…"

"I fear you are misunderstanding me." Ino shot a frustrated glare at Kiyomura. He was clearly struggling to keep his composure. He put his fist to his mouth and cleared his throat before going on. "This is not a joke. It might be the first of April today, but I would never play such a distasteful prank."

Kiyomura paled visibly. "But… you mean, you are serious?"

Ino nodded gravely. "I am terribly sorry to inform you, Mr Miyagaki has passed away."

Once again, the room fell silent. What thoughts were passing through the minds of all the guests at that moment?

Utayama carefully prised Keiko's hand from his sleeve and got up from the sofa.

"Sorry, just to be clear. You mean to say, Mr Miyagaki passed away this morning… and he committed suicide?"

"Indeed," the secretary briskly replied.

"You are *sure* it was suicide?"

"There is absolutely no possibility of a mistake. He was in bed in his bedroom. He had taken a large quantity of his sleeping medicine."

Several long sighs could be heard in the room. Utayama took a step towards Ino. "Did he leave a suicide note?"

"Yes."

"And a doctor? Did you have a doctor examine him?"

"A doctor is present. He wrote out a death certificate."

Utayama immediately thought of the extra car parked outside. It must be the doctor's car.

"And the police?" Suzaki looked up at Ino. "Have you informed them already?"

Ino took a step forward. He looked round at everyone in the room with a troubled expression.

"Regarding that matter… of course, under normal circumstances, a situation like this should be reported at once. However, these are very unusual circumstances, which require some consideration concerning how to act next."

"I'm afraid I don't understand what you mean."

"It's difficult to explain here."

"An unnatural death has occurred in this house and we need to report it to the police," Suzaki said, getting up from his chair. "Where's the telephone?"

But Ino raised his hand to stop him.

"Please wait. You are absolutely correct. The police must be informed. But as I told you just now, the circumstances are rather unusual… Mr Miyagaki himself asked us not to inform the police for the time being."

"He did what?"

"How? What do you mean?" Madoka got up from the sofa now too.

"Please, calm down," Ino said in response to the barrage of questions. "I can't explain the circumstances here. I would like to ask you to join me in Mr Miyagaki's study. I shall explain everything there."

"I can't believe it," Utayama heard Shimada Kiyoshi mutter. As the lean man got to his feet, he threw something black on the table in front of him.

61

"And I had promised to teach him how to make one of these…"

The thing on the table had two arms and two legs, horns and a spear-like tail. A pair of wings spread from its back. Utayama had never before laid eyes upon such a creation, so intricately crafted out of just one sheet of black paper: an origami creature.

2

The group left through the door leading into the interior. Outside the door, the hallway came to a dead end to their right after barely a metre. A life-size bronze statue stood against the wall. A young woman, clothed in ancient Grecian style.

Her left hand rested on her well-endowed chest, while her right stretched forward, palm up. Everyone besides Keiko, who had never visited the house before, knew who this woman was supposed to be.

A rectangular bronze plate was attached at eye level to the dark-purple-painted door of the reception room. On it a name was etched: Ariadne.

Ariadne appeared in the Greek myth of Theseus and the Minotaur. The daughter of King Minos of Crete, she fell in love with the young Athenian Prince Theseus. Before he entered the labyrinth to defeat the Minotaur, the princess gave Theseus a ball of thread so he could find his way out again.

The drawing room in the deepest part of the house was called Minotaur, and this reception room Ariadne. In fact, there were over a dozen rooms in this house named after a character connected to the labyrinth of Minos.

Ino led the way, with the eight guests following him down the dark hallway, which was barely a metre wide. Unlike in the rooms themselves and on the stairs leading from the entrance level, there was no carpet, only bare, dark brown vinyl floor tiles. The high ceiling was made up of square windows, each side as long as the width of the hallway. They were the undersides of the low pyramids made of steel and glass Keiko had seen from above earlier. The low sun shining through the blue-tinted glass told the group it was already dusk.

A twisting maze of hallways took up a large part of the building, forming the labyrinth that gave the house its name.

"It really is like a labyrinth here," Keiko whispered, sticking close to her husband. "I can still hardly believe Mr Miyagaki actually lives in a place like this all by himself…"

She fell suddenly silent in mid-sentence. Of course, she had just been informed of their host's death, but still hadn't fully absorbed the news.

As they walked along the hallways, their footsteps ringing out, it was as if they were walking through a valley flanked by steep, sandy slopes. With the setting sun shining through the windows above, and the internal lights not switched on yet, Utayama was overcome by a strange sensation, as if this weren't the Labyrinth House he had visited before. He almost felt as if he had truly wandered into an unknown labyrinth.

His thoughts turned to its owner, and his sudden suicide…

Utayama thought back to what Miyagaki had said to him three months ago. Miyagaki had told him he had no intention of becoming the world's oldest living person. Utayama wondered if, back then, he was already thinking about what had happened today. He also couldn't help thinking about Ino's strange announcement.

Ino seemed very calm. That might just be his manner, but why had he waited so long to tell them? What had he been thinking about all this time? And what did he mean when he said Miyagaki himself had asked them not to inform the police?

The light faded increasingly quickly from the windows above. They turned right, left… and so on until eventually the party arrived at their destination: Miyagaki Yōtarō's study.

Before them was a sturdy-looking dark brown door. Like the door to the reception room, it bore a bronze nameplate. This one read: Minoss.

King Minos ordered the architect and inventor Daedalus to create the labyrinth. For some reason, an extra "s" had been added to the name on the plate. It must be a mistake.

Ino pushed the door open. The guests silently followed him into the room with heavy hearts.

The room was spacious, but gloomy. There were two doors: in the right rear and the left rear corners. The right door led to the bathroom and toilet, the other to the bedroom.

Ino felt along the wall to the left of the doorway and flicked a switch. Lantern-shaped lights affixed to all four walls filled the room with a yellow glow. This finally released Utayama from the illusion that he had been wandering in an unfamiliar labyrinth.

"Please, it's this way," Ino said, as he proceeded to the back of the room and opened the door on the left. The lights in the bedroom were already on.

The guests glanced at each other. They were all apprehensive about what would confront them.

"Please," Ino repeated, standing next to the door. Samejima was the first to go through. Kiyomura followed with a resigned look on his face, then Shimada. Hand in hand, Utayama and Keiko entered the room last.

"Sorry for the wait, Doctor," Ino said as he shut the door behind him.

The man he spoke to was standing in the back of the room, next to the bed, in front of a full-length mirror fixed to the wall.

"This is Dr Kuroe Tatsuo. He's the head of the Department of Internal Medicine of Miyazu's N— Hospital. He's the physician who has been taking care of Mr Miyagaki these last few months."

The man gave a shallow bow of greeting. He was somewhat overweight and looked to be in his fifties or thereabouts. He wore a white coat over his bulging body. His head was egg-shaped, and balding, and he examined all the guests with round, friendly-looking eyes as they came into the room.

"I am terribly sorry to have to inform you of the sad news," he said in a hoarse voice, and glanced at the bed. "Mr Miyagaki was the last person I would ever have expected to commit an act like this…"

A human form could be seen lying under the duvet. A white sheet covered the head resting on the pillow. Kuroe's hand reached out towards the sheet. Utayama looked on silently, noticing a glass and a bottle filled with white pills on the bedside table, alongside the writer's gold-rimmed glasses and various other objects.

Kuroe pulled the sheet away.

"Oh… no…" Madoka groaned. Sighs and gasps could be heard in the room.

Utayama thought Miyagaki looked very peaceful. But he could not understand why the aged writer had gone this far.

Looking at the closed eyes, Utayama placed his fingertips on his own eyelids, fighting against the tears welling up behind them.

3

The party returned to the study. Ino Mitsuo stood before them.

"Allow me to explain. This is very important, so please listen carefully."

A magnificent-looking desk was up against the right wall (seen from the entrance) of the room. On it stood a black telephone and a word processor. Ino pulled out a leather chair from the desk and offered it to Kuroe.

"Please have a seat, Doctor."

He then addressed the rest of the party:

"This will be rather complicated, so please make yourselves comfortable. I am afraid there are not enough chairs in this room for all of you, however."

There was a small table with two stools against the wall opposite the desk. Utayama urged his wife to sit down, while he himself leant against the wall. The second stool was taken by Suzaki Shōsuke who sat on it hunched over, his back rounded. The other five guests stood scattered about, forming a semi-circle around Ino.

"Now, I shall explain everything in order," the secretary went on. "First, regarding how I found Mr Miyagaki's body this morning…"

Ino neatly folded his hands in front of his stomach and looked at the guests as he began his account.

"I arrived here two nights ago, to prepare for today's party and to take care of other arrangements. Yesterday, I was busy the whole day with tasks like preparing your rooms and going food shopping, so I wasn't able to talk properly with Mr Miyagaki. But looking back now, I do think he was acting somewhat curiously. He was pale and barely spoke to me. At the time, I simply assumed he was not feeling well, and hoped he'd be better in time for the party.

"Last night, Mr Miyagaki retired to his room at eleven o'clock. Before he went, he made sure I was aware of everything I had to take care of today.

"This morning, when he hadn't emerged from his room by noon, I began to worry. At that moment, Dr Kuroe arrived. I had met him before and I knew Mr Miyagaki would occasionally go to the hospital in Miyazu for a check-up."

Utayama was shocked by this, because he knew Miyagaki hated going to doctors. He realized Miyagaki's situation must have been far graver than any of them had known.

"The doctor told me Mr Miyagaki had called him at home last night, asking him to come here at noon. That is correct, Doctor, is it not?"

Kuroe gave a slow nod.

"Indeed. At first, I was rather reluctant to come, because I was needed at the hospital today, but he was very insistent. He pressed the matter so strongly, I couldn't refuse. Because…" Here he paused for a moment to think. "I might as well tell you now, considering the circumstances. You see, Mr Miyagaki was suffering from his lungs… he had cancer. It was in a very advanced state, with an extremely small chance of him making a recovery. He himself was aware of his condition."

Utayama thought back to three months ago, when the writer had coughed every time he smoked a cigarette. So he had had lung cancer…

"When the doctor arrived, I came here to the study for Mr Miyagaki. But there was no reply to my knock. The door was locked from the inside. I returned to the reception room and made a call to the study. But he didn't answer the phone either. I started to fear something had happened, so I used my spare key to let myself in. And in the bedroom, I found Mr Miyagaki lying in his bed, like you just saw…

"I immediately summoned the doctor, but it was already too late for any help. Near the pillow, next to the bottle of sleeping pills he used to commit the act, was a suicide note, which I have here."

The secretary took a white envelope from the inner pocket of his suit and showed it to everyone.

"The envelope was addressed to me. It is without any doubt Mr Miyagaki's. The letter itself was written on a word processor, but it is signed by hand at the end and dated today."

Inside the envelope was a sheet of paper folded in four. The secretary carefully unfolded it and read the contents out loud:

"I have chosen my own death, at my own hand. Do not panic. Do not inform the police at once. Dr Kuroe should have arrived at the house by the time you read this. Have him act as a witness and listen to the cassette tape on the desk. Everything I wish for after my death, has been recorded on that tape. Follow my instructions.

  "Signed 1st April 1987. Miyagaki Yōtarō."

Ino then suggested they all read the note for themselves. He handed the envelope and letter to Kiyomura, who was standing the closest.

"… Yes, this is his handwriting…" Kiyomura nodded with a grim look and handed them on to Hayashi.

An oppressive silence filled the room as they were passed around.

Eventually, the note and envelope were returned to Ino. The secretary placed them on the desk, from where he picked up a cassette tape.

"You have read the note. This is the tape mentioned in it. I'll ask you to listen to it now."

Audio-visual equipment had been set up on customized wooden racks on the wall opposite the entrance. The racks also held an enormous number of records, CDs and VHS tapes. Miyagaki had been a great fan of classical music and films and was proud of this collection.

Ino removed the tape from its case and briskly walked to the rack. He switched on the amplifier and placed the tape in the cassette deck.

A second later, a voice came abruptly from the speakers. They all tensed as they recognized the voice of the master of the Labyrinth House: Miyagaki Yōtarō.

"Dear all. By the time you listen to this message, I will no longer be an inhabitant of your world. For once I have finished recording this message, I plan, of my own free will, to end my life.

"Dr Kuroe may already have informed you that I am suffering from cancer. I first found out about my condition after an examination in September last year. I feel terribly sorry for Dr Kuroe, who informed me of my illness and so strongly believed in me, but I do not intend to try to live on and fight against a disease I have so little chance of beating. It is already too late for an operation, so at best I can only hope to extend my life slightly through radiation treatment or anti-cancer drugs. However, it is against my own philosophy of life to cling so desperately to the little time left to me. Therefore, I have decided to end my own life on the morning of my sixtieth birthday. We all have to face whatever is coming to us."

The voice broke off for a brief chuckle.

"Anyway. I have accepted my approaching demise. But there are two matters that still weigh heavily on my mind. The first is the question of who should inherit my rather sizeable estate. The other concerns four of you present here: Suzaki, Kiyomura, Funaoka and Hayashi.

"I shall explain myself on this second matter first. I am in a way a very prideful person. I like to think that when it comes to the love and dedication I have shown towards my profession these past forty years, I have no equal.

"The literary form that is the detective story, originated by Poe and since developed through the contributions of countless fellow writers, is something I cherish more than anything else. You may think I sound conceited, but I have devoted my whole life to the creation of this wonderful form of literature. At the same time, I also pride myself on having spent a lot of my time and energy looking for those worthy to be my successor.

"The four of you I have invited here for my sixtieth birthday, Suzaki, Kiyomura, Funaoka and Hayashi: you are my favourites of the many writers who have made their debuts in *Reverie*. However, and this is extremely important to note: do not presume your accomplishments up to now have been enough to satisfy me.

"I do not intend to list my criticisms here, but I will say this: you are all still far from where you need to be. I hope you are all aware of that yourselves. None of you has managed to tap into your true potential yet. As I look at the four of you now, I feel you still have to mature a lot as writers before you will be able to truly make full use of your talents. But when will that day come? This is one of the matters that have been troubling me."

The four writers exchanged uneasy glances.

"I shall now address the other matter of concern: my estate. I do not know its exact worth, but I am still in possession of the properties in Tokyo left to me by my parents, so I trust it will be quite considerable. Another property of mine is, of course, the Labyrinth House. I won't mention how much it cost to build the house, though I can imagine a curious building like this might have trouble finding a buyer. In any case, taking into account those properties together with my securities, bank savings and the rights to my books, I believe my estate will easily amount to several billion yen.

"However, as you all know, I have no living relatives. Nor have I have ever been married. That is why, for some time now, I have said that after my death my estate shall be used to fund and manage a literary prize bearing my own name. I had been planning to get started on the practicalities of arranging that soon. However, I now wish to alter my plans somewhat.

"I wish to use half of my legacy to fund the prize as mentioned earlier. However, I wish to leave a bequest of the other half to one person.

"I have not decided yet who this person shall be. The candidates must be judged first.

"I can imagine the puzzled looks on your faces as you hear this. Allow me to explain myself. The real reason I invited you here, on the pretext of celebrating my sixtieth birthday, is to determine which of you shall inherit half of my fortune. And you yourselves will make that decision for me. The candidates are of course the four previously mentioned, whose future careers I am concerned about: Suzaki, Kiyomura, Funaoka and Hayashi."

71

The voice paused for a second, as if Miyagaki was savouring the looks on the four writers' faces at that very moment.

"What does he mean?" Madoka asked, looking around the room in shock. "What… does he want us to do?"

"There's more," Ino said, cutting her off. "Please listen first, and you can ask questions later."

"Imagine how pleased I was with myself when the idea first came to me! An entirely new kind of game. The plan made me realize my grey matter still had something of worth left in it.

"Now it is time to explain myself properly. This is what I want you to do after… after you have found me.

"One: Inform the police of my suicide five days from now, at noon on the sixth of April. Do not allow any outsiders to enter the house until then. I trust my body will not decompose too badly in a mere five days.

"Two: During those five days, nobody is to take even one step outside the house, save for Ino and Dr Kuroe. Some of you may have plans—I am particularly sorry for the ever-busy Utayama—but I hope you will manage. I have also asked my housekeeper Kadomatsu Fumie to remain in the house from the first until the sixth. Dr Kuroe, I ask you to respect the wishes of a dead man and not inform anyone of this affair until noon on the sixth of April. I thank you.

"Three: During these five days, the judging and selection of my heir shall be carried out. The candidates are the four persons mentioned earlier.

"Each of the four candidates shall, during this period—which, to be exact, lasts from now until ten o'clock on the evening of the fifth of April—write a story, which will be your entry for the judging process. The four completed works shall

72

be read by my editor Utayama, the professional critic Samejima and Shimada, who is to act as the 'representative' of the general fan of the mystery genre. These three shall judge all the works by noon on the sixth of April. The author who is judged the best shall be appointed heir to my estate. The judges..."

A murmur spread through the room. The unexpected contents of the recording had caught everyone by surprise.

"Quiet, please," Ino said, and paused the tape.

"Ino, this is just too crazy..." Utayama said.

The secretary blinked his small eyes. "I agree this is quite a shocking story. But I implore you to listen to the end. The most important part is still to come."

He rewound the tape a few seconds, and then hit play.

"... shall be appointed heir to my estate. The judges shall of course also be rewarded for their efforts.

"Four: The required length of the written work is roughly fifty pages. I would have preferred a full-length novel, but considering the specific circumstances, I can't be too demanding. Fifty pages in five days. Some might find that a lot to write; others will find it easy. Suzaki, for example, who is a slow writer, might struggle. When it comes to my own writing pace, incidentally, I would like to offer the excuse that there's a difference between a slow writer and a writer who simply doesn't publish much.

"Five: The theme of the work. I'm sure I don't need to tell you that I want you to write a detective story. The judging shall also be conducted based on that criterion. But I have a few more conditions to add.

"Ah, yes, now we come to what might be the most interesting point of this contest. First of all, the story must be set in this house, the Labyrinth House. Furthermore, you are to use the people gathered in this house today as characters in your story. That includes myself, Miyagaki Yōtarō. You can decide for yourself if you want to include me dead or alive.

"One final condition relating to the theme: the mystery at the centre of the story must be a murder, and every author must be the victim in their own story.

"What do you think? Sounds fun, doesn't it? You'll write a detective story set in the curious building you are in at this very moment, and you'll be the victim in your story. An irresistible idea! I only regret I won't be able to read your stories myself.

"Now, where was I? Seven… no, six: You must write your stories on the word processors prepared for you in your rooms. This is to ensure that identification of your handwriting does not affect the reception of your stories. I believe all four of you have started using word processors for your work lately anyway, so using them here should not pose any problems for you.

"I assume you all understand that if any foul play is detected, the offender will be immediately disqualified. Leaving the house during the designated period will be considered a contravention of the rules. Furthermore, if even one person decides to not participate in this contest or refuses to cooperate, the contest will be cancelled, and this testament will be void.

"The proper legal documents that guarantee all I have explained now have already been prepared and are in my safe. I hereby request Ino to confirm the contents and promptly arrange for the contest to start.

"Anyway… it's been a long time since I have spoken so much. I feel rather exhausted.

"I hope from the depths of my heart you will dedicate all your talent and skill to winning what might be the biggest prize ever awarded for a story. I shall await you in the nether-world."

4

Ino stopped the tape and pushed the rewind button. All ten people in the room were silent this time; eight were slowly repeating the terms of Miyagaki's will in their minds and watching each other.

When Ino had finished rewinding the tape, he removed it from the cassette deck and put it back in its case. He then turned to the party.

"The situation is as you have all just heard. I was delayed in telling you about Mr Miyagaki's death because I had to consider the contents of the tape myself. I have gone through the documents mentioned at the end of the recording. The legal arrangements are all in place."

Ino had first been employed in his late twenties by Miyagaki Yōtarō, and had been his loyal secretary for almost a decade now. Not only was he utterly devoted to his employer, he was also qualified as a solicitor, though he chose not to work as one as he found the profession didn't suit him. He was usually employed at a tutorial college in Tokyo that focused on the bar examination.

"As Mr Miyagaki's secretary, I feel it's my obligation to do everything I can to make his last wishes come true. I had Dr Kuroe listen to the tape earlier, and he was kind enough to agree to cooperate."

"Of course, I have never before been involved in such a peculiar business..." Kuroe said. He placed the brown bag he had been resting on his knees on the floor. "I want to respect the wishes of the deceased as much as I can. Even if I do feel a bit apprehensive about the whole thing."

"I will ensure you do not suffer any problems once the affair is concluded," Ino said confidently. "This is a unique case, and I think the authorities will realize that too once I have explained it to them."

Ino returned to the desk and placed the cassette tape on top of the envelope, then looked around at the guests.

"If you have any questions, feel free to ask them now."

A few people opened their mouths. Utayama was one of them. There were lots of things he wanted to ask, but he couldn't seem to put his questions into words. The others seemed to be having similar difficulties.

Eventually, Madoka spoke up. "I'm scheduled to appear on television the day after tomorrow… It's my first time, so I was looking forward to it…"

"A TV appearance?" Kiyomura asked scornfully. "My dear Ms Funaoka, I hope you realize what's more important here."

"There's no need to talk to me like that," Madoka retorted with a red face. "I know what you're getting at: you want to remind me how much money is at stake here."

"I'm pleased to see you do understand after all."

"Don't patronize me. I understand, but… this isn't normal. To decide where so much money goes, based on a mere fifty pages."

"But don't you think it's just the kind of thing you'd expect of Mr Miyagaki? Of course, I'm shocked by his suicide, too, but he was never one to simply die and… anyway, we should be honoured Mr Miyagaki has such high hopes of us." Kiyomura pushed himself away from the wall where he had been leaning, and turned to Ino. "Of course we'll take part in the game. Absolutely. Suzaki, Hayashi, you don't have any objections, do you?"

"I'd like to hear from the two gentlemen themselves," the secretary said.

Suzaki, still hunched over on the stool, simply nodded. Hayashi assented too, stroking his moustache pensively.

"And now for our judges." Kiyomura looked at Samejima, Shimada and Utayama in that order. "I assume you will all be happy to oblige?"

Samejima nodded, with eyes closed:

"If this is what he wanted, all I can do is follow his wishes."

Kiyomura then turned to look enquiringly at Shimada, who was leaning against the bedroom door.

"I don't have anywhere else I need to be, so okay," the priest's son agreed. "But I have to admit, this is quite the responsibility..."

"Excellent. And how about you?" Kiyomura asked Utayama.

"Well, I..." Utayama hesitated, glancing over at Keiko. Ino noticed the look.

"Are you worried about your wife?" the secretary asked.

"Yes, that's it," the editor replied.

"Let me see... Yes, I think we can consider your wife an exception, as no role in the contest has been specified for her. She can leave the house with Dr Kuroe if she wishes to do so."

"No, I'll be fine," Keiko spoke up. "I've come all this way, I'm not going back all alone, I'd feel awful. I'll be all right."

"All settled then!" said Kiyomura in high spirits. The shock of what they had seen in the bedroom had now been completely swept away by the unexpected turn of events.

"A contest: The Labyrinth House Murders. And with perhaps the biggest prize sum ever awarded for a story to boot. The old man really was a genius!"

CHAPTER THREE

EVENING

1

Ino locked the double stone entrance doors once Kuroe Tatsuo had left the house. He also locked the lattice door in the upper entrance hall, at the top of the stairs leading down to the house.

Next, the guests began hurriedly reorganizing their plans until the sixth. For some time, the phone in the reception room was in near-constant use, mainly for long-distance calls to Tokyo.

It was nearly seven in the evening when all of the guests were finished, and Ino summoned them to the table in the middle of the room.

"Please gather round, everyone. Did any of you have trouble rearranging your schedules? No? Glad to hear it. Now, I have a few points that require your attention. Please have a seat."

Ever since he had appeared in the reception room less than two hours ago, Ino had been very calm, as precise and careful in word as in deed. Was it simply because he was keen to make sure his master's will was executed as instructed, out of a sense of professionalism? No, Ino's attitude must also have owed something to a sympathy with Miyagaki Yōtarō's outlook and his projects. Or, to use a grander word: ideology.

Whatever the case, Utayama couldn't help but be impressed by how composed Ino was. He felt a newfound respect for the loyal secretary, who was quite a bit younger than Utayama himself.

But, of course, the most impressive person in this affair was the man who had come up with this incredible inheritance game: Miyagaki Yōtarō.

"First of all, the rooms you are to stay in have already been decided. Mr Suzaki, Mr Kiyomura, Ms Funaoka and Mr Hayashi—you will find identical-model word processors in your rooms. You should also find three floppy disks for saving your manuscripts and 500 sheets of B5 printer paper, along with an instruction manual for your word processor. If anything is missing, please let me know.

"As for your rooms: the layout of this house is rather complicated, so I have marked their locations on floor plans."

Ino got the copies out of his black briefcase, and handed one to each guest.

The map was printed on an A4-sized sheet of paper and annotated in neat handwriting to show who was staying where. Utayama and Keiko were in Poseidon and Dionysus, two rooms on the eastern side of the Labyrinth House and closest to the reception room.

"I believe you have all stayed in the house before, apart from Mrs Utayama. Most of you will already be familiar with the following, therefore, but allow me to explain just in case.

"Each room has its own toilet. There is a communal bathroom adjoining this reception room, which you are free to use at any time. The library, drawing room and games room are also accessible day and night. However, the study shall be kept locked, so is off-limits.

"All meals shall be served here in the reception room: breakfast at ten o'clock, lunch at one and supper at eight. I understand that for some of you this schedule might differ from your usual habits, so I apologize for the inconvenience. You may help yourselves to any and all of the drinks in the sideboards in the reception room and the drawing room.

"I have locked the entrance doors and will look after the key, but allow me to stress once again: please do not leave the house on your own. We do not want to go against the terms of Mr Miyagaki's will for some trivial matter. If a pressing situation does arise, I urge you to contact me first. Is this clear?"

Keiko poked her husband and whispered: "Hey."

"What?"

"I didn't bring that much spare underwear with me."

Ino overheard her, and spoke to the whole group, as if in response to her concern: "I shall leave by car tomorrow to do some shopping. Please write a list of any necessary items you wish me to buy. I shall be happy to purchase them for you."

The secretary then glanced at the gold mantel clock on the sideboard.

"For now, you may wish to settle into your rooms. The keys have been left in the doors. Supper will be ready at eight, so please be back here by then."

2

At this point, it becomes necessary to briefly explain the layout of that curious building, the Labyrinth House. (See Figure 1.)

The above-ground entrance building, the staircase and the reception room (Ariadne) are all located in the southern part of the house. On the other side, the northern end, is the drawing room named Minotaur. To the west of the drawing room is the games room, to the east the library, named after the architect of the Labyrinth of Minos and his father, respectively, Daedalus and

Eupalamus. The study and bedroom named after King Minos adjoin the library.

Eleven more rooms encircle the labyrinth, four on the eastern side, seven on the western. As mentioned earlier, each is named after a character connected the myth. To get from one room to another, it is necessary to enter the labyrinth. This is why each room has its own toilet. Polycaste, the room usually used by the housekeeper, is the odd one out, as it can only be accessed through the kitchen and is not directly connected to the labyrinth.

After Ino had finished his explanation, all the guests picked up their luggage to leave the reception room, with the copies of the floor plan in their hands. Some of them had visited the house more than a few times, but of course none had completely memorized the convoluted labyrinth. Without a map, they would get lost sooner or later.

Keiko started to get up from the table, but Utayama told her to wait until the other guests were gone. It was obvious there'd be a traffic jam in the cramped hallways if they all went out at the same time.

When the room had cleared, Utayama and Keiko finally left too. Outside the door they found someone still in the hallway: Shimada Kiyoshi. He stood there, slowly swaying his sports bag back and forth, as he looked at the bronze statue to the right of the door.

"Is something the matter?" Utayama asked.

"Oh, no, it's just…" Shimada gestured towards the statue with the hand that was holding the floor plan. "I assume this is Princess Ariadne, from the Greek minotaur myth."

"Yes, I think so."

"Hmm... Well, I was looking at her hand," Shimada said, softly touching her fingers with his own. "She's holding it out with the palm up, as if offering something."

"Yes."

"Don't you think that's odd? I mean, she's not holding anything. Shouldn't she be holding out the ball of thread to give to Theseus?"

"Aha, I see what you mean. But perhaps this is the moment after she has given him the ball of thread?"

"Hmm... After she's given it to him...?" Shimada mumbled somewhat hesitantly, stroking his chin. When the Utayamas started to walk on, he too finally stepped away from the statue and followed them.

From the reception room, the three first turned left, and then immediately right again. Then they continued straight on at the first intersection, down a long corridor leading northwards. There were wall lights on both sides, but their illumination was weak, and the corridor was dim. As they walked, they looked up at the ceiling. Through the glass pyramids, they could see the dark night sky.

After a while, they came to a right turn, which Utayama and Keiko would need to take to get to their rooms—there were no double rooms in the Labyrinth House, so they would be sleeping separately, albeit in neighbouring rooms.

"Ah, yes. Your room is down that way. Poseidon, isn't it? The god of the sea responsible for the birth of the Minotaur," Shimada said. "Let's see, I'm in Cocalus. So I'll take the next left... Do you know who this Cocalus was?"

"He was a king in Sicily who offered shelter to Daedalus."

Shimada was closely examining the floor plan.

"Hmm. There are quite a few names here I don't recognize. I'll have to look them up later."

It was probably Miyagaki himself who, with the contest in mind, had decided where everyone was staying. The writers were grouped on the western side of the house, while the judges were on the east, with the exception of Shimada, who was on the west, presumably simply because there were fewer rooms on the east.

After they had bid him goodbye, Keiko took her husband softly by the hand.

"What's the matter?" Utayama asked, to which she replied weakly:

"Knowing Mr Miyagaki's still in his room, I…"

"Oh," he gasped, and felt his heart sink again. What with all the strange developments surrounding the will, he had completely forgotten the harsh reality of Miyagaki's death. In his mind, he recalled the peaceful look on his face.

"And the more I think about what's happening now," Keiko went on, "the more I realize how unusual it all is."

"Are you afraid?"

"I don't think so," Keiko said, stopping and looking around her. "But walking down these hallways I get the feeling there's something lurking somewhere. It's all a bit creepy. Take those masks for example…"

White plaster masks hung from the walls here and there. The faces of youths, old men, women, beasts… Perhaps it was a trick of the light, but it seemed as if all those faces with their white eyes were staring at them blankly. Perhaps they were meant to act as guides through the labyrinth, but they weren't exactly cheery decorations.

The couple quickened their pace.

"The person my room's named after, Dionysus…" Keiko ventured after a moment. "Who is that?"

"He's the god of wine-making, believed by the Greeks to be the first person in the world to make wine. He's also known by the name Bacchus."

"Oh, yeah, I've heard that name."

"Do you know the myth of the Minotaur?"

"Yes, more or less."

"After Theseus defeated the monster in the labyrinth, he fled to Crete together with Ariadne, but he then abandoned her there. In another story, Dionysus appears on the island and takes Ariadne as his wife."

"Oh. Those myths are quite confusing, aren't they?"

"It's the same with our Japanese myths, and those from all over the world—lots of convoluted relationships. Oh, well, I guess that's why there are enough characters related to the Minotaur myth to name all these rooms after them. Perhaps you could ask Suzaki to fill you in on the topic later?"

"He does look like he knows his stuff. But I don't think I'd get along with him. He's a bit gloomy."

Utayama accompanied Keiko to her room first, then went to his own. Fortunately, the route between their rooms was quite straightforward, so he didn't feel too bad about being separated from her.

Just as Ino had promised, the key to his door was in the keyhole. It had a small black tag attached to it, on which "Poseidon" was written in white-outlined characters.

Shimada had called the god of the sea the one responsible for the birth of the Minotaur, and that was true in a sense. Pasiphaë, the wife of King Minos, had harboured an abnormal love for the snow-white bull that Poseidon had sent them, and as result, the monstrous Prince Minotaur, part-man, part-bull, was born.

Utayama's guest room was decorated in Western style and at the back, to his right, was the door to the toilet. On the left was a bed, with a desk placed next to it against the near wall. Opposite the other end of the bed, a large full-length mirror was fixed to the wall. The sky beyond the glass ceiling was already dark.

Utayama fished his cardigan out of his bag. It wasn't cold, but he was starting to feel chilly for some reason.

He placed his jacket on the bed and put on his sweater, before examining his face in the mirror. He was swarthy, with boyish features. Dark rings had formed under his bloodshot eyes.

He looked exhausted, he thought. He had been very busy with work lately, and that coupled with his daily drinking… He might not have been as bad as Miyagaki, but he realized now he had been neglecting his health for the past decade.

The face of the old writer, eyes closed, flashed through his mind.

Why had Miyagaki chosen such a sudden death? An unbearable pain filled Utayama's heart. And yet… he couldn't help but wonder what kind of stories would be written under these unusual circumstances. His inner editor was excited, looking forward to what might come.

What would those four writers come up with? And which of them would win the enormous prize?

3

"I'm in trouble… Oh, this won't go well…"

"Oh, shut up. You can complain as much as you like, but there's nothing I can do about it."

"But this is important to me."

"You'll get used to it soon enough. Don't give up now, the game has just only started."

"That's easy for you to say. You always were a fast writer."

"But this game isn't about speed. And, think about Suzaki for example. At least you're not as slow as him, right?"

"I guess not…"

These were the voices of Hayashi Hiroya and Kiyomura Junichi. Their footsteps echoed through the sand-coloured corridors of the labyrinth.

Utayama and Keiko stopped just ahead of a turning and looked at each other.

"But with a keyboard like mine…"

"That's just a minor matter. When it comes to speed, I'm actually faster writing by hand."

"It's not a matter of speed as much as how it really hinders my work…"

"You know, it's actually none of my business anyway. Don't forget, the four of us are rivals now. If it's really a problem, complain to Ino."

The sounds of the pair's voices and footsteps were drawing nearer to the couple, so Utayama stepped out from the corner just as the two writers arrived from their right.

"Hello there, you two. What's going on?" he asked.

"Oh, hi," said Kiyomura. "Hayashi here won't stop complaining, so I told him it won't help crying to me about it."

"What's the matter?"

"Well, you see…"

Hayashi was looking at the floor, scratching manically at his curly hair. "It's about the word processor in my room."

"Yes?"

"We all got the same model, but Hayashi's having problems with his," Kiyomura explained.

Utayama nodded. "I see. I seem to remember you usually use a word processor to write, don't you?"

"Yes, I do, and I've got pretty good at touch-typing too, even if I do make a mistake now and then," Hayashi said in a weak voice. "That isn't the problem. It's the keyboard. I tested it just now, and there's a problem with some of the keys. A few, like the 'R' key, sometimes seem to get stuck, and the letters don't show up on the screen right away when I hit them. So then I have to bang them a few times before the letter appears."

"Oh, that does sound rather troublesome. I suppose you'll have to pay extra attention to make sure what you type appears on the screen." Utayama then tried to cheer up the frowning young writer. "But the letters do appear eventually, right? I'm sure you'll manage."

"I guess so…" Hayashi said, not very convinced.

Utayama could sympathize with Hayashi's worries, but he also thought his defeatist attitude was exactly his weak point as a writer. Hayashi's mystery works were greatly appreciated for their minute attention to detail and solid writing, but they lacked youthful energy, a reflection of the author's own nature.

The four went into the reception room together. Suzaki and Samejima were already there, chatting on the sofas. Madoka and Shimada had not showed up yet. Fumie was already laying out food on the table.

Ino was sitting in the armchair near the door. Hayashi went over at once and explained the problems he was having with his word processor, but the secretary coldly shook his head.

"I understand of course this might be inconvenient for you, but I'm afraid I am not able to provide you with a replacement at this stage."

Hayashi sighed, his shoulders sagging in dejection.

Kiyomura took the opportunity to mention something to Ino. "Oh, that reminds me, there's no nameplate on the door of my room."

Ino picked up the floor plan from the small table next to him.

"Let me see. You are staying in… ah, yes, Theseus. Last year, the brace from which the plate was hanging started to loosen, so we removed the whole thing from the door altogether and never got around to replacing it. Will that be inconvenient?"

"Oh, no, not really. But earlier, I was a bit confused when I arrived at what I thought was my room but didn't see the nameplate on that door. Fortunately, the name was on the key tag."

"If you like, I could write it down on a sheet of paper for you and—" Ino offered, but Kiyomura cut him off:

"Don't trouble yourself. I'm sure I'll remember the way after I've come and gone a couple of times." Kiyomura licked his thin red lips. "But it's a bit sad knowing the room of the hero who defeated the monster remains nameless."

Utayama had something to ask the secretary too: "Tell me, have you explained what is going on to the housekeeper?"

Ino stole a glance at the kitchen door. "Fumie had already agreed to stay here and prepare our meals until the sixth anyway, so I thought it wise not to tell her about Miyagaki for now."

"Won't she think it odd that he never shows himself?"

"I told her he's staying in bed because he's unwell. I said I'd take his meals to his room."

"I understand. So we'd better watch what we say when she's around."

"Oh, no, I don't think you have to worry too much about her."

At that very moment, the kitchen door opened, and Fumie appeared carrying a tower of plates and bowls.

Ino lowered his voice. "She's a bit hard of hearing. And she's not very interested in us in the first place. Spending five days here might be a bit boring for her, but she can watch television in her room and she's not the type to complain anyway."

"Dinner smells good," Kiyomura said, walking over to the table. "It's eight already, isn't it? Perhaps it's just because of the atmosphere of this place, but I am absolutely famished. Who's missing? Madoka and Shimada?"

That nonchalant shrug of Kiyomura fits his personality perfectly, Utayama thought.

"Oh, look at this," Kiyomura said, as he picked up something from the table and turned around to Utayama. He was holding the black origami figure Shimada had put there earlier.

"Ever see one of these before? I think I saw it in a book once, but never the real thing. It's brilliant."

"Oh, let me see."

Kiyomura approached Utayama, so he could take a closer look at the figure.

"Is it... a devil?"

"It has ears and wings, a mouth, feet and even five fingers on each of its hands. And this is all folded from a single sheet of paper, without cutting it."

"Wow, that is amazing."

Kiyomura balanced the origami devil on his palm and stared at Utayama. "That Shimada's supposed to be representing the general mystery reader, but I wonder how he got to know Mr Miyagaki? Did you hear anything about that?"

"Oh, no, not any specifics."

"I'll have to ask him myself later on then. I'm sure you'll understand that all four of us are very curious as to how reliable our judges are."

4

"Funnily enough, it was the reverse of what happened today," said Shimada in reply to Utayama's question, pouring a generous amount of milk into his coffee. "Mr Miyagaki was having trouble with his car, and I just happened to be passing by."

Utayama had to resist the urge to smoke a cigarette after supper. He leant back slightly in his seat.

"Oh! So you just met by complete accident?"

"Yes. Well, to be honest, I was actually heading towards the Labyrinth House, because I wanted to have a look at it.

"It was December, the season when it pays to be careful driving in the snow, so I had taken the same route as today from Miyazu. And on my way here, I came across a broken-down Mercedes. Not in exactly the same spot as you found me today, of course. I believe Mr Miyagaki must have been on his way back from the hospital."

Shimada took a sip from his coffee, and continued:

"It turned out he just had a flat tyre, but he had difficulty changing it. I'm the type who can't just pass by these things, so I helped him out. Of course, at first I hadn't the faintest idea that I was talking to none other than Miyagaki Yōtarō, but after a while I realized who he was. I recognized him from his photographs in his books.

"And that's how we got acquainted. All I did was give him a helping hand, but he was very grateful, and said that he would like to invite me to his house for dinner, if it was convenient. Seeing that the house had been the whole point of my visit in the first place, and more importantly, it was a dinner invitation from a great writer whose work I had been reading for many years, I of course happily accepted. I even stayed the night here."

"How lucky for you," Kiyomura said with interest. "Mr Miyagaki could be a difficult man at times, so for him to be so friendly to you, I assume there is much more to you than meets the eye."

"Really?" Shimada said, and pouted his thick lips. That seemed to be his way of showing embarrassment. "Anyway, fortunately he did seem interested in what I had to tell him."

"Might that have involved Nakamura Seiji?" Utayama asked.

"Indeed. If Mr Miyagaki did find me interesting, it's only because I spoke to him about Nakamura."

"Could you tell us about him too?"

"Of course, it's not a secret," said Shimada, and sniffed.

"Nakamura Seiji?" said Kiyomura, cocking his head. "I think I've heard that name before. But where?"

"It's the name of the architect of this house," Suzaki responded in a low voice. His elbows were resting on the table, his fingers folded in front of his mouth. His eyes, behind their strong square-rimmed glasses, were fixed on Shimada. This writer seemed interested in Nakamura too.

"You may have heard about the Blue Mansion, the Decagon House and the Mill House," said Shimada. "These buildings were all built by the architect Nakamura Seiji. He passed away a year and a half ago in an incident that occurred in his own residence, the Blue Mansion in Kyūshū."

"I remember now," Madoka cried, one hand raising a cup of coffee to her lips frozen in mid-air. "It was on some island in Ōita Prefecture. Some murder case? Six months later on the same island, in the Decagon House, it happened again…"

Shimada sniffed again. "Yes. And then the Mill House in the mountains of Okayama Prefecture also became the scene of a unique murder case.

"Call it fate, but I happened to be involved in some way in all three incidents. During the one at the Mill House, which came to its conclusion last autumn, I was actually at the house, having been stuck there along with all the others involved. It's a bit embarrassing to say this out loud myself, but I did play a role in solving that case…"

"Wow, this is the first time I've met a real-life 'great detective'," Kiyomura said, clapping his hands with over-the-top excitement.

"Mr Miyagaki said exactly the same thing."

"He must have been thrilled. So I assume you're the capable assistant of your brother the inspector? And now you have travelled all the way here to the Labyrinth House on secret orders, to prevent a tragedy from happening in another of Nakamura's creations?"

Shimada chuckled. "No way. My brother and I honestly are not connected at all when it comes to this matter. I came here purely on my own initiative, and once again I seem to have got tangled up in something.

"After the events at the Mill House last year, I learned that the famous Miyagaki Yōtarō's Labyrinth House was also designed by Nakamura, and couldn't resist coming here to admire it for myself. I am nothing if not nosy."

Utayama nodded as he listened to Shimada's story, imagining the childish delight that must have beamed on Miyagaki's face as he listened to Shimada's tales of detection. The writer would probably have loudly applauded his near-magical origami creations too.

"By the way, what did you do about your car?" Utayama asked, suddenly recalling how they had arrived at the house.

"Oh, I phoned the rest area earlier. I came up with an excuse, so they'll look after my car a bit longer."

Shimada sniffed once again.

"Coming down with a cold?" Utayama asked.

"Perhaps. I hope not."

"Maybe Keiko should have a look at you," Kiyomura said.

Shimada looked at Keiko and her husband in puzzlement:

"Oh, are you a nurse or something?"

"She used to be a doctor, didn't you, Keiko?" Kiyomura butted in.

Shimada looked surprised. "Really?!"

"After medical school I worked in the Ear, Nose and Throat department of a hospital for a while. But I quit after I got married," Keiko said bashfully.

"Oh, you must be very smart."

"I always find it pretty embarrassing when people say that."

"Oh, I–I'm sorry," stammered Shimada. "I'm sure you're not smart really… I mean… Oh, I'm sorry, I didn't mean it like that…"

Keiko laughed as Shimada ruffled his hair in embarrassment.

When Keiko first met Utayama five years ago, she had been losing sleep over her career. Because her grades had been exceptional, she had entered a medical programme at a national university to become a doctor. But once she started working, she found herself unable to cope. The main reason was the pressure of interacting with patients. She'd met her husband around the time she realized she wasn't suited to the profession, and had been seriously considering quitting.

Utayama was not against her quitting after their marriage. The people around them all thought it would have been better if she had carried on working. But seeing how much calmer and more peaceful Keiko had been since giving up her job, Utayama knew it was the right choice.

"Anyway, I think I'll excuse myself for the evening," Suzaki said, getting to his feet. It was half-past ten.

"Are you getting started right away?" Kiyomura queried, shrugging. There was a hint of sarcasm in the way he had asked the question. "We should hold a wake for our beloved Mr Miyagaki tonight. Sit down and have a drink first."

Suzaki ignored Kiyomura and shuffled to the door.

"Oh, boy," Kiyomura said once he had disappeared, suppressing a yawn, "I suppose even someone like him becomes desperate when there's billions of yen at stake."

5

"I'm going to get some rest too."

It was nearly a quarter to eleven o'clock when the secretary announced his departure.

"Please remember to write your shopping lists. I'll see you tomorrow at ten for breakfast."

After the table had been cleared, Kiyomura asked the stony-faced housekeeper to fetch glasses and ice for everyone, before going over to the sideboard and examining the many bottles, a look of glee on his face.

"Don't go drinking too much now. You're on your own if you can't find your way back through the maze," Keiko warned her husband. Utayama didn't quite know how to respond, so settled for rubbing his hands in anticipation.

"Your good lady is right. I don't want to see the caterpillar again either," Madoka laughed.

"The caterpillar? What's that?" Shimada asked.

Madoka pouted her luscious red lips.

"When Utayama here drinks too much, he becomes a caterpillar. Doesn't matter where he is, he suddenly drops on the floor and starts rolling around, saying he's a caterpillar or that he's regressing to his primordial form. I honestly haven't a clue where it comes from…"

"That's… rather unique."

"In Mr Miyagaki's old place in Seijō, there was a pillar we used to tie him to whenever he got too drunk."

"That sounds rather serious," said Shimada, laughing heartily. He had been folding paper again. The figure, at first impossible to make out, had now become a pterodactyl, with outstretched wings. "I myself would quite like to meet this caterpillar."

Utayama tried to temper his expectations.

"They're exaggerating. Don't take them too seriously. Now I'm forty I should watch my drinking."

"Don't forget what you just said," Keiko whispered with a mischievous smile. "Our baby heard you too."

*

By the time Madoka made to leave, it was past eleven.

"You're going already too?"

Kiyomura placed his hand on Madoka's shoulder as she started to rise from her chair. His face was already flushed after a few drinks.

"I can't sit here boozing all night," she replied, shooting a cold look at him and brushing his hand away. She could hold her alcohol quite well—she wasn't flushed at all despite the several drinks she'd knocked back.

"Ah, don't be so cold. Be gentle with me!"

"Oh, don't be such a baby."

"Can I stop by your room later?"

"I'll take that as a bad joke," she said flatly, and got up from the table. "If you do stop by I'll treat you to the sound of my personal alarm."

"Huh? Why did you bring one to this place?"

"Because you never know what could happen. Goodnight, everyone."

Kiyomura watched Madoka leave, a dark look on his face. I'm right about those two, Utayama thought.

Kiyomura and Madoka had been married until the previous summer. They had first met at the Miyagaki residence in Seijō. Madoka had won *Reverie*'s Newcomer Award one year, followed by Kiyomura the next. That had been in the spring four years ago.

Initially, Madoka had been attracted to the smooth-talking, handsome Kiyomura. After a period in which romantic rumours about the two spread, they got married, to the great surprise of their friends and family. But it didn't even last two years.

There were also many rumours about the reason for their divorce. Some said Kiyomura never stopped chasing other women; others pointed at Madoka as the unfaithful one. But ultimately it was her who had wanted the split more. There had been no trouble resolving the financial side of things, but Kiyomura had been very reluctant to agree to the divorce.

Looking at the scene unfolding before him, Utayama suspected Kiyomura still hadn't moved on from Madoka. It was actually the first time he'd seen them together in a long while, he realized.

The cold attitude of his ex-wife seemed to hurt Kiyomura, but eventually he resumed his usual cheerful manner.

"How about a game of pool?" he proposed to Hayashi.

"Now? I was thinking it's about time I got to bed too," said Hayashi, clearly not interested.

"Really?"

"Yes. I have my stubborn word processor to get used to, remember…"

"Hm. Okay, suit yourself," Kiyomura said with a disappointed shrug.

"Will you be all right yourself? You seem to be taking things rather easy. Even for someone like you, it can't be a trivial task to write fifty pages from nothing," said Samejima, who had also been drinking.

Kiyomura grinned.

"Should I consider that a warning from one of our dear judges?"

"Oh, no. Nothing as serious as that."

"No, I get what you mean. But unfortunately, I still haven't come up with the oh-so-important plot for my story. I could go sit at my desk now, but I wouldn't be able to write a single word. That's the type of writer I am. Shimada, how about you then? Just one game."

"Oh, sorry, I don't know how to play pool."

"That is a shame."

Kiyomura downed the remainder of his whisky and water and got up.

"I'll play by myself then. Or perhaps the ghost of Mr Miyagaki will pay me a visit and have a game with me."

6

After Kiyomura had set off for the games room alone, Hayashi retired too.

Once they had gone, Shimada spoke up, in a slow, steady voice:

"Assuming all four manage to submit their stories by the deadline, what criteria do we need to judge their works? I'm sure you'll understand, I have no experience with such things. That's what I'm concerned about. Especially since the inheritance of such a large fortune rests on our decision."

"Of course, it is a big responsibility, but I don't think you should fret about it too much," said Samejima, who was also quite the drinker and not flushed in the face at all. Like Utayama, the critic usually craved nicotine with alcohol, but the pack of cigarettes on the table remained unopened, out of respect for Keiko's condition.

"The evaluation of any work of fiction is to a large extent based on one's personal preferences. I suggest we all frankly share our opinions, and from there we can discuss fully each other's views and arrive at a joint conclusion.

"For example, an often-quoted theory holds that a good mystery story depends on three things: one, the seeming impossibility of the opening; two, the suspense in the middle section; and three, the surprise of the ending. But there are plenty of excellent exceptions to that rule that I can think of. And of course there are elements of writing style that one could consider objective marks of quality, up to a point, but I suspect all of our authors are accomplished enough that their stories will not be lacking in that department."

"That is true," agreed Shimada. "I have read books by all four of them and each has their own unique qualities. But when compared to Mr Miyagaki's works, it feels like they lack something."

"Yes, that must have been what was weighing on his mind. I suppose Utayama here would call that missing element a certain extravagant flourish," Samejima said. Utayama leant forward in his seat and nodded.

"Indeed. I probably shouldn't say this out loud as an editor, but, to put it bluntly, I don't care about how well-rounded a story feels or whether it will sell or not. I also don't have any time for those reviews that only can only pick holes by pointing out minor problems, like how a certain trick wouldn't work in real life, or how the real police conduct investigations differently from how they do it in a book. What matters to me is the degree in which some kind of excessive, over-the-top element in the work resonates with me. In that sense, I think the Japanese mystery writing scene is really in the doldrums at the moment."

Utayama could feel himself getting tipsy, probably because he was tired. He started to speak faster, and began drinking faster too.

He didn't know how to exactly define this notion of an "extravagant flourish" himself, but of the four writers, he had the highest hopes for Suzaki. Would he be able to produce a fifty-page story in five days, though? Considering his incredibly slow writing, it was unlikely.

Although he admitted that Suzaki held the most promise, in such unusual circumstances who could predict what kind of tales the other three would come up with? Perhaps one of them might be able to write an unexpected masterpiece.

"What kind of mystery fiction do you like?" Samejima asked Shimada, who sniffed again.

"I don't have really strong preferences myself. I can enjoy anything, from classic puzzlers to suspense and hardboiled. But if I had to pick one genre, I guess I'd say I'm a *honkaku* fan."

"I see. And which *honkaku* writers do you like?"

"I usually tell people I am a Carr fan. I also like Queen, and Christie. Lately, I've started considering Colin Dexter and P.D. James as must-reads too. But in the end, I always return to Carr. I love the good old atmosphere of the golden age detective story."

"I notice you didn't name any Japanese writers."

"Well, I'm a big fan of Miyagaki Yōtarō."

"Aha."

"I believe you're a Queen devotee yourself?" Shimada asked in return.

"Devotee is putting rather strongly," said Samejima, who, finally unable to resist the urge, took a cigarette out, apologizing to Keiko:

"Forgive me. It'll be just this one cigarette."

Keiko smiled back. "I appreciate your consideration. It's okay, it's a big room."

"Thank you," said Samejima, before lighting it and turning back to Shimada. "It's true that even now, after all this time, I find myself entranced by the meticulous logic displayed in Queen's works. I first read them when I was young and was utterly bowled over. Of course, one has to be careful not to be too focused on logic, and logic alone. To be honest, the analytical structure of the early Queen novels tends to be like a house of cards."

"I think that as a reader, I value surprise over logic," said Shimada. "I can forgive a little bit of unfairness towards the reader, as long there's a big surprise awaiting at the end that turns everything on its head."

"You must enjoy Madoka's short stories then…"

"Of course. And as someone who appreciates intricate logic, I guess you are a fan of Horinouchi… excuse me, I mean Hayashi's style."

Shimada had started to utter Hayashi Hiroya's pen-name. He was well aware of the unspoken rule not to refer to any of the writers by their noms de plume in Miyagaki's home. They were all still following his wish, out of deference to the master of the house.

The three judges continued their discussion of the mystery genre for quite some time. Keiko left just before midnight, and

Utayama escorted her to her room. Then he headed back to the reception room, but got lost a few times.

Just look at yourself, he thought, wandering around a gloomy labyrinth in the dead of night…

The plaster masks on the walls seemed to be watching him with their creepy white eyes as he passed. Perhaps Utayama was simply drunk, but he couldn't help but quicken his pace. He found himself confronted with dead ends on more than one occasion, and might even have ended up talking to the floating faces on the walls… he couldn't quite remember afterwards.

When Utayama eventually found his way back to the reception room, he saw Shimada had been folding origami figures with Samejima. He joined them and opened a new bottle of whisky, which he set to drinking straight. The next moment, he found himself enthusiastically orating with bloodshot eyes about how wonderful Miyagaki's detective stories were.

The night slowly went by. The last time Utayama looked at the clock, it was past one.

Later, as he lay sprawled across the sofa in the reception room, he dreamed about wandering a labyrinth.

CHAPTER FOUR

THE FIRST STORY

1

Steel ribs criss-crossed the Stygian ceiling in geometrical patterns. The thick glass between the beams steadily turned from dark to light. Then the first rays of sun shone through, tinted light blue. The shadow of night was about to take its leave and give way to day: a routine repeated since the age of myth.

Thus came the morning. The room was released from the grip of darkness, in which the evils of the world could run rampant. But one person was unable to escape from the dark. Instead they were left cold and alone in the room.

The Labyrinth House: inside which lay a tangled web of paths, a symbol of life and rebirth since ancient times. At the very centre of the web was a square room.

A body lay on its back on the thick ivory-coloured carpet, its four limbs strangely stiff. All ten fingernails were dug into the carpet pile, the fingers frozen rigid. The body was simply a lump of flesh now, its life already taken by the chaos of darkness.

The reek of death is uniquely distinctive. But in one way this corpse was more singular still. It seemed a cruel, infantile prank. A bizarre decoration.

A wound gaped on the corpse's neck, like a poisonous snake opening its mouth wide. The neck was twisted at an impossible angle, like the broken stem of a chrysanthemum. The body floated in a dark red sea of blood. But where the head should have been, an unusual object sat instead.

Was this a representation of the beast who lived in this labyrinth? The beast the room was named after? The grotesque black object had been hanging from the wall only the previous night: a bull's head.

2

"Utayama, wake up! Please, wake up!"

Utayama felt himself being shaken by the shoulders. Eventually he managed to open his eyelids. He couldn't focus, but at the centre of his field of vision, he recognized Samejima Tomoo's blurry face.

"Utayama!"

"Oh… good… good morning," said Utayama feebly. He tried to get to his feet, but felt his head spinning, so quickly sat back down again. A dull pain ran from the crown of his head to the back of his skull.

"I drank too much again… Where am I? Oh, the reception room?"

Utayama had apparently fallen asleep on the sofa. His cardigan was unbuttoned and his trousers wrinkled.

"What's the matter?"

"Something terrible has happened. You have to get up now and come with me," replied Samejima hurriedly. The critic's face was pale and clearly troubled. It must be serious.

"What happened?" Utayama asked, rising from the sofa. His head began to spin again, so he clutched at the sofa arm for support.

"Are you all right?"

"Yeah, well, I'm used to hangovers. But tell me what has happened."

Samejima's eyebrows furrowed deeply. "I'm afraid it is something terrible: Suzaki is dead. In the drawing room."

"He's… what!?" Utayama couldn't believe his ears. Was this real? Perhaps he was still in a nightmare.

"But, how…"

"I am afraid it was clearly a murder."

"No way…"

But judging by the look on Samejima's face, this didn't seem to be a prank. Utayama's hangover was gone in a second, but instead, he was overcome by an even worse feeling of nausea.

Had Suzaki Shōsuke really been murdered? Utayama hurried after Samejima from the reception room into the hallway. It was already light outside since it was nearly midday. The sun was high in the sky, shining through the tinted glass and lending the labyrinth a different atmosphere from what it had had the night before. However, although the corridors now were brightly lit, Utayama could still feel a darkness lurking somewhere in the maze.

Samejima was practically running, wearing a thin cardigan over pyjamas. Utayama could barely keep up.

When they arrived at the room in question at the northern end, they found Kiyomura Junichi, also in pyjamas, leaning his back on the dark purple door, as it to keep something inside from breaking out. A look of relief came over his face when he saw them.

"Shimada woke me up. What the hell is happening?" barked Kiyomura.

"Where's Ms Kadomatsu? She was here, wasn't she?" Samejima asked, at which Kiyomura nodded.

"I found her cowering outside the door. She looked so pale, I told her to go back to her room and lie down."

"And Shimada?"

"He's gone off to wake up Madoka and Hayashi."

At that moment, multiple footsteps reverberated through the cold, stale air of the labyrinth. Shimada and Hayashi had arrived. Shimada was wearing a sweatshirt beneath a tracksuit, while Hayashi, like Kiyomura and Samejima, was wearing pyjamas. Apparently, everyone had been woken from their sleep.

"What about Keiko?" Utayama asked, suddenly remembering his wife.

"I woke her up too," said Samejima. "But I thought it best not to bring her here. I asked her to wait for us in the reception room instead."

"I see, thank you."

"Well, we'd better take a look inside," said Shimada, going to the door. "Is Suzaki really dead?"

"He sure is," Kiyomura said, covering his eyes with his hand and shaking his head lightly. "I warn you, it's not for the faint-hearted in there."

"Excuse me," Shimada said, gently pushing the other man away from the door, while his long arm reached for the knob. "Is it locked?"

"I came when Ms Kadomatsu woke me up. The door wasn't locked when I got here," Samejima explained.

"I see," Shimada mumbled, then he turned the knob and slowly pushed the door open.

"Uurgh!"

Shimada wasn't the only one to give an involuntary cry of horror at what was revealed. Utayama and Hayashi peered past him into the room, shocked looks on their faces.

The room was square, with a thick ivory-coloured carpet, surrounded by cool terracotta walls. It was the drawing room,

Minotaur, where three months ago, Utayama had spoken with Miyagaki for the last time.

In the centre of the carpet was an antique sofa set. On the floor in front of one sofa, to their left lay the body of Suzaki Shōsuke.

He was dressed as he had been when he left the reception room last night: black trousers and a plain brown sweater. His skinny, weak-looking body was lying on its back, motionless. The dark red pool that had spread around his head made it clear he was dead.

But the group in the doorway were staring at something quite apart from the blood.

There was a terrible, gaping wound in Suzaki's neck, and his head had been violently twisted—no, practically torn off.

But that was not all. Where Suzaki's head had once been, now sat the black head of a bull, crowned by two horns.

"No…"

"Oh, this is too horrible…"

Shimada, Utayama and Hayashi all had to step back and look away. Kiyomura and Samejima had stayed outside, obviously not wanting to be confronted with the horrifying sight a second time.

"This is clearly a murder… But why…" Shimada said, his voice trembling. He wanted to enter the room, but Utayama held him back.

"No, you shouldn't go any closer. We have to contact the police first," he finally managed to say.

"Of course, you're right," Shimada said, taking one step inside, and glancing around. "Was that bull's head in this room before?"

"It used to hang on the opposite wall. Anyway, we need to call the police…"

"No, wait, hold it, we're going to call the police?" Kiyomura burst out. "But that'd go against Mr Miyagaki's wishes."

Utayama stared at the writer in surprise. "What... but that's not important now!"

"I know this is a serious matter. But if we call the police in, the contest will be cancelled, and then that fortune will just 'poof!' disappear. Please try and see this from our position."

"You can't be serious..."

But Kiyomura looked very determined. He shot Utayama a fierce glare, then turned to Hayashi.

"What do you think?"

"Err, I... well..." Hayashi was astonished by Kiyomura's attitude too. He looked away, at a loss for words.

"It's unthinkable. Someone has been killed. How can you even suggest continuing?" Utayama protested, fighting the nausea rising in his throat.

"Hey, what's this about Suzaki?"

Funaoka Madoka finally made her appearance, holding the floor plan in one hand. She rubbed her eyes sleepily, looking up at the five gathered in front of the door.

"What? Come on, tell me!"

She was wearing a gaudy floral dress. She had got dressed after Shimada's knock woke her up.

"I suppose we'd better ask your opinion too. What do you think—"

"He's in there, is he?" Madoka cut in, ignoring Kiyomura completely. "Surely, it's just some kind of prank?" She went to the doorway and peered in over Shimada's shoulder. Then she let out an ear-piercing scream, stumbled backwards and would have collapsed on the floor if Utayama hadn't caught her.

"Are you okay? Oh, dear. She's passed out," said the editor, concerned.

"Truth be told, I feel like fainting myself," Samejima added grimly.

"Let's all go to the reception room," Shimada suggested, closing the door behind him. Then he turned to Samejima. "We will need to inform the police of course, but perhaps we should talk with Ino first. Where is he?"

A troubled look appeared on the critic's face.

"I couldn't find him in his room. He said yesterday he was going to do some shopping, so perhaps he has already left the house."

3

The six guests made their way through the labyrinth, the unconscious Madoka being carried by Shimada and Utayama. No one spoke.

The gruesome scene Utayama had just witnessed would not leave his alcohol-clouded mind. He was constantly fighting the urge to vomit.

In the reception room they found Keiko waiting for them. She stood up from the armchair as they came in.

"Has someone really been killed?" she asked, pale-faced. "Wait… Is that Madoka? No, she can't be—"

"Suzaki was murdered. Fortunately, Madoka only fainted," said Shimada. He and Utayama laid Madoka, who was heavier than she looked, on the sofa. Keiko went to the sideboard and got a bottle of brandy.

"Could you look after her?" Utayama asked his wife, before going over to the telephone stand, which was located at the inside corner of the backwards-L-shaped room. But before he could lift the receiver, a hand was placed firmly on his shoulder. The hand belonged to Kiyomura.

"Please wait."

"No," insisted Utayama, shaking his head and looking the taller Kiyomura straight in the eye. "This might go against Mr Miyagaki's will, but considering the circumstances…"

"You're so stubborn."

"This isn't about me," Utayama snapped back. He looked at Samejima. "What do you think we should do?"

"I think you're right."

Kiyomura raised an eyebrow. "I get it. It makes no difference to you, does it? Go on, call the police and have the contest cancelled. You won't lose out anyway."

Utayama ignored this outburst, reached for the telephone and immediately started dialling the emergency number. He could feel his finger trembling. His head was pounding, he still felt sick and he was sweating too. When he put the receiver to his ear, he realized there was no dial tone.

"What's the matter?" Samejima asked, noticing Utayama's shocked face.

"The phone. It's not working…"

Utayama hung up the receiver and tried again, but there was still no dial tone.

"It's either broken… or the line's been cut."

"No…"

If the line had been cut, it meant someone had done it intentionally. But who? Utayama's nausea suddenly got the better of him. He slammed the receiver down and ran to the kitchen, covering his mouth with his hands. He stood bent over the sink with the tap running while it all came out.

Eventually, he realized Keiko had been standing behind him for some time, rubbing his back.

"Are you all right?"

"Yes… thanks. I think I'll be okay now. How is Madoka doing?"

"She's come to."

Utayama drank some water straight from the tap. When he finally felt better but still with a heavy head, they returned to the reception room.

Madoka was conscious, curled up on the sofa. Samejima was sitting opposite her, staring at the floor. Kiyomura and Hayashi were sitting at the table, completely silent.

"Where's Shimada?" Utayama asked. Samejima pointed towards the double doors in the south wall, which led to the stairs. "He went to investigate the upper entrance doors."

Utayama wanted to go after him, but at that moment Shimada returned. The lanky man closed the doors behind him.

"No good. The lattice door is still locked. I can't tell whether Ino actually went out or not, though. Could there be any spare keys?"

"If there are, I imagine Ino has those too," Samejima said.

"Is there any other way out, besides the front entrance?"

"No."

Shimada sniffled. "So there's nothing we can do. We'll have to wait for him to return."

4

"The upper entrance is the only way in or out of this house. Ino locked the door yesterday after the doctor left, and it is still locked. If he left this morning to go to the shops, he must have locked the door behind him on his way out," Shimada muttered, looking at the door leading into the labyrinth. "And

110

sometime last night or this morning, Suzaki was killed in the drawing room…"

Shimada sat down at the corner of the large table and looked around at the others.

"Perhaps we should discuss the murder ourselves," he suggested. "At least it'll give us something to do until Ino returns. We'll end up going crazy if we just sit here in silence."

"I see our 'great detective' can't wait to step onto the stage," Kiyomura said. He was frowning anxiously, but forced a sneer on his face. "Well, please yourself."

"This matter concerns all of us. This house has essentially been one gigantic underground locked room since last night. A murder has occurred here, so logically speaking, the murderer has to be one of us."

"One of us? You mean one of us did… something horrible like that?" Madoka shrieked from the sofa.

"Yes," Shimada said without any hesitation. "I don't believe this could have been the work of an intruder. I think it's best not to even entertain that possibility for the time being."

"But why would someone want to kill Suzaki?" Madoka asked.

"You mean what would the motive be?" said Shimada, raising a quizzical eyebrow. "I'm surprised to hear you ask that question. There is a very obvious motive, at least for three people among us."

"No!" Madoka shrieked again and shot up from her seat. "You're suggesting one of us killed him to get rid of the competition?"

"Oh, come on, that's nuts," Kiyomura said dismissively. "How would the murderer be able to claim the prize money once the police get here?"

"That is why the line was cut, so we can't contact the police."

"But that's only delaying things until Ino returns."

"Indeed. But…" Shimada trailed off and leant his slender body back in his seat. "Perhaps we should leave that discussion for later. For now, we have no means of contacting the outside world, so I think it would be a good idea for us to try to get a better idea of what happened ourselves." He paused for a second and looked at Samejima. "You woke me up and told me what had happened. And I believe you said it was the housekeeper who discovered the body?"

"Yes, that's right." Samejima got up from the sofa. "Should we call her in, too?"

"Yes, it would be rather discourteous to exclude her."

The critic nodded to Shimada and headed to the kitchen. Kadomatsu Fumie's room was named Polycaste, after Daedalus' younger sister. It was different from the other rooms, as it was accessed through the kitchen and was not directly connected to the labyrinth.

After a few moments, Samejima came back with the wrinkled old woman. She was wearing a grey skirt and an olive-green cardigan and seemed to be moving somewhat stiffly, no doubt due to fear. She came silently into the room behind Samejima and stood staring at the floor. Shimada asked her how she had found the body, but she asked him to repeat what he said, speaking in a strong accent. It appeared she was indeed hard of hearing.

"He'd like you to tell us how you found the body in the drawing room," Samejima said, speaking directly into the woman's ear.

"I know nothing, nothing at all!" she replied, weakly shaking her head, but after a while they managed to get the following out of her.

That morning at nine, the housekeeper had gone to the kitchen to prepare breakfast. It was not quite ten o'clock when she finished. Utayama was still asleep on the sofa in the reception room,

112

but nobody else had showed up. She figured that at this rate, nobody would be there on time for breakfast.

So after clearing the glasses and bottles left in the reception room from the previous night, she went into the labyrinth, as Ino had also asked her to clean the games and drawing rooms. She went to the games room first, and then the drawing room. And that was when she stumbled upon the awful scene.

"Was the door locked?" Shimada asked.

Fumie shook her head. "The drawing room is always unlocked."

"I see. A different question then. Do you have a spare key to the entrance doors?"

"I gave my key to Ino last night."

"I see. And have you seen him this morning? Has he gone out for shopping?"

"I have not seen him today."

"Hmm…"

"Where is Mr Miyagaki?" the housekeeper asked. "I'd like to go home…"

"Oh, he's… You see, right now…"

Would she even understand if he tried to explain what had happened yesterday? Shimada didn't know how to answer her.

"Mr Miyagaki is still feeling ill," Samejima said, coming to the rescue. "But you will have to stay here for now, until the police have arrived."

Fumie seemed to accept that and returned to her room. Shimada sat down once more and looked at Samejima.

"So, in shock after discovering the body, she came to wake you up?"

"Well, I believe she went to Mr Miyagaki's room first, but when there was no reply she went to Ino's room. There was no reply there either, so she came to me."

113

"Was she given a copy of the floor plan with all our names on it, too?"

"No, but I think she knows the labyrinth by heart. Ino always stays in the same room. She must have come to my room because it is the nearest to his."

"I see. So then you hurried to the drawing room."

"At first, I didn't really understand what had happened. Her explanation didn't made much sense. But she dragged me over there, and when I actually saw what was inside the room, I nearly collapsed."

Samejima was ashen-faced. It seemed Utayama was not the only one to have that terrible scene seared in his memory.

"At that point, I could tell Fumie was exhausted, mentally as well as physically, so I decided to wake the rest of you. I couldn't find Utayama in his room, so I got his wife out of bed, and then I went to your room."

Shimada took over: "Aha, yes. Then I said I'd wake up Kiyomura and the others, while you went to the reception room in search of Utayama…

"That at least clears up what happened after the body was discovered. Anybody have anything to add?" He looked around the room, as if he were leading a discussion.

The writers, the critic, the editor and his wife… This sort of scene was very familiar to all of them, but only within the pages of murder mystery novels. What they were confronted with now was like something out of a whodunit, but it was a real-life murder case.

"Now, why did the body end up like that…" Shimada muttered to himself under his breath.

"Huh, what do you mean? Like what?" Keiko asked, looking at her husband. He seemed to hesitate to tell her.

"His head was cut half off," Kiyomura broke in coldly. "And

114

then, for some reason, the murderer put a stuffed bull's head on his neck. That's 'what'!"

"Stop it," said Madoka, glaring at Kiyomura. "I don't want to think about it any more."

"I don't like thinking about it myself either."

"Actually, I think you have touched upon a very important matter," said Shimada gravely. "We can't tell what the cause of death was without an examination. Was it the partial decapitation that killed him, or was that done after death? I noticed the axe used to inflict the wound lying behind the sofa."

"Oh, you saw it too?" Kiyomura said. "I think it used to hang on the wall in the drawing room, along with a sword."

"Hmm, so it was already in the room? Still, it's the bull's head that interests me the most."

Shimada stroked his thin chin pensively, but Kiyomura was quick with an answer:

"Isn't it obvious? It was an allusion to the name of the drawing room. Minotaur, the monster with the bull's head."

"Of course, that's part of it, but…"

"That's all there is to it… I hope… I hope you are not trying to suggest that just because the 'Minotaur' was slain, the person responsible must be the one staying in the Theseus room—in other words, me?"

5

It was already past one o'clock, but Ino still hadn't returned. The guests had asked the housekeeper to prepare some lunch for them, but they didn't eat much. At two o'clock, Hayashi finally broke the lengthy silence.

"This is odd… How can he be gone for so long?"

"Indeed," Shimada said, stroking his chin. "Even considering he had to buy things for all of us, he's been away far too long."

Hayashi ran his fingers through his long, curly hair. "What if he's had an accident?"

Shimada got up. "That's certainly possible, but I would like to check his room. Would someone care to join me?"

"I'll come," Utayama said. Keiko looked anxiously at her husband, but he assured her he would be all right. His headache and nausea were finally gone.

The two left, Shimada with his copy of the map in his hand.

"You know, from the start, I had my doubts about whether Ino had really gone out to the shops," he said.

Utayama had been wondering about it, too. First of all, it would be strange for Ino to leave the house without telling anyone. At the very least, you'd expect him to have said something to the housekeeper, who had been in the kitchen at nine.

But then why hadn't the secretary shown up yet? Utayama couldn't help but ask Shimada:

"You don't think… he's been murdered too?"

"It's impossible to say yet. But I can't deny that it's possible…"

Ino's room, Europa, was located in the east, south of Miyagaki's study. Ino's neighbour to the south of his room was Samejima, in Pasiphaë. Despite Europa and Pasiphaë being adjacent rooms, the distance between them door to door wasn't that short, as they were separated by the labyrinth.

Shimada had to check the floor plan a few times, but eventually they found themselves at their destination. He examined the name etched in the bronze plate: Europa.

"The mother of Minos, daughter of the Phoenician King Agenor. Zeus loved her, and took the form of a bull to trick her.

116

When she got on the bull's back it leapt into the sea and brought her to the island of Crete. There she gave birth to Zeus' son Minos," Shimada said.

"You know your Greek mythology."

"Oh, no, I just did a little bit of research in the library last night before I went to bed. I have to admit, I was once again amazed at how convoluted the relations between gods and man could be," he said, knocking loudly on the door.

No answer came, so he reached for the knob.

"Huh, it's not locked."

"Oh…"

"I was prepared to force the door open if necessary, but I guess we won't have to."

He pushed the door open and stepped inside. The room had the same basic layout as the others: a bed, a writing desk and chair, a small table, two stools and a full-length mirror on the wall.

But there was no sign of Ino. As they went to check the toilet, for a second, Utayama expected them to stumble upon Ino's body there, but fortunately, his fears did not come true.

"Empty there, too…"

Shimada looked under the bed, but found nothing. Then he checked the built-in wardrobe on the south wall.

"His suit is here," he said, pointing inside it. "Wasn't he wearing this yesterday?"

"Yes, I believe he was," agreed Utayama.

"Hmm. Oh, that's odd, his wallet is in the inside pocket. I'm afraid that is a bad sign."

He looked around the room one more time and went over to the desk, next to the head of the bed. There was a black briefcase on the seat of the chair.

"He left his briefcase here too."

Shimada picked it up, placed it on the desk and without any hesitation, started examining its contents. He eventually found a brown leather cardholder.

"Hm. It's his driving licence."

Considering Ino's punctilious character, it was inconceivable that he would go out in the car without his licence.

Shimada riffled through the briefcase some more, and eventually took out a few sheets of paper.

"Look, here are the shopping lists we gave him. I'm afraid there's no longer any room for doubt."

Shimada then checked the drawers of the desk and the suitcase next to the bed. If Ino had indeed been in possession of a set of spare keys, they were nowhere to be found. Utayama helped Shimada search the room thoroughly, but to no avail.

Shimada frowned and crossed his arms. "It is almost certain Ino never left the house. That explains why he never 'returned'. But without him, we are completely trapped in this sealed underground space."

6

After leaving Europa, the two entered the labyrinth to return to the reception room, when Shimada suddenly said:

"I want to make a small detour. Would you join me?"

"Where to?" Utayama asked.

"I think we can ignore the rooms currently in use by ourselves for the moment, but I'd like to have a look at the other rooms. Perhaps Ino is one of them."

Shimada didn't say it out loud, but Utayama was aware that neither of them was expecting to find him alive.

"There is the library," Shimada went on, "Suzaki's room of course, and I think there is an unused guest room too. The housekeeper cleaned the games room this morning, so I think we can skip it."

Shimada unfolded the floor plan. "Let's see. Suzaki's room is Talos and the unused one is Medea, but the library is closest."

The library was named Eupalamus, to the east of the drawing room. The two made their way through the sombre hallways, illuminated by the blue afternoon light shining in from above.

Shimada stopped when they arrived at the intersection. The right passage would take them to the library, while the left led to the drawing room. Utayama froze for a second, fearing Shimada would suggest having another look at the crime scene.

An image of the terrifying sight flashed through his mind once more. He never wanted to see it again if he could help it.

Suddenly a thought occurred to him: if the murderer was one of the other guests, how could he be sure it wasn't Shimada?

Utayama felt a shiver run down his spine. It couldn't be Shimada... could it?

Just then, Shimada shot Utayama an inquisitive glance.

"What's the matter? Aha, are you getting suspicious of me?"

"Oh, err, no, of course not..."

Shimada grinned. "I can tell from the look on your face. But you don't have to be afraid. Even if I were the murderer, I wouldn't attack you now. Everyone would know it was me. I would never be so foolish."

The library was a gloomy room, filled with rows of high bookcases. All the books from Miyagaki's Seijō home had been moved here. The collection was easily larger than the library of an ordinary middle school.

Between them, the pair searched every nook and cranny, but failed to find anything out of the ordinary. Then they headed to the western part of the house.

A long hallway led northwards from the reception room. If one took the western turning at the far end, the corridor made a U-turn and headed back south in the direction of the reception room. But at the end of that hallway, the corridor turned back on itself again to head north.

Shimada was peering at the floor plan.

"Compared to the eastern side, the western side looks much more complex. There are a lot more branching paths here."

Along the left-hand side of the northwards-running hallway they were looking down were the entrances to sixteen side-corridors.

"Medea is... err, the tenth corridor on our left."

Shimada started to walk north, going more slowly now. Utayama had stayed on this side of the house before, and he remembered how easy it was to get lost.

As they walked, Utayama looked at the white plaster masks hanging on the walls, one next to each of the sixteen side-corridors. They weren't so bad during the day, but at night he remembered shuddering at the sight of those eyes staring down at him.

They took the tenth corridor. On the wall, a lion bared its teeth as if to warn them off. When they came to the unused room, Medea, they found it unlocked. There was no one inside. They checked beneath the bed and inside the wardrobe too, but found nothing of interest.

The two then headed to the last place they wanted to search: Suzaki Shōsuke's room, which was between those of Hayashi and Madoka.

The name on the door plate read Talos, which referred to Polycaste's son, and Daedalus' nephew, rather than the identically named giant bronze automaton that was the guardian of Crete. Daedalus had been so jealous of Talos' talents that he murdered his nephew.

Thankfully, this room was not locked either, which spared them searching Suzaki's body for the key.

The lights had been left on. Suzaki had probably only intended to leave his room for a short while, but he had never returned.

They searched this room as they had the others, but again found nothing of interest. Everything in this room was the same as in the other guest rooms, even the light switch was in the same place on the wall immediately to the left of the door. The only differences from the other two rooms were the presence of the word processor to be used in the competition and of Suzaki's luggage, now without an owner.

"Nothing here either," muttered Shimada. He looked a bit feverish. Perhaps he had a cold. He was about to leave the room when Utayama noticed that the word-processor screen on the desk was giving off a dim light.

"Look at this," the editor called to Shimada, as he went over to the desk. "He must have set the display brightness to the lowest level before he left the room."

Shimada turned around sharply. "Had he been writing?"

"Yes, I think it's the beginning of his story."

Utayama turned the dial to adjust the brightness and looked at the screen.

"Yes, you see."

They were looking at rows of text. The page counter said 'Page 1': Suzaki had only just started. At the top of the screen, written in large font, was the title: 'The Minotaur's Head'.

The story started with the numbered section 1. A strange sensation came over Utayama as he saw the title. He read on, and then cried out:

"What!?"

Almost simultaneously, Shimada groaned: "Ah… But it's impossible…"

THE MINOTAUR'S HEAD

1

Steel ribs criss-crossed the Stygian ceiling in geometrical patterns. The thick glass between the beams steadily turned from dark to light. Then the first rays of sun shone through, tinted light blue. The shadow of night was about to take its leave and give way to day: a routine repeated since the age of myth.

Thus came the morning. The room was released from the grip of darkness, in which the evils of the world could run rampant. But one person was unable to escape from the dark. Instead they were left cold and alone in the room.

The Labyrinth House: inside which lay a tangled web of paths, a symbol of life and rebirth since ancient times. At the very centre of the web was a square room.

A body lay on its back on the thick ivory-coloured carpet, its four limbs strangely stiff. All ten fingernails were dug into the carpet pile, the fingers frozen rigid. The body was simply a lump of flesh now, its life already taken by the chaos of darkness.

The reek of death is uniquely distinctive. But in one way this corpse was more singular still. It seemed a cruel, infantile prank. A bizarre decoration.

A monstrous black helmet had been placed over the head of the body, hiding its face. Was this a representation of the beast who lived in this labyrinth? The beast the room was named after? The grotesque black object had been hanging from the wall until the previous night: a bull's head.

CHAPTER FIVE

THE REASON FOR THE DECAPITATION

1

Utayama and Shimada returned to the reception room and told the other guests what they had found. When they reached the end of their account, Kiyomura cried out in bewilderment:

"What!? Are you sure? It was exactly like his story?"

"Yes," Utayama confirmed, even though he himself couldn't quite believe it. "He had only just started, but what he wrote described the crime scene... There was a description of a body lying in the Minotaur room, with a stuffed bull's head where the person's head used to be."

"According to the will," added Shimada, "each writer was supposed to be the victim in their own story. That means the body Suzaki wrote about was his own, so he was murdered exactly as he described in his story."

"It can't be!" Kiyomura barked, pouring himself another glass of brandy. He had started drinking after Shimada and Utayama had left. "It's similar to what happens in *The Tragedy of Y*, I suppose. But why would the murderer do it?"

Shimada wrinkled his large nose. "Who knows? But if the allusion of the scene isn't just to the Minotaur myth, but also to Suzaki's story, it tells us a great deal about the murderer's actions last night. They must have read Suzaki's story on the word processor before 'arranging' the body like that in the drawing room. But we can't tell whether the murderer read the story before the actual murder itself or not."

"Isn't it likelier they read it before the murder?" Hayashi suddenly spoke up. He was sitting, hunched up on his chair. "It would seem the more natural order if the murderer first read the opening of the story, then lured Suzaki to the drawing room and murdered him there."

Shimada frowned. "I agree. It seems a bit far-fetched to imagine the killer read the story only after committing the murder."

"Wait," interrupted Kiyomura, slamming his glass down on the table. "Shouldn't we worry about Ino's whereabouts first?"

On their way back, Shimada and Utayama had remembered to look inside the bathroom and toilet just outside the reception room, but Ino wasn't there either.

"You say it doesn't seem like he went out, because you found his driving licence and our shopping lists. But if we can't find him and all the entrance doors are locked, there's nothing we can do. We can't call the police and there's no way for us to get out of the house."

"Indeed."

"So what are we going to do?" Kiyomura asked, looking around the room.

When his eyes fell on his ex-wife Madoka, she suddenly started to cry out hysterically:

"No! I can't bear it any more, staying here under the same roof as his dead body!"

"But there's nothing we can do."

"The murderer's here in the house too. How can you all stay so calm?" she wailed.

"I'm not calm at all. I never wanted to come across a dead body outside the pages of a book."

Madoka's cheeks started to redden. "Really? I know you never liked Suzaki. You were always complaining about him. Saying how you couldn't stand the way he flaunted his knowledge."

"Oh, be quiet!" Kiyomura snapped, but she didn't stop.

"And of course you've had a pretty miserable time on the stock market recently, haven't you? Yes, I can see it now: you're killing the competition to get your hands on the money…"

Kiyomura tutted loudly. "You can stop your fantasizing right there. You're one to talk about money troubles. You know, I've heard stories too. Hooked up with the wrong man and spent a fortune on him, right? Hayashi here has his problems too."

Kiyomura turned to the small man who was nervously stroking his moustache. "The other person in that car accident of yours didn't come out unscathed, did they? Must have been quite the shock to you."

"I… err…" Hayashi mumbled.

"And I know Suzaki wouldn't leave you alone either. I think you finally told him to back off a while ago, didn't you?"

Everyone in the industry knew about Suzaki Shōsuke's behaviour. Utayama was aware that he'd been making passes at Hayashi for the last two years.

Kiyomura carried on: "Anyway, regardless of what personal motives we might have, there are billions of yen at stake in this competition—that's surely motive enough for any one of us."

Hayashi's head dropped. Madoka bit her lips. Kiyomura looked at them for a moment before turning to Shimada.

"However, that does not necessarily mean one of us murdered Suzaki to take out a rival in the competition. Personally, I'd like to think I'm not so short-sighted. Actually…"

"Yes?" Shimada prompted with a raised eyebrow.

"Actually, what if someone besides the three of us decided to take advantage of this unique situation? Yes, there is a competition going on involving the inheritance, that's true. But what if someone had a completely unrelated motive to kill Suzaki and determined to use this occasion to divert suspicion onto us authors? I find that much more believable myself."

"Aha, so you mean it could have been one of the rest of us: myself, the Utayamas, Samejima or the housekeeper?"

"Nonsense, why would I ever do something like that?" Samejima said in an offended tone. Utayama felt the same, but he couldn't deny Kiyomura had a point.

"You know what?" said Kiyomura to Shimada, another sneer on his face. "If this were one of my stories, I'd make you the murderer."

An enigmatic smile appeared on Shimada's face. "You mean I might have a surprising motive that lies in my past, for example?"

"Something like that."

"Well, please do write that story one day."

Shimada went over to the glass table in front of the sofa. Everyone watched his movements. He bent over and took a tissue from the box on the lower shelf, then excused himself before blowing his nose. When he had done so, he looked around the room.

"But, as you just pointed out, we should think about what we're going to do. The phone doesn't work. The way out is locked…"

"We might be able to force the door open," Utayama suggested. "We have to leave this place one way or another."

"I'm afraid that's impossible," said Kiyomura, immediately shooting the idea down. "You've been here often enough yourself. First of all, there's that sturdy bronze lattice door that seals off the entrance hall, then the stone doors and another lattice gate after that. How are we going to force those open?"

"But…"

"It'd be a different story if we at least had a hacksaw to hand, but I'm guessing any tools are kept in the storeroom upstairs. We'd have to get through the inner lattice door before we could get in there. The murderer must've thought of that."

"What about breaking through the roof then?"

Kiyomura looked up at the ceiling. "I don't see that happening either. Even if we managed to break that thick glass, those steel frames would stop us from even sticking our heads outside."

"But that means—" Utayama began, but it was Madoka who finished the sentence:

"—we're completely trapped here!"

She ran her hands wildly through her hair, but Kiyomura just shrugged.

"I don't think we need to worry about starving. Lots of people know we're staying here. When none of us has returned home after the sixth of April, somebody will get worried and call the house. Then they'll find out the line's dead."

"So all we can do is wait until somebody finds us?"

"Yep," said Kiyomura. "So that means we have enough time to follow the instructions in Mr Miyagaki's will," he added, shooting Utayama a serious look.

Kiyomura was clearly determined that the contest should continue as planned. Utayama didn't know how to answer and could only shake his head non-committally.

"I agree you have a good point," put in Shimada, leaning with one hand on the table. "For the moment, it seems unlikely we'll be able to escape the house on our own, and the police won't be coming of their own accord any time soon. All we can do now is wait. But it is also very likely that the murderer is still in the house. So I propose—"

"I know exactly what you're going to say, oh great detective," cut in Kiyomura, looking up at the slightly taller man. "Let the game of detection begin at last, right?"

2

It was three in the afternoon.

Shimada had made it clear that he did not consider the affair to be a game in any way, but that he did indeed think they should start to investigate the murder. The others agreed, and he left the reception room along with Utayama, Samejima and Keiko.

They were heading for Minotaur, and Suzaki's body. Since they didn't know when the police would arrive, Shimada had suggested they have a better look at the crime scene and the body themselves.

He had also asked Keiko to join them. Of all the people present, she obviously had the most medical knowledge, so he wanted to know what she could tell them. Utayama wasn't sure she should come, but to his surprise, Keiko calmly accepted the task.

"I only studied the basics of forensic medicine in medical school, so I might not be of much help," she said, resting her hand on her bulging stomach. "Perhaps it's not something our baby should hear, though…"

"It's you I'm worried about," Utayama said.

"I know, and of course I'm afraid, but this is no time to be scared of a body. I'll be all right."

"But—"

"I'm sure I'll be able to handle this better than the first time I had to dissect a body in class," Keiko joked, but Utayama could see the tension in her features.

Kiyomura, Madoka and Hayashi had decided to stay in the reception room, as they had no wish to see the body again. Utayama hadn't been too keen to do so either, but he couldn't let Keiko go on her own. He was surprised that Samejima had decided to join them. Like the couple, the critic seemed apprehensive as they approached the crime scene.

When they opened the door, the stench of blood hit them like a wave. In the middle of the room lay Suzaki's disfigured corpse. His precious glasses had fallen on the floor. His purple tongue protruded from the corner of his mouth. His eyes were rolled back in his skull. And on his neck: the black bull's head.

Shimada was the first to enter, skirting around the sofa set and observing the body from a short distance.

Although Keiko hesitated on the threshold for a second, Utayama was amazed at how calm she stayed. While he and Samejima stood in the doorway averting their eyes from the sight, Keiko slowly approached and studied the mangled corpse, taking care to avoid the blood on the floor.

"Can you make out the cause of death?" Shimada asked. "Loss of blood from his neck?" He was examining the dead writer from the other side of the sofa.

"Yes," Keiko confirmed, but then she noticed something, which made her shake her head. "No, wait, that's not it."

Surprised, Shimada went round to her side.

"Look here. There's a fairly deep wound on the back of his head. As if he was hit with the corner of some heavy object."

"Aha, indeed. So that injury was what…"

Keiko shook her head again. "No, I don't think it killed him. It probably only knocked him out. But look here, on his neck…"

In spite of himself, Utayama joined them. Timidly, Samejima did likewise.

"It's hard to tell because the wound has bled so much, but can you make out those narrow bruises?"

"… Yes," Shimada said, peering at the corpse's neck. "Are those… ligature marks?"

"I think so."

Keiko was right. Just above the horrendous open wound was a dark, bloody line, running around the neck. This was clear evidence—some kind of thin cord had been wrapped around Suzaki's neck to strangle him.

Shimada had been bending over, but now he straightened up again.

"So first the murderer caught him off guard and knocked him out with some kind of blunt instrument. For example, perhaps they used that ashtray from the table to hit him on the back of the head. Then they wrapped a cord around Suzaki's neck and strangled him. And then they used the axe to cut the head off, or almost off… Can you give us an estimate of the time of death?"

Keiko looked down at the body doubtfully.

"It's difficult to say, I never studied this that much…"

"Just a rough estimate will do."

Keiko seemed to come to a decision. She reached out and took hold of Suzaki's left arm by the wrist, carefully picking a spot not covered in blood, and lifted it.

"He feels cold and his arm has started to stiffen. How about his legs?"

Shimada followed Keiko's example and tried to lift the legs but gave up right away.

"I can't. They're completely stiff."

"It's supposed to take about five or six hours for rigor mortis to affect the lower half of the body. It takes about twelve hours for it to spread through the whole body."

"Twelve hours would set the time of death before three in the morning."

"I'm afraid that's all I can tell you."

"No, sorry for asking you do this. Thank you."

Keiko stepped away from the body. As she made her way back to the door, she staggered, and for a moment Utayama thought her legs would give way. The stress and the shock must be taking a toll on her, but she had suppressed her unease in order to answer Shimada's questions. This was a side of his wife that Utayama had never seen before.

Shimada began pacing around the room, watched by the others who had returned to the doorway.

"This looks rather heavy," he said, peering down at the axe lying on the floor behind one sofa. Utayama was glad that he didn't try to lift it.

"Even so, I suppose even a woman could've done it," continued Shimada. "The cut has not gone completely through the bone, and with a little help from gravity, I suppose a single strike would have been enough…" He looked at the wall at the back of the room. "And I suppose this is where the stuffed head was?"

There was an L-shaped hook on the terracotta wall above the sideboard, which was indeed where the stuffed bull's head had hung.

"And the axe was over there, was it?" Shimada asked, pointing at the west wall. "Yes. I see, along with that sword, right?"

Shimada started to go over to the spot but stopped halfway and turned to look at the north wall, to the left of the doorway.

"Oh, there's a full-length mirror here too. That's rare in a drawing room."

"Haven't you seen enough?" asked Samejima, white as a sheet. "I can't take being in this room any more."

"Oh, of course, I'm sorry…" apologized the "great detective", scratching his head.

He made as if to head back over to the door but stopped, his gaze lingering on the body.

"But why like this?… That's the important question." He stared for a moment longer at the body lying in the pool of blood, then he turned to Utayama: "Don't you agree?"

Utayama cocked his head. "Isn't this all just an allusion to the story written on the word processor?"

"That's not exactly what I meant. Why did the murderer set up the scene to imitate Suzaki's story?… Well, yes, one explanation could be that the killer is not quite right in the head, or that they have some kind of fetish. But why set it up like this in particular? That's what's troubling me."

"What do you mean, 'like this in particular'?"

"Oh, haven't you noticed yet?"

"Noticed what?"

"Think back to the manuscript. In the opening scene on the word processor, we read about a dead body arranged to resemble the Minotaur. But the story only said that a bull's head 'had been placed over the head of the body'. It never mentioned that the head had been cut off and a bull's head put in its place."

"Oh, that's right."

"It's true that, if you wanted to invoke the Minotaur, cutting off the head and substituting the bull's is more effective. But if that was the aim, why not cut the head clean off? Why did the murderer only go halfway?"

Shimada looked expectantly at the puzzled Utayama, then at Keiko and Samejima, but no answer came.

"I believe this question is key to understanding the murder. And I think I may be able to answer it."

"And how is that?" Samejima asked.

"Let's go back to the reception room. I will explain everything there," Shimada said. He headed for the door, but then turned to Keiko. "I might need your help again later. Please be so kind as to oblige."

3

"Oh, where's Kiyomura?" asked Shimada. It was twenty to four when they returned to the reception room and found him gone.

"He went to get dressed. Apparently he couldn't relax in his pyjamas," Hayashi said. He was sitting at the table, still wearing pyjamas.

"Of course. I see you don't have the same problem."

"Oh, no. It's not that," muttered Hayashi. He glanced at Madoka who was lying on the sofa. "She just didn't want to be left alone."

"Aha."

After a while, Kiyomura returned. He was wearing a light purple long-sleeved shirt and stonewashed jeans.

"Done with your crime scene investigation then?" he asked jokingly. He sat down at the table, and crossed his long legs. "Let me guess: now you're going to interrogate the suspects?"

"Something like that," Shimada said with a mischievous smile. He sat down opposite Kiyomura and called the others to the table.

"But first allow me to tell you what we learned."

Shimada briefly explained about the crime scene and the body to the three writers.

"... and the estimated time of death could be any time between late last night and early this morning," said Shimada. "You're sure you can't narrow it down any further?"

Keiko shook her head. He sighed, and then asked everyone where they were at that time. Of course, nobody had an alibi that could be corroborated.

Kiyomura tutted. "What lousy luck. If only I'd crawled into someone's bed last night."

Utayama felt a twinge of suspicion towards Kiyomura. Here they were, locked in a house where a murder had just taken place and with the murderer probably still among them, and he was cracking jokes? Utayama knew Kiyomura was the type to make light of serious situations, but even so, how could he be acting so relaxed? Unless...

Shimada then brought the conversation around to the mystery that had been troubling him earlier.

"Yet, the biggest question remains: why did the murderer take an axe to Suzaki's neck?"

He then repeated the thoughts he had voiced in the drawing room. It was clear the killer wanted to allude to the content of "The Minotaur's Head", as found on Suzaki's word processor. However, why did the murderer go further than they needed to?

"I have come up with an answer to this question. If I'm right, I think it'll give us an important clue as to who the murderer is."

"Haha, well, do please enlighten us," Kiyomura said. He seemed a bit taken aback by how confidently the "great detective" spoke.

Shimada looked at everyone around the table.

"It's something we're all familiar with from murder mysteries: a body displayed in a bizarre way. In Suzaki's story, the corpse

135

was made to look like the Minotaur. We'll never know why, since he died before he could finish it. Meanwhile, after our real-life murder, the killer arranged the body so as to allude to Suzaki's story.

"Now, here is what I want you all to consider: what effect did the near-decapitation have on the crime scene?"

"What effect did it have?" Utayama parroted.

"Yes. Of course, one effect was to make the body look even more 'half-man, half-bull', and I suspect that is what the murderer wanted us to focus on. But there has to be another intention—the real reason the killer did it. Now, this might sound crazy, but I think the reason was the blood. The red blood, which was never mentioned in Suzaki's story."

"You mean, you think the killer wanted to use the colour of the blood somehow?" asked Utayama.

Shimada nodded and looked slowly around the group.

"Indeed. I think the murderer might have sustained a wound in committing the crime and left a bloodstain. Red blood on an ivory carpet. It would have attracted our attention instantly. And these days it's practically suicidal for a murderer to leave their blood at a crime scene—when the police analysed it, they could trace it back to the culprit."

"I see," the editor muttered.

"But as you all know, the carpet in that room is thick, and bloodstains are hard to get out. So that's why the head had to be cut off."

"It's the same reasoning as in 'The Sign of the Broken Sword'," Utayama said. "Hide a leaf in a forest, and if there's no forest, create one."

"Indeed. You hide a bloodstain in a pool of blood."

Everyone froze as they watched Shimada's eyes dart around the table. Nobody knew what he would say next.

"With that in mind, I've been inspecting you all carefully, and I can't see any obvious wounds."

"I hope you're not suggesting carrying out a full bodily examination or anything," piped up Kiyomura.

"No way! What right do you—" Madoka began to cry, but Shimada raised his hands to cut her off.

"I would never suggest anything of the sort. You see, there are no indications at the scene there had been a scuffle between the murderer and the victim. Suzaki was likely caught off guard.

"With no big struggle, the murderer could only realistically have sustained an injury to some uncovered part of their body: the face, hands and arms, that is. Maybe the lower legs, too, if the murderer were a woman wearing a skirt or dress. But it's unlikely Suzaki could've inflicted an injury deep enough to draw blood from the killer's stomach or back, for example."

"Well, have a good look at me then," said Madoka, throwing her arms on the table and rolling her sleeves up. "Not so much as a scratch, you see. Want to see my legs too?"

"Oh, no, that's all right. The women can check each other."

"What a gentleman you are."

"However, could you all roll up your sleeves at least? I'll go first."

Shimada rolled up the sleeves of his tracksuit jacket.

The other five followed his example, and soon twelve bare forearms lay on the table: a curious sight.

"No cuts here that I can see," Utayama said.

Shimada nodded. "Nobody has suffered a wound to their arms. And there are no cuts on our faces or necks, either, as we can all see."

"Perhaps you should lift your hair and show us your neck," Kiyomura suggested to Madoka. She sighed and glared at her ex-husband, but did as asked.

"There you go. You can see for yourselves. It's not me."

The women then checked each other's legs, but found nothing suspicious.

However, Shimada didn't seem disappointed. "There is one possibility remaining."

Madoka raised an eyebrow. "Oh, really?"

"Of course. And fortunately we have a doctor here to help us investigate."

Keiko looked up enquiringly. "What's that?"

"Well, you see, if the murderer bled enough to stain the carpet, we also need to consider that it could have been... a nosebleed."

Kiyomura spread his arms theatrically. "And so you want our resident ENT doctor to examine all of our noses."

"What do you say, Keiko?" Shimada asked. "It's been over ten hours, but could you still find the traces of a nosebleed if you examined us now?"

Keiko hesitated.

"If I could do an intranasal exam, then yes, I think it'd be possible."

"Then that is what I would like to ask you to do."

"But I don't have my instruments with me."

"I'm sorry, but there's nothing we can do about that."

"At the very least, I need some light."

"I have a penlight, if that's any help."

"That's enough!" Madoka cried out, shooting up out of her seat. "Examining our noses? I refuse to submit to such humiliating treatment!"

"If you refuse, I won't force you of course," said Shimada. "It might indeed make for quite a silly spectacle, Keiko staring up all of our noses." Then he added in a lower voice, "But you should

138

be aware that some of us might become suspicious if you don't want to go through with it."

*

After Shimada had brought the pen-shaped miniature torch from his room, Keiko began the examinations. Madoka had agreed to take part, despite her initial objection, after Shimada's not-so-veiled threat.

He stood by the telephone, observing the almost comical procedure as Keiko examined her patients one by one, with the sofa serving as an examination table and the "suspects" awaiting their turn seated around the dining table. Utayama also kept a close eye on the writers' faces and behaviour.

Kiyomura had stopped his quips and theatrical gestures. Madoka sat quietly with a pout on her face. Hayashi was hunched up miserably on his chair. Samejima was silently playing with a pack of cigarettes.

Nobody seemed to be behaving particularly suspiciously.

Keiko examined Kiyomura, Hayashi, Samejima and Madoka in that order, but she could find no signs of a nosebleed. Then it was Utayama's turn. Slightly nervously, he sat down in front of his wife.

"Your mucus doesn't look right. You should quit smoking," the doctor said.

Madoka glared at Shimada.

"I do believe it's your turn now," she said.

"Indeed it is." Shimada seemed puzzled by the fact that nobody fitted his profile of the killer. He frowned, but underwent his examination. Keiko pronounced him clear too.

"We're forgetting someone. That old lady. And of course, someone needs to examine the doctor's nose too," Kiyomura said.

Keiko promptly offered the penlight to Shimada. "Please examine me."

"Huh?"

"I don't want everyone to suspect me either."

"But I'm no doctor."

"Don't worry, it's easy," Keiko said, and placed the penlight in his hands. "You'll see the nasal septum—the part of your nose that divides the nasal cavity into two nostrils. At the lower end of the septum, there's a cartilaginous part that's called Kiesselbach's area. If you put your finger in your own nose, you'll feel it immediately."

"Ah, yes."

"Over ninety per cent of all nosebleeds occur there. So you just need to check it for an injury, or dried blood."

"Okay, let's see…"

Keiko lifted her chin, looking up at the ceiling. Shimada, somewhat hesitantly, aimed the penlight up her nose. After his inspection, he thanked her and shook his head.

"Seems all fine to me."

They then fetched Kadomatsu Fumie, who had been in her room all this time. They checked for injuries on her arms and legs, and eventually managed to convince her to undergo a nasal exam, telling her how important it was. But they found nothing.

Kiyomura glared at Shimada.

"All right. We've wasted enough time playing your games. It takes more than the logic of a whodunit to dissect a real murder case."

4

"Anyway, I still say we should follow Mr Miyagaki's will and continue with the contest," Kiyomura continued, planting his hands

140

on top of the table. "One person has been killed, and another has gone missing. This is a very serious situation, but we shouldn't forget the conditions of the contest as stipulated by the will still hold. Of course, if one of the competitors killed Suzaki in order to get rid of a rival, they would be disqualified. But since, for the moment, we don't know who the murderer is…"

"But—" Utayama tried to interrupt, but Kiyomura ignored him.

"Are you saying I should simply give up on my chance to inherit an enormous fortune? You've got to be kidding. All we can do now is wait for help to arrive. So rather than sitting here sucking our thumbs, we might as well concentrate on continuing the contest as best we can. I'm sure that what's Mr Miyagaki would've wanted us to do."

Utayama spoke up again, louder this time: "But surely you can't write under these circumstances."

"Oh, I can," Kiyomura said with an impish grin. "And I can't imagine Hayashi or Madoka giving up either."

The other two authors looked at each other uncertainly. Clearly, neither of them knew what to say.

Eventually, Hayashi spoke up. "Suppose we did proceed with the contest. Wouldn't Ino's absence be a problem?"

"He was only the coordinator. The cassette tape and the will itself should still be safe in the study, so the contest is still valid."

Kiyomura shot a glance at Shimada, who had been sitting silently at the table, running his fingertips over the grain of the wood. Having his deductions proven wrong so easily must have been a shock to him.

"I'm sure you all think I'm making light of the situation, or that I'm just obsessed by money, but I've been thinking about the murder too, you know. It's not just Shimada here who can play detective."

Shimada's fingers stopped moving.

"Murder mystery authors try to make their murders as complicated as possible, so as to overwhelm the reader. But that's not how things work in real life. Real murders don't tend to make use of ingenious tricks, and they rarely turn out to be the least likely suspect.

"Consider Shimada's argument about the reason for the decapitation. It made sense and sounded plausible, but you saw how that turned out. So there's still room for other interpretations.

"Perhaps the killer simply cut the head off to make the allusion to the Minotaur stronger. Perhaps the sight of all that blood frightened them and put them off completing the job. Or perhaps the murderer hated Suzaki and just felt like mutilating his body."

Shimada frowned, but didn't say a word.

"So what do you think happened?" Samejima asked, playing with an unlit cigarette. Kiyomura coughed, and then turned his head to the double doors leading to the staircase.

"I don't think the murderer is in the house any more."

A ripple of gasps went through the room. The others watched Kiyomura with puzzled looks on their faces.

"Judging by Shimada's words earlier, it seems he thinks the reason he couldn't find Ino is that he has been murdered too. But I have my doubts about that."

"So you are suggesting Ino is in fact the murderer?" Samejima asked.

Kiyomura grinned.

"There has been one murder in this house. And one man has gone missing. And that man just happens to hold the keys to the entrance doors. Just think about it! Isn't he the most likely suspect? I can't understand why none of you pointed this out earlier."

"And his motive? Why would he kill Suzaki? And why make the allusion?" Utayama asked.

"Anything could be a motive. Perhaps it's something we don't know about. I could imagine plenty of possible reasons why Ino might have a personal grudge against Suzaki.

"Like I said earlier, these are unusual circumstances. A fortune is at stake in this contest. What if Ino made use of this situation to finally act on his desire to kill Suzaki? Perhaps he originally planned to remain in the house with us afterwards—acting innocent—but after committing the murder decided to flee instead. By cutting the phone line and locking us in here, he can prevent us from calling the police for a few days, giving him time to make a run for it. How does that sound? A lot more likely, wouldn't you say?"

Kiyomura put his hands on his hips and awaited their reactions.

Hayashi and Madoka seemed quite impressed by this new theory. They were clearly less suspicious of Kiyomura now. Shimada didn't say anything, just stared down at his fingers on the tabletop.

Finally lighting the cigarette, Samejima said: "Supposing that's true… Shimada's theory about the reason for the decapitation could be correct too."

Kiyomura nodded gravely. "If his theory is correct, it would indeed be further proof of Ino's guilt. None of us has any injuries, so the only person left who could possibly fit Shimada's profile of the wounded killer is Ino."

"That makes sense…"

Had Ino Mitsuo murdered Suzaki? As their discussion continued, it seemed to be heading towards that conclusion. Utayama still felt that something was a little off, but began to come around to Kiyomura's theory. He glanced at Keiko next to him. She seemed convinced too and was observing the others.

Kiyomura smiled brightly, knowing he had won the audience over.

"And so, I repeat that I believe we should continue with the contest to decide which of us will inherit Mr Miyagaki's fortune, at least as long we are within the set time-frame and no help from outside arrives. What do you say?" he asked, looking confidently around the room.

Madoka closed her eyes, as if she had made up her mind. "All right. I don't want to miss this opportunity either."

"And you, Hayashi?"

Hayashi averted his eyes, but grunted in the affirmative. "All right. I'm in too."

Kiyomura gave a satisfied nod and looked at Samejima, Utayama and Shimada one by one.

"Well then, since the three of us are all agreed, I trust that our judges will not object?"

CHAPTER SIX

THE SECOND STORY

1

He found himself wandering in a dark labyrinth. Narrow hallways with lights flickering weakly on the grey-painted walls. With each step he took, the shadow extending from his feet changed length and shape, dancing to the sound of footsteps echoing in the darkness.

Utayama was overcome by questions.

"What is this place…?"

He stopped walking and turned around. The long hallway stretched away behind him into darkness. He looked up at the ceiling, but again saw only blackness. The longer he looked, the darker it started to feel; a darkness pressing down on him.

"Where am I?"

A maze… a labyrinth… The Labyrinth House? Was this the underground house of Miyagaki Yōtarō, built by Nakamura Seiji?

No… The lights on the walls here were different. Those glimmering lights… those weren't lamps. Weren't they… torches?

The floor here was also different. The hallways of the Labyrinth House were laid with dark brown vinyl floor tiles. But Utayama was now walking on stone flags.

Where on earth was he?

Utayama was standing at an intersection. A white mask hung on each of the walls leading off to the left and right. On the right was a lion's head, baring its teeth. On the left was a unicorn's head with a long horn protruding from the centre of its forehead.

Which turning should he take? Right? Left? Or continue straight on?

Tac-tac…

The sound of approaching footsteps.

Tac-tac, tac-tac…

Where was it coming from? In front? Behind? Right? Left… Impossible to tell.

Utayama felt an instinctive urge to flee. He had to get away immediately. He turned right without thinking, tripped over his own feet and stumbled, then started to run as fast as he could.

Tac-tac, tac-tac…

He could hear the sound of footsteps echoing over his own. He didn't know who it was, but they were following him. He had to escape. He couldn't let himself be caught. He absolutely had to get away.

After a while, he came across a Y-shaped fork. Two passages: one going to the left, the other to the right.

Now Utayama was sure he wasn't in the Labyrinth House. There were no junctions like this in its labyrinth.

He could still hear the footsteps. Slowly but surely, they were drawing closer.

How had Utayama ended up in this mysterious maze? There was no time to consider this question, so he took the left passage.

He followed it through countless twists, turns and intersections, and eventually found himself standing in front of a door.

Utayama was puzzled to see the word "Minotaur" etched on the bronze plate on the door. He knew this door. It belonged to the drawing room. But that would mean this was the Labyrinth House after all.

Tac-tac, tac-tac…

The footsteps were still getting nearer. They had followed him determinedly through the maze, as if his pursuer knew the route Utayama would take.

He opened the door and burst into the room. The body of the murdered Suzaki lay inside…

"Hey," said Kiyomura Junichi, raising a hand in greeting. "What's the matter? You look like you've seen a ghost."

The writers were chatting on a sofa. There was Kiyomura, Hayashi Hiroya, Funaoka Madoka and Samejima Tomoo. Opposite them, leaning against the terracotta wall were Shimada Kiyoshi and Keiko, who was staring at Utayama in puzzlement.

Astonished by this sight, Utayama's eyes darted about the room. To his left, on the carpet, lay Suzaki's bloody corpse. He was lying on his back, his half-severed head twisted unnaturally, but for some reason the stuffed bull's head above his neck was missing.

He was about to ask everyone what was going on, when suddenly he heard a loud bang behind him.

He spun around. Someone was standing in the doorway. No, not someone—a monster. It was easily over two metres tall. A hairy, muscular body. And on top of its neck rested a black bull's head…

"We're the sacrifice," said Suzaki's half-severed head in a rasping voice. "We're the sacrifice for the beast in the labyrinth. Of course, a proper sacrifice should really consist of seven young men and seven maidens."

"It's crazy if you ask me," said Kiyomura dryly. "We're neither young men nor maidens, and there aren't enough of us either. Oh, well."

The monstrous half-man, half-bull was holding a bloody axe in its hand. Its cold glass eyes flickered mysteriously as it raised its brawny arm high.

… A dream. That's it. This has to be a dream, or rather a nightmare. But despite this realization, the axe didn't stop. It came down in a slow arc towards Utayama's head.

A dream…

Suddenly, his vision turned crimson.

A dream…

*

Utayama was woken by his own cry of fear. He shook his head a few times, trying to rid himself of the after-images of the nightmare lingering in his mind.

He pushed himself up in bed. He was covered in cold sweat, his heart was pounding fast, and he was breathing heavily.

The starlight shining through the glass in the ceiling helped drive away some of the darkness in the room. He took a deep breath and swung his legs around to sit on the edge of the bed. As his eyes adjusted to the dark, he noticed someone only a few metres away, staring right at him. For a second, he froze in shock, but then realized he was looking at his own reflection in the full-length mirror.

"Ah…"

The air in the silent room was stuffy, so he got up and switched on the small ventilation fan. Then he took a cigarette from the desk and lit it. His eyes followed the smoke rising up to the ceiling.

Was it really okay? Would it really be all right after this?

Doubts and worries swirled in his mind. He began to ponder what had caused them.

2

What had happened after they had agreed to continue with the contest, as Kiyomura had insisted?

The discussion had ended just before five o'clock, after which the three writers left for their own rooms in order to work on their stories. It had been agreed that supper would be ready and laid out in the reception room at eight. The housekeeper kept saying she wanted to go home, but Samejima patiently explained the situation to her, and she eventually agreed to stay to prepare their meals.

In the meantime, Samejima left to get changed. Utayama and Keiko remained in the reception room, sitting quietly together. Shimada didn't need a change of clothes from his tracksuit and sweatshirt. He stared down at the tabletop with his head in his hands. From a distance it was impossible to tell whether he was deep in thought or sleeping.

When eight o'clock came and supper was served, Utayama helped himself to a little food without waiting for the others. Then he took a bottle of whisky from the sideboard and signalled to Keiko that they should go to their rooms.

Just then, Shimada called out to him:

"Utayama."

"Yes?"

"Do you truly believe Ino murdered Suzaki, and has already left the house?"

Utayama was momentarily lost for words. He wanted to say "Yes," but when he started to speak no sound came out. Deep down inside, he realized he was still unsure. "... Probably," was all he could manage.

Shimada's brow furrowed deeply. "Are you sure it isn't just what you all want to believe? Kiyomura's theory makes sense in a way. Perhaps it's even the most straightforward interpretation of what happened. But look at it from a different angle. Isn't it all a bit too obvious?"

"I don't really know," was Utayama's honest answer.

"But—"

"I'm sorry, but I'm very tired. I don't want to think about it now."

That was how he honestly felt. He looked at Keiko. She was exhausted too. Right now, all he wanted to do was go back to his room and get some sleep.

The pair said goodnight and moved to leave the reception room, but Shimada spoke up once again:

"Please allow me to ask you one last thing then."

"Yes?"

"Has Mr Miyagaki ever mentioned any kind of gimmick in the construction of this house?"

"A 'gimmick'?"

"Yes. Like a secret passageway, hidden doors or rooms, that kind of thing."

Utayama cocked his head pensively. He knew why Shimada had asked. The architect Nakamura Seiji's buildings often had quirks in their construction of the types Shimada had named. But Utayama was not aware of any such oddities in the Labyrinth House, and he told Shimada so.

By now it was nearly nine. Samejima had just returned after getting changed and having a rest, and the couple said goodnight once more and set off back to their rooms.

Utayama took Keiko's hand.

"What a day," he said. "Are you feeling all right?"

"Yes."

"So, what do you think?"

"About what?"

"What Shimada asked me. Whether we're going along with Kiyomura's theory because it's what we want to believe."

"I'm not sure," Keiko said with a sigh. "He might say that, but… I did all those nasal exams, and nobody showed any signs of a nosebleed, or any other injury. Ino is the only one who wasn't examined, so doesn't that mean he must be the murderer?"

"I guess so…"

Utayama suggested to Keiko that it might be better if they slept in the same room tonight, but she said she would be okay.

"I'll be fine. How do you expect both of us to fit in a single bed anyway? Three of us, actually, with the baby."

"I know, but…"

But what if Ino was the murderer and was still lurking in the house? Or what if he had indeed left the house at some point, but had returned? He had spare keys to all the rooms. Wouldn't it be dangerous for Keiko to be on her own?

Utayama explained his worries, but she reassured him once again.

"I can bolt the door from the inside. Besides, why would I of all people be targeted?"

"Aren't you scared?"

"Of course I'm a bit afraid, but I'll be all right. And you can't smoke if we share a room, can you?"

In the end, after loudly and repeatedly begging her to be careful, Utayama said goodnight to Keiko and went to his room alone.

He was both physically and mentally exhausted. He didn't even open the bottle of whisky he had brought with him. Instead he just switched the lights off, fell on his bed, closed his eyes and was asleep within a few minutes.

*

He wondered what time it was and looked at his wristwatch, pushing a button to light the LCD screen up with an orange glow.

It was 1.40 a.m.

As he stood in the dimly starlit room, the same thoughts kept running through Utayama's mind:

Was it really okay? Would it really be all right after this?

After his few hours of sleep, he could now think things over with a refreshed mind, and he was starting to worry.

Did he truly believe Ino had murdered Suzaki and had already left the house?

Shimada had asked him this question, and he had not been able to give a clear answer.

If Shimada's theory about the reason for the decapitation was correct, the murderer could not be one of the remaining seven guests (or the housekeeper). But what if the murderer hadn't been obeying the rules of Shimada's logic puzzle?

What if Suzaki's body had been mutilated out of pure hatred? What if the murderer had simply lost their mind? Or what if there was some other explanation…

Perhaps Ino being the murderer was indeed, as Shimada said, the most straightforward interpretation of what happened, but also a bit too obvious. The possibility remained that someone else could be the killer.

Perhaps Suzaki had really been murdered because he was one of the competitors with a chance of winning the fortune. After all, Suzaki had probably been the favourite. Utayama himself had thought so.

Perhaps the killer was Kiyomura. He had pointed the finger at Ino and insisted on continuing the competition. Did the seemingly feeble Hayashi have it in him to kill someone? Or Madoka, who had fainted when she saw the body?

On the other hand, if the motive was something they hadn't thought of yet, then Samejima, Shimada or even the housekeeper might be the murderer. And of course the others might suspect him and Keiko.

If Ino was not the murderer, he had probably already been killed by the real murderer, just as they had feared initially. And that would mean the murderer now had of all the spare keys that had been in Ino's possession.

And yet, they were carrying on the competition. Yes, they were respecting Miyagaki's will, and yes, they had no way of contacting the outside world at the moment anyway, but was it really okay to go on like this?

This was not normal behaviour, and Utayama knew it. Whatever the justifications they came up with: someone had been murdered. It was unforgivable of them to blithely continue with the contest.

He picked up the bottle of whisky and took a swig.

"This is all wrong," he muttered. "We have to do something."

Wasn't there some way of breaking down the entrance doors? If they could at least force the lattice door at the top of the stairs, they might find a useful tool in the storeroom. Or what if, as Shimada was thinking, there really was a hidden passageway somewhere?

At any rate, they should stop this crazy contest at once and concentrate on getting out of the house.

Once this thought had occurred to Utayama, there was no stopping him. Perhaps the pressure of the circumstances was getting to him too. He took another sip of whisky and pulled on a cardigan over his wrinkled shirt.

"First I have to talk some sense into him," he said to himself. He was thinking of Kiyomura Junichi: the one whose idea it had been to proceed with the contest. He was the one who was absolutely against trying to find any way to contact the outside world or working out a means of escape. So, Utayama needed to talk with him first. And if necessary, yes, he could even put an end to the competition by refusing to be a judge.

He looked at his wristwatch once more. It was nearly two in the morning. At this time, Kiyomura was likely still in front of his word processor, working on his story.

Utayama made up his mind, and left his room.

3

The lights in the hallway were on. Utayama took out his floor plan from his trouser pocket and worked out the route to Kiyomura's room, Theseus.

He started walking, but stopped after a few steps and listened carefully. The echoes of his footsteps faded, and thankfully, there were no others to be heard,

He gave a sigh of relief and set off once more. He felt strange, as if he were floating across the floor. He was still both mentally and physically tired, so those few pulls of whisky had had an exaggerated effect.

After a couple of turns, he found himself in the long southward-running corridor that led to the rooms in the western side. The lights gave off a yellow glow that shone down onto the dark brown vinyl floor tiles. And the ceiling…

He knew he was in the Labyrinth House, but he couldn't resist looking up to make sure.

What was he afraid of? That he was still in his nightmare? How could he be so ridiculous?

"'We're the sacrifice. We're the sacrifice for the beast in the labyrinth,'" Suzaki's raspy voice echoed through his mind.

He began to feel as if his own echoing footsteps were following him and sped up. When he reached the southern end of the corridor, he stopped and listened again. Silence.

He couldn't shake the feeling someone else was roaming the labyrinth, walking whenever Utayama did, stopping whenever he stopped...

He started walking again, following the corridor as it turned back north. Masks stared down at him from the walls next to each of the sixteen passages on the left.

The first passage led to Shimada's room, Cocalus. What was Shimada doing at the moment? Utayama wondered. Maybe it would be better to speak to him first, then the pair of them could go to Kiyomura together? He considered the idea for a second, but then decided against it. He should see Kiyomura on his own. For some reason he felt that this was his task alone.

He looked at the floor plan again. Theseus was the thirteenth passage on the left.

One, two, three... He counted the masks on the wall as he went. Myriad blank eyes stared down at him, the emotion in their gazes seemingly changing with the flickering light.

Six, seven, eight...

How would Kiyomura react? If his previous behaviour was any guide, he would probably laugh in Utayama's face. "What are you talking about? You know Ino's the murderer. He's gone now, so what is there to be afraid of?" Yes, doubtless he'd say something like that.

But did Kiyomura himself really believe that? Perhaps, deep down, he had doubts about his theory too. Or perhaps... What if Kiyomura had killed Suzaki?

Eleven, twelve, thirteen.

This is the one, Utayama thought. He glanced at the lion baring its teeth, and turned into the passage. At the end of the corridor he turned left, then right, then left…

Eventually, he arrived at the dark purple door. He wanted to check whether he was at the right room, but he could not see a bronze nameplate. Then he remembered what Kiyomura had mentioned earlier: it was missing from the Theseus door.

Even so, he still couldn't help but feel something was off. But if it wasn't the missing nameplate, what was it?

He knocked on the door and called out:

"Excuse me. It's me, Utayama. I'm sorry to bother you so late at night."

There was no reply. He knocked once more, a little louder this time.

"Hello?"

Still no answer. Utayama listened carefully, but could not hear anything from inside. Nor was there any light spilling from the crack under the door.

Had Kiyomura already gone to sleep? That seemed very unlikely. There were only three days left until the deadline, the evening of the fifth. Kiyomura might be a fast writer, but even he wouldn't have gone to bed already.

Had he gone somewhere else perhaps, to clear his head? To the reception room or the games room?

Taken aback by Kiyomura's apparent absence, Utayama tried the doorknob on a whim. To his surprise, he found it was not locked.

That's very odd, he thought. A murder had occurred in this house. Even if Kiyomura did believe Ino was the murderer and had already fled, would he really have gone to sleep in his room, or left without locking the door?

Utayama couldn't help but push the door open.

"Hello…?" He called out once more, stepping across the

156

threshold and searching blindly for the light switch on the wall to his left. When the lights came on, he found Kiyomura's body... But no... for a moment Utayama had been completely overwhelmed by his own imagination, but in fact, there was nobody in the room.

Utayama noticed the word processor on the desk was still on.

"The toilet perhaps?"

He quickly went over to the door at the back of the room, knocked and opened it. There was nobody inside. Of course, it would have been strange to go to the toilet with the lights in the room switched off. So Kiyomura had gone somewhere. The situation still made Utayama a bit queasy, though.

Feeling slightly tipsy, Utayama went unsteadily over to the desk. He felt the seat of the swivel chair. It was cold. So some time had passed since Kiyomura had last sat there.

On the desk, next to the keyboard of the word processor, lay a copy of the floor plan, folded out. If Kiyomura had left it, this suggested he had gone to the reception room or games room, or somewhere he could easily find his way.

Utayama looked at the screen. Apparently, Kiyomura had been working on his story before he decided to switch the lights off and leave the room.

A story competition with the biggest prize ever awarded: Miyagaki Yōtarō's fortune. A detective story set in the Labyrinth House. And the murder victim in the story had to be the author himself: Kiyomura Junichi.

What kind of story had he been writing? Utayama wondered. No, there were more important matters to deal with right now...

But what should he do first? Go look in the reception room or games room?

"A Yearning for Poison".

Utayama unconsciously read the title at the top of the screen.

Suddenly, his mind was filled by a horrifying suspicion. Something he had never considered before.

It can't be, he thought. Fearfully, his eyes ran over the lines below the title.

A YEARNING FOR POISON

She was waiting for the man. It was night. The lights were out in the room. The woman lurked in the darkness, holding her breath.

She felt determined on what she was about to do. She could not be absolutely sure she would succeed, but she did not fear failure.

She had only one thing in mind. To win this game.

"Hello?" A man's voice came from the other side of the door.

She intentionally waited a second before she replied, "Come in. It's not locked."

The doorknob turned. The man stepped inside.

"Oh, but it's pitch-dark in here."

The man was puzzled to find the lights were off.

"Why don't you switch the lights on?" he asked.

"I like the darkness," the woman replied. "And you can look up at the stars like this."

The pale starlight shone through the glass ceiling.

"Haha, a little rendezvous beneath the starry sky... in an underground house. How stylish."

His eyes had grown accustomed to the darkness. He closed the door behind him.

"Let's have a drink first." The woman poured some wine into the two glasses she had prepared and handed one to the man.

"Here you go," she said.

"Thanks."

"By the way, do you happen to know the name of this room?"

"Of course, the name was written on the door. Medea."

Medea was the character from Greek mythology after which the room was named.

"Yes. And do you know who she was?"

"A witch?"

"Yes. She was the daughter of King Aeëtes of Colchis, and had magical powers. She ended up marrying Aegeus, King of Athens. She then tried to poison Aegeus' son Theseus."

"Oh…"

"So, you see, this room is Medea. And yours is Theseus."

The man didn't say a word.

"Let's have that drink now." She raised her glass.

"What a strange story to tell me just now," the man said, his face twitching in the darkness. "Don't tell me my glass has been poisoned."

The woman smiled.

"I'll leave that up to your imagination."

4

Utayama rushed out of the room. There was no time to think.

The suspicion in his mind was a foolish one, but the more he tried to deny it, the more it grew.

Medea was the witch who had tried to poison Theseus…

The word processor had been left on. The story was unfinished. The door was not locked. The room was empty…

Utayama was back in the long corridor with the sixteen branching side-passages. The room he was heading for now—Medea—was directly south of Theseus. It was unused. He and Shimada had visited it yesterday during their search for Ino.

159

Which passage should he take? Not bothering to look at his floor plan, Utayama took the first turning on his right, but that branching corridor did a U-turn and brought him back to the main corridor again. Frustrated, he took out his map.

Coming from Theseus, he should have taken the third side-passage to his right. He went to it now. Hanging from the wall next to the turning was the mask of a beast with a horn in the middle of its forehead. Its hollow white eyes seemed to be ushering Utayama down the passageway.

The passage wound this way and that. Every time Utayama turned a corner, he found himself facing a wall, but eventually he came to the door.

"Ah!" Utayama cried, frozen on the spot.

The door to Medea was open. The light inside was on. And in the middle of the room, lying face down on the floor, was a man, his long legs pointing towards Utayama. He wore stonewashed jeans and a light purple shirt. It was Kiyomura Junichi.

"Kiyomura!"

Utayama suddenly felt dizzy, as if he were being sucked into the crack between reality and fantasy. He lifted his two arms in front of him and, as if he were swimming through the air, staggered his way into the room.

"Kiyo… mura?"

The man on the floor did not move a muscle. Utayama held his breath as he crouched near the body and examined the face. Kiyomura's features bore the traces of excruciating pain, and his hands were clutching at his neck, the nails digging into the skin. Had he suffered so much that he had clawed at his own throat?

Utayama's trembling hand reached out to check for a pulse, but Kiyomura was already dead. Utayama got up and looked around the room. There was nothing different from when he and Shimada visited the day before.

"Is… somebody here?" he called out, looking around to make sure he was alone. "Anyone?"

It was eerily silent. All he could hear was the sound of his own breathing.

Coming to his senses, he realized he had to wake the others up right away and let them know about this new death.

His hands still shaking, he unfolded the plan. Whose room was closest? It was Shimada's room, Cocalus.

Just then, he heard the sharp sound of footsteps approaching behind him. He shuddered and turned around.

"It's you!" a voice cried. In the darkness beyond the open door, stood a tall, slender shadow: Shimada Kiyoshi.

"I heard someone cry out in the room next to mine— Ah!" Shimada let out another cry when he noticed the body lying next to Utayama. "Is that… Kiyomura?"

"Yes."

"Is he dead?"

"Yes. He was dead when I found him."

Shimada came into the room. He was wearing a black sweatshirt. Utayama began to explain in a muddled manner how he had discovered the body. Shimada's deep-set eyes flicked between Kiyomura's body and Utayama while the latter talked.

A long moan escaped Shimada's throat when he was told about the opening of the story on Kiyomura's word processor.

"So it was about a man and a woman meeting in this very room, Medea? And that's why you came here."

Utayama nodded vehemently. "Yes. It was only the start of the story, and nothing had really happened yet, but it seemed very suggestive, describing Medea as a witch who tried to poison Theseus."

"And now he's really dead."

Shimada looked down at the body, running his eyes over it carefully.

"It's impossible to tell what the cause of death is just by looking. We can't even tell if it was murder or not. We should examine him first."

"But…"

"Don't forget there's still no way for us to contact the police," said Shimada, getting down on one knee. He put his hands on Kiyomura's shoulders and turned the body face up.

"… No visible injuries. He dug his nails into his throat here, but I can't see any other marks to suggest he was strangled. I'm afraid your wife will need to have a look at him."

"Was he… poisoned?" Utayama managed to utter. Shimada shrugged.

"Perhaps. If so, that would make this murder very similar to… what was it called, 'A Yearning for Poison'? So, once again, the murderer has made an allusion to the story written by the victim."

Shimada looked away from the body. "But, assuming that is true, the question remains: how did the murderer manage to give him the poison?"

"Indeed…"

"Suppose the murderer somehow learnt the contents of the story Kiyomura had written, or what he planned to write, and poisoned Kiyomura in this room to allude to the story. How could the murderer have set it all up? Kiyomura of all people would have known what his own story was about. Wouldn't that have made it difficult to poison him in the Medea room?"

Utayama saw something out of the corner of his eye, and his attention was drawn towards the door. Shimada noticed the strange look on the editor's face.

"What's the matter?"

Utayama pointed to a spot on the wall immediately to the left of the door for anyone entering the room. Shimada went over and examined it.

"Aha, so that's it."

A square plastic panel was built into the panelled wood wall. And surrounding the light switch in the middle of the panel were...

Utayama followed Shimada to scrutinize the panel up close and saw what they were: pins. Dozens of them had been stuck around the light switch, like a pincushion, but with the sharp ends facing outward.

"There's a thick layer of putty that the pins are stuck in. And I fear..."

Shimada carefully brought his nose close to a pin. A brownish substance had been smeared on its sharp end. Shimada sniffed it.

"It smells like stale tobacco. It's probably concentrated nicotine."

"Nicotine?"

"Yes, the stuff in cigarettes. It's pretty poisonous in the right concentration. It affects the autonomic nerve system, resulting in respiratory paralysis."

Shimada went back to Kiyomura's corpse. He got down on one knee again, carefully removed the left hand from the throat and opened it.

"Look here. Just as I thought."

A couple of little red wounds could be seen on the pad of one finger.

"This is how the nicotine got into his blood. I don't believe he smoked, so it would have affected him very swiftly. It must have stopped his breathing before he even had time to cry for help..."

Shimada put the hand back where it had been and glared at the doorway.

"The killer had prepared that booby trap in advance. They must have summoned Kiyomura to this room. So when he arrived here and found the room pitch-dark, what did he do? He tried the light switch of course. And because all of the guest rooms have the light switch to the left of the door as you come in, he didn't even look, just felt for the switch with his left hand. And when he switched it on, his finger was pricked by the nicotine-laced pins."

Utayama remembered he had once read a mystery with a similar murder method: Ellery Queen's *The Tragedy of X*. Perhaps it had been the inspiration for this murder?

Utayama explained his suspicions to Shimada, who nodded gravely.

"Yes, you may be on to something. That housekeeper is probably the one person here who might not be familiar with the book, but everyone else, including you and me, will have read that Queen masterpiece."

"But how would the killer have got their hands on such a poison? They must have prepared it beforehand…"

"Nicotine is used in concentrated form as a component in agricultural insecticides. It would be difficult to refine concentrated nicotine from cigarettes, but you might be able to obtain it by boiling down insecticides easier than you'd expect."

"But are there any insecticides in the house?"

"They wouldn't necessarily have to be in the house."

Only then did Utayama realize Shimada was right. The murderer (whether it was Ino or not) was very likely in possession of the keys to the entrance doors. Unlike them, the murderer had always been able to leave the house. So they could easily have brought the insecticide, pins and putty from outside.

Shimada gave Kiyomura's body a pitying look.

"How ironic. He disproved his own theory that the murderer was no longer in the house by falling into the murderer's trap himself. By the way…"

"Yes?"

"I wonder how the murderer managed to lure Kiyomura to this room."

"Maybe the murderer simply summoned him somehow?" Utayama suggested.

Shimada shook his head. "I think that is unlikely. Don't forget, this room is Medea. Would he be so oblivious to the fact he had been summoned to the unused room which functioned as the setting of the opening scene of his own story?"

Utayama didn't know what to think.

"And while Kiyomura was really persistent in pushing his theory that the murderer had left the house, I don't think he can have been truly sure of it himself. Part of it was just him wanting the contest to continue. I don't believe he was absolutely confident about his safety. And yet, he fell for this trap so easily. It somehow doesn't really make sense to me… Hey, what's this?"

Shimada's hand reached out to grab a piece of white paper that was sticking out of the chest pocket of Kiyomura's shirt.

"Is this his map? Oh, no, it isn't," said Shimada, shaking his head, when he had unfolded the paper. "It's…"

Utayama leant forward and peered past Shimada: it was a short note, written on a word processor.

I'll be waiting for you in the games room at 1 a.m. I have something important to discuss with you about the contest, so don't be late. Do not tell anyone about this.

Madoka

CHAPTER SEVEN

THE THIRD STORY

1

Had Funaoka Madoka arranged a secret meeting with Kiyomura?

Utayama stared down at the neatly typed black letters while his confused mind tried to make sense of it all.

She had something important to discuss about the contest. This suggested she wanted to strike some kind of agreement with Kiyomura. For example, if either of the two were to win, they would split the inheritance.

That was quite possible, Utayama thought. Kiyomura and Madoka had been a couple, even if they were no longer together. Considering the enormous fortune at stake, they might have thought cooperation was the best policy.

"But this is the wrong room," Shimada mumbled, folding up the note again and replacing it in Kiyomura's chest pocket. "It would at least make some sense if the note had instructed him to come to this room."

Utayama understood that Shimada suspected this note had played a role in Kiyomura's death. But if it was fake, created to lure him into the trap, it should have mentioned Medea. Instead, it had directed him to the games room.

"We'll have to ask Madoka whether she wrote it or not. Of course, she'll deny either way. Anyway, we should wake everyone up first. We can sort out the note later."

Shimada got to his feet.

Utayama left the room, but spun around when he heard Shimada give a cry. He had just closed the door and was standing before it with a puzzled look on his face.

"What's wrong?" Utayama asked.

"It's missing," Shimada said, shaking his head.

"What's missing?"

By way of answer, Shimada simply pointed at the door. Utayama let out a long, understanding "Oh…"

The bronze nameplate was indeed missing. Utayama clearly remembered seeing it with the name "Medea" on it when they had checked the room yesterday. But now the nameplate was gone, leaving only a screw hole behind.

"Did someone remove it?"

Shimada gave no answer and turned away from the door.

"Let's go. We've already wasted too much time."

2

It was nearly three in the morning. They were agreed it might be dangerous to split up, so decided to wake everyone up together.

The closest room on the map was Aegeus, directly north of Kiyomura's room, where Hayashi Hiroya was staying.

First Suzaki had been murdered and now Kiyomura, ruminated Utayama. If their deaths were motivated by the desire to inherit Miyagaki Yōtarō's fortune, the murderer surely had to be one of the remaining two writers: Hayashi or Madoka. Or was the murderer the missing Ino after all? Or perhaps even Samejima?

Or what if, whatever his motive might be, Shimada was the killer? Utayama could not really believe that, but still couldn't entirely ignore his suspicions. For that reason, he intentionally trailed a few steps behind Shimada as they walked.

They kept the white masks on their left as they went down the long hallway, their steps echoing through the dark labyrinth. As they checked their floor plans and made their way to the passage leading to Aegeus, Utayama could feel something nagging at him. What was it? He had experienced the same feeling earlier when he made his way from his own room to Kiyomura's. A minor dissonance. A slightly unsettling, uncomfortable feeling. Something was wrong. Something was not as it should be...

He followed Shimada, who was walking briskly and scratching his head.

What was that feeling?

By the time they arrived at Hayashi's room and Shimada knocked on the door, Utayama's question was still unanswered.

"Hayashi?"

Shimada's hand froze mid-knock.

"What's the matter?" Utayama asked, finally forgetting his odd feeling.

Shimada gestured towards the door with his chin.

"It's open."

"Oh, you're right."

They didn't even have to try the knob. The door, with its bronze "Aegeus" plate, was slightly ajar.

Shimada called out Hayashi's name again, but there was no reply.

Light was shining from the gap between the door and frame. That was the single difference from how Utayama had found Kiyomura's room earlier.

Was Hayashi not in his room either? What if he had suffered the same fate as Kiyomura? Or what if Hayashi was the murderer?...

"Coming in!" Shimada cried loudly, and he pushed the door with his right hand. It swung partly open with a creak.

"Ah!"

"What on earth?!"

As their eyes processed the sight inside, each let out a muffled cry.

To the left of the entrance, in front of the desk with the word processor on it, was Hayashi Hiroya.

He was wearing an off-white vest and lay face down on top of the overturned swivel chair. His hands were resting on the edge of the desk, his head hanging down. The dark brown object sticking from the middle of his back was the reason why he was no longer moving.

"I can't believe it…" Shimada whispered, stepping into the room.

Utayama felt dizzy once more and had to lean against the door. When his head cleared somewhat, he realized it wasn't moving, despite him putting all his weight on it: something was preventing the door from opening fully.

He had to gather all of his waning strength to peek behind it. He saw that the small table and two stools that would have been originally at the rear of the room had been moved there.

"Look at this," Utayama called out to Shimada, who had gone over to desk. Shimada turned around and raised an eyebrow.

"How odd," he muttered. "It looks like he barricaded the door."

"Oh, yes, a barricade…" said Utayama, now realizing why the furniture had been moved.

Hayashi had agreed to continue with the contest, but he was a timid man. He might have blocked the door out of fear. But the barricade had already been pushed aside when they came into the room, and the door had not been shut much less locked…

169

Shimada turned back to the desk and examined Hayashi. He shook his head.

"He's dead. This wound must've been what did him in."

The handle of the weapon, perhaps a kitchen knife, was sticking out of Hayashi's back. His vest was stained red. Judging from how bright the blood was, not too much time had passed since he had been stabbed.

Shimada looked around the room. "There are scratches on his arms, shoulders and elsewhere. The room is a mess too, even if we ignore the furniture he moved for his barricade. The bed sheets are lying on the floor, and look at his bag—it's all the way over there."

Next to the full-length mirror on the back wall lay an overturned cork-coloured travel bag.

"This indicates he must have struggled with the murderer. He was attacked with that knife and ultimately got trapped against the desk."

"But why would he make that barricade, only to open the door and allow the murderer to come inside with a knife?" asked Utayama.

"That is indeed very puzzling." Shimada stroked his narrow chin. "Did the murderer somehow manage to convince Hayashi to open the door? If so, it would be someone Hayashi trusted..."

It would be difficult to open a door with the latch bolted, and a table and stools acting as a barricade, even if the murderer had the spare keys. As there was no sign the door had been forced open, that meant Hayashi himself had let the murderer into the room. That seemed to indicate the killer was not Ino Mitsuo at least. Hayashi would never have opened the door for him.

While Utayama was considering these scenarios, Shimada started to examine the word processor. Utayama went over to him, trying to ignore the blood seeping through Hayashi's vest.

"Same thing again?" he asked timidly.

"I don't know yet," replied Shimada. "Have a look at this," he said, pointing at the screen. "What do you think it means?"

Utayama peered at the screen. The last paragraph of Hayashi's story broke off abruptly. Then there were four blank lines and, at the very end, what Shimada was pointing at:

nuei

3

THE GHOST IN THE GLASS

It is the night of 2 April 1987. Location: one of the rooms in Miyagaki Yōtarō's mansion.

I light a new cigarette, while staring at the square screen of the word processor. Lately, whenever I hear about how dangerous smoking is, I make up my mind to finally quit, but I'm not sure I can do it. I can fight the urge most of the time, but the moment I'm faced with one of my manuscripts, I unconsciously reach out for a smoke.

Smoke rising to the ceiling. An ashtray full of butts. A grey fug hangs in the air.

We all came to this underground house to celebrate Mr Miyagaki's sixtieth birthday, so I never expected to be working on a new story like this. I'll explain the details later, but I have to write a story over the next three days, before 10 p.m. on the 5th.

The theme is a difficult one. The story must be about a murder committed in this very building: the Labyrinth House. The characters must be the people currently in the house. Furthermore, the murder victim must be none other than myself.

Will I able to write such a story, in such a short time?

I have been racking my brains since yesterday and have finally come up with an idea. It's a dying message, left by a murder victim in their final moments. Now I only have to figure out how I'll use it.

Anyway, let's get writing. Yes, let's start with the scene where, I, Hayashi Hiroya (better known as Horinouchi Kazuhiro) am murdered…

*

To the left of the entrance, in front of the desk with the word processor on it, was Hayashi Hiroya.

He was wearing an off-white vest and lay face down on top of the overturned swivel chair. His hands were resting on the edge of the desk, his head hanging down. The dark brown object sticking from the middle of his back was the reason why he was no longer moving.

A word processor sat on the desk, still switched on. It seemed he had been attacked while working on his manuscript on it.

This was one of the rooms in the Labyrinth House, the residence of Miyagaki Yōtarō. In the room Aegeu

nuei

172

Utayama and Shimada couldn't help but gasp as they finished reading the opening of the story on the screen.

The prologue was written from Hayashi's perspective, as he was getting started. The story thus featured a narrative-within-a-narrative structure. It was impossible to tell how it would have developed further, but, according to the narrator, the story would feature a dying message.

And what caught their attention the most, was of course the description of the crime scene.

Shimada began: "It's the same once again… It's all the same: the room, the body in front of the desk, the partly written manuscript on the word processor, the way he's lying there…"

"So does that mean his hands were deliberately placed on the edge of the desk after the murder to allude to the story?" Utayama asked, baffled.

Shimada stroked his sharp chin. "For the moment, I can't say anything for sure. If this scene was set up to allude to the manuscript, it means the murderer first killed Hayashi by stabbing him in the back, then moved the body here and rested his hands on the edge of the desk. Of course, it's possible the murderer did indeed go to all that trouble to remain as faithful to the story as possible.

"However, it is also possible this is all just a coincidence. It could be a coincidence the murderer used a knife with a dark brown hilt, and that it hasn't been pulled out of his body. It could be a coincidence the murderer ended up stabbing Hayashi in this spot. It's certainly not *impossible*."

"But what is the truth?"

"Who knows? It's impossible to say now."

Shimada peered at the screen. "But these letters: 'nuei'. I think that's something we should consider carefully."

"You mean you think it's a message left by Hayashi?"

"Yes, more or less," Shimada answered vaguely. "Allow me to present one theory. As you just read, Hayashi was working on the opening part of his story in which he himself would be murdered. The victim in the story-within-the-story was also working on a manuscript when he was killed. And in the prologue, we are told that the story-within-the-story would include a message left by a murder victim.

"But then Hayashi was attacked by the murderer for real, in this room. Having been fatally wounded, what would he have been thinking? Of course, as a victim he would naturally want to identify his killer for the other people here, but he had also just been working on a story about his own murder. Wouldn't it be conceivable he would want to leave some kind of dying message on his word processor?

"So, Hayashi's body being at the desk, in this pose, could either be the handiwork of the murderer or just a coincidence, but either way, let's say the murderer assumes their victim is dead and leaves the room. But Hayashi isn't quite dead, and uses his last reserves of strength to pull himself up onto the desk, type something on the keyboard, and then collapses and dies, with his hands resting on the edge of the desk."

Shimada pointed at the screen.

"'*This was one of the rooms in the Labyrinth House, the home of Miyagaki Yōtarō. In the room Aegeu.*' You see how it just stops mid-word? Then there are four empty lines, and suddenly it says 'nuei'. At the very least, I think we can safely assume those four letters are not supposed to be part of the story he was working on.

"And look at the keyboard too," he went on.

Utayama glanced down at it. A black ashtray full of cigarette butts sat next to it on the desktop.

"First, note the position of the keyboard. It has been shifted away from the screen of the word processor. And see the smears of blood here and here? I think they prove Hayashi handled the keyboard after he had been wounded by the murderer."

Utayama was impatient for Shimada to get to the point:

"So you do think it's a dying message?"

Utayama couldn't help but feel excited. Perhaps the shock of the macabre deaths he had encountered over the past two days had numbed him, preventing the normal reaction to yet another death. His feelings of fear and sorrow for the victim were being drowned out by his growing curiosity about the "mystery" before him. If they could solve the dying message, they'd know who the murderer was.

"What do you think these letters could mean?" Utayama asked, gazing wide-eyed at the message. He couldn't make any sense of them.

"Nuei". Those were obviously not the initials of anyone in the house. Nor did it resemble any of the writers' pen-names.

He knew there was an island country called Niue, but the closeness of the name to the letters on the screen must just be a coincidence, he thought. None of the people here came from Niue or had any other ties with it as far as he knew.

What if the victim had wanted to write a longer word, but died midway through? But Utayama couldn't think of any word that started with "nuei". Perhaps it was another language?

Suddenly, a loud noise rang out, destroying the silence that filled the underground labyrinth. Utayama started and straightened up.

"What was that?" He could feel all the hairs on his neck standing on end.

It was a shriek, but not one produced by a human. It was piercing, metallic and continuous: "bee-boo, bee-boo…"

"It's Madoka!" Shimada cried. "Don't you remember what she said on the first evening? She brought a personal alarm with her."

"Oh!"

"Let's go," said Shimada, already rushing to the door. "I'm afraid something horrible may have happened already."

CHAPTER EIGHT

THE FOURTH STORY

1

Utayama knew roughly where Madoka's room was located, having looked at the floor plan so many times. He had not memorized the route, but there was no time to check the map as he barely managed to keep up with Shimada, who was running down the corridors.

Shimada didn't know the way either.

When they arrived back in the long hallway with the branching side-passages, they headed north, following the noise, but came up against dead ends twice. Even so, they arrived at Madoka's room sooner than if they had carefully examined the floor plan first.

"Ms Funaoka!" Shimada cried, as he reached for the doorknob.

The nameplate read "Icarus". The son of Daedalus. When King Minos learned that Theseus had killed the Minotaur and fled the island of Crete, he suspected Daedalus had assisted the hero, so he imprisoned Daedalus and Icarus in the labyrinth. Daedalus then crafted two sets of artificial wings, which he and his son used to fly away to make their escape. However, the wings were made from birds' feathers held together with wax, and Icarus did not heed his father's warnings not to fly too close the sun. The sun melted the wax, and Icarus fell into the sea.

The famous myth flashed through Utayama's mind as Shimada knocked on the door, calling out to Madoka.

Bee-boo, bee-boo...

On the other side of the door, the alarm was an unrelenting reminder of the urgency of the situation. The constant wailing echoed in their heads, merging in Utayama's mind with the cry of Icarus as he plunged out of the blue sky down towards the sea.

Shimada shouted Funaoka's name louder and louder, but there was no reply. He twisted the knob repeatedly with both hands, but the door was locked and would not budge.

Shimada turned to Utayama:

"It's no good. Give me a hand."

"With what?"

"We're going to have to break it down."

The two started to shoulder-charge the door, using the full length of the short corridor for their run-up. After a few attempts, the door creaked, but did not open. They charged it a fourth time, then a fifth, to no avail. At this rate, the pair of them would break before the door did.

"It's no good," Utayama said weakly, rubbing his smarting shoulder. The alarm was still ringing.

"There's no other option then," said Shimada. "I'll go to the drawing room."

"Why to the drawing room...? Oh, the axe!?"

"That's the only way we'll be able to open this door. Please wait here for me. If anything happens, give a loud shout."

Shimada turned and set off back down the corridor, running as fast as he could. His echoing footsteps slowly faded into the labyrinth.

Left alone, Utayama twisted the knob once more in desperation. The door still did not move. What with the ringing of the alarm in his ears and his aching shoulder, he could feel a headache coming on.

Was Madoka inside the room? Had she too been turned into a lifeless corpse? Utayama leaned his back against the door and covered his ears with his hands.

He couldn't take any more of this. The strange feeling of excitement that had come over him when he read the dying message in Hayashi's room had dissipated completely. He shook his head, trying to rid himself of an overwhelming feeling of dread.

It used to be thought that mazes and labyrinths could ward off evil. The ancient Chinese believed evil could only fly in a straight line, so city walls were built in rows, but with the entrances out of line with each other so as to create a mini-maze. Similarly, in England, labyrinth patterns used to be drawn on doorsteps to ward off demons and witches.

But evil had not been warded off from this house, Utayama thought. The complete opposite had happened. A bloodthirsty devil was now lurking in this labyrinth.

Who was the killer? First Suzaki had been murdered, followed by Kiyomura and now Hayashi. If the murders had been committed to get rid of rivals in the story competition, the last writer remaining was also the only suspect: Madoka. But it appeared she was in trouble now too.

This had to be the work of a lunatic, Utayama thought. An insane killer, murdering for the thrill of it. Was it Ino, who had disappeared? Or Samejima? Or was it the housekeeper, or perhaps Shimada…?

No, there was one other possibility: an unknown third party might be hiding in the house. Perhaps a murderous madman had snuck in without anyone knowing and was lurking somewhere. In that case there would be no motive for the killings, of course. All those carefully arranged crime scenes might just be part of a sick game.

As Utayama slowly convinced himself of this theory, he began to worry about Keiko. What if she became the next victim?

The alarm seemed to be getting fainter now. Were the batteries running low, or had his ears just got used to the noise? Utayama could hear the sound of running footsteps approaching, and a breathless Shimada appeared around the corner. When Utayama saw the axe in his hand, he shrank back against the door involuntarily. What if Shimada swung it at him?

"Please get out of the way," Shimada ordered, almost angrily. Utayama moved behind Shimada, as he took his position in front of the door, holding the axe in both hands and starting to swing it.

The door squeaked as it was slowly split open. The sound of the personal alarm grew louder. The only light inside the dimly lit room was the yellow glow of the nightlight.

One axe swing followed another. The steel blade that had severed Suzaki's neck was now slowly destroying the door.

Eventually, the hole was big enough for Shimada to stick his arm through. The door could be unlocked by turning the knob from inside, and Shimada did so.

He rested the axe against the wall and pushed the door, but it still wouldn't open.

"The bolt…" he groaned irritably, and reached through the splintered hole once more. He undid the latch and opened the door.

"Ms Funaoka, are you here…?"

Shimada stepped into the dark room. His left hand reached out automatically for the light switch, but then froze in mid-air. He remembered the booby trap in Medea. He carefully examined the switch and made sure it was safe before he pushed it.

"Oh, no…"

The pale fluorescent light revealed Funaoka Madoka, lying on the ivory carpet, her head turned towards the door.

She was wearing a rose-pink negligee, suggesting she had been attacked after getting ready for bed. Her long hair was spread out on the carpet. Her right hand was reaching out towards the door, and in front of it lay a yellow heart-shaped pendant: her personal alarm.

Shimada slowly approached the body. He picked up the small wailing object and switched it off. Silence returned, but they could still hear the alarm echoing in their minds.

"I think she was hit on the head with something," said Shimada, pointing at the back of Madoka's cranium, where there was a small patch of dark blood in her hair. "But this is very curious…"

"What's that?"

Shimada went to the back of the room. "Think about it. The personal alarm was going off, meaning presumably that she had been attacked by the killer and switched the alarm on in response. We immediately ran here from Hayashi's room."

Shimada nervously reached out to the toilet door, and pulled it open. "Nobody in here either."

Utayama watched silently as Shimada went on talking.

"The door of the room was locked, and it was also bolted." Shimada walked over to the built-in wardrobe. "So we break the door open, and as you can see, there is nobody in the room besides the victim."

The only clothes in the wardrobe were two of Madoka's dresses: one black and one pink. Utayama had been standing near the doorway, observing Shimada's movements, and now he finally realized what Shimada was trying to tell him.

"So… that means this is… a locked room mystery."

Shimada looked under the bed. "How did the murderer escape from this room while it was locked from the inside? And how did they manage to get out in the short time it took for us to arrive from the branching passage?"

At that moment, from the corner of his eye, Utayama saw Madoka move.

"Ah!" he cried and ran over to her side.

"What's the matter?" Shimada asked.

"I–I think she moved!"

"What!"

Utayama held her right wrist and felt for a pulse… She was still alive! The pulse was weak, but definitely there!

"She's not dead yet," he declared, looking up at Shimada. He didn't have to wait for instructions before saying what he did next:

"I'll get Keiko!"

2

It was ten past four in the morning. The personal alarm had started ringing at around half-past three, and they had been in the room for roughly ten minutes, so it had taken them about thirty minutes to get to Icarus and to eventually break the door open.

The killer had attacked Madoka after she was in bed, leaving only the nightlight on. She had activated her personal alarm, which had been lying ready near her pillow. Surprised by the sudden noise, the murderer struck Madoka once on the back of the head, but did not finish her off, and quickly fled the scene. But the question remained: how?

182

The house was mostly underground, and of course had no windows. The only way to get out of a room was through the door, but the door to Madoka's room, Icarus, had been locked. This was built into the doorknob, so that the door could be locked by pushing the button into the knob and pulling closed the door behind you from the outside: you didn't need a key for that. But how could it have been bolted from outside the room?

Could the killer have employed some kind of mechanical trick, using the small gap between the door and the frame?

It had taken Shimada and Utayama about two or three minutes to reach the door of Icarus after first hearing the alarm. Would it really have been possible for the murderer to use such a trick to engage the bolt from outside in such a short time, all the while knowing that people might arrive on the scene at any moment, brought running by the sound of the alarm? Furthermore, even if it were possible—what purpose did it serve?

Utayama went past the long corridor with the branching side-passages and turned back on himself at the end. He ran as fast as he could through the dark labyrinth to reach Keiko. Once he got to the long straight hallway leading to the reception room, the rest of the route was easy. He had gone back and forth between that room and his own room countless times over the last two days, and by now he could get his bearings by checking the branching corridors and the masks.

He was running so fast that he went face first into a wall a few times, but eventually made it to Keiko's room, Dionysus. His heart was thumping in his chest. He was drenched in sweat, both from the stress of the situation and the physical effort. He didn't think he had ever run so much since he left university.

"Keiko."

He was so out of breath he could hardly speak. He tried to steady his voice as he knocked on the door.

"Keiko? It's me. Open up."

He stopped knocking. There was no answer. It couldn't be…

An immense fear filled his mind. Looking at the bronze name-plate with the name of the god of wine etched into it, Utayama cried out his wife's name, hoping he was wrong:

"Keiko!!"

He knocked hard again and twisted the knob, and was finally set at ease when a reply came.

"Who's there?" The voice sounded weak and sleepy.

"It's me. There's an emergency. You have to get up. Could you open the door?"

"… Okay, just a second."

After a brief wait, Utayama could hear the latch being gently unbolted and then the door opened. Keiko stood in the doorway, wearing a white negligee and looking sleepy.

"What's the matter? What time is it?"

"It's an emergency. More people have been killed."

"What?"

Keiko stopped rubbing her eyes, and opened her mouth in shock, though she did not cry out. She had not really been awake until she heard the word "killed".

"Kiyomura and Hayashi, they… no, I'll explain later. But first you need to help Madoka. She's been hit on the head and—"

"All right."

Keiko cut off Utayama's confused explanation, walked over to her bed and picked up her cardigan, which she hurriedly threw over her shoulders. Then she took a yellow pouch out of her bag on the desk. This was the first-aid kit that she always took with her when travelling.

"Where to? The reception room?"

"Her room."

"Show me the way."

Utayama didn't want his pregnant wife to run, so he had to stop her from going too quickly as they made their way back to Madoka's room as fast as they sensibly could.

"How bad is the wound to her head?"

Utayama shook his head weakly.

"I can't say. At first, I even thought she was dead."

"Did someone attack her?"

"Yeah."

"And Kiyomura and Hayashi? You mentioned them first…"

"They're both dead."

"No…" Keiko gripped her husband's hand tightly.

"I'll explain later. Though a lot of it is still a complete mystery," he said.

"And the others?"

"Shimada's waiting in Madoka's room."

"And Samejima?"

"Oh, I don't know…"

"And the housekeeper? Will they be all right alone? Ino is the murderer, isn't he?"

"… I don't know."

They had arrived at the long straight hallway leading to the reception room and turned north at the intersection.

"Who's that?"

A voice echoed through the long tunnel-like space. The Utayamas turned around in surprise and spotted Samejima towards the far end of the hallway, wearing a blazer over pyjamas.

"What's happened?" Samejima asked, jogging towards them. "Did you hear that noise just now? It sounded like an alarm ringing. It didn't stop, so I went to the reception room to have a look."

Utayama understood now why Samejima was there. The racket must have travelled through the labyrinth to the eastern side.

"You're right, that was an alarm," Utayama said, observing the expression on the other's face. "Madoka's personal alarm…"

Samejima froze and turned pale. "Huh? Do you mean she…"

"She was attacked by the killer."

"What?"

"I'm afraid it's true. You should come with us."

3

By the time Utayama had brought Keiko and Samejima to Icarus, it was half-past four, about an hour before sunrise.

Madoka was still lying in the same position on the floor.

"I thought it'd be better not to move her, so I left her lying there. She's still breathing. I tried talking to her, but she doesn't react," Shimada quickly explained. "Please, could you examine her, Keiko?"

Keiko let go of Utayama's hand, and crouched at Madoka's side. The writer was lying with her left cheek pressed against the floor. Keiko checked her pulse, then examined the wound on her head and looked at her face.

"Could you move her to the bed? Lay her on her back, but keep her face sideways," she instructed the other three.

"Sure," said Shimada, snapping into action. He signalled to Utayama. "Could you take her shoulders? I'll take her legs."

"All right."

"I'll help too," Samejima quickly offered.

186

"Be careful. Make sure you keep her head as still as possible," urged Keiko.

Following her instructions, they picked up Madoka and laid her on the bed. Shimada pulled the duvet up, which had been rucked against the wall, to cover her to her chest.

Madoka's eyes were still closed, her brow furrowed. Keiko put an ear to her mouth to listen to her breathing, then loudly called out Madoka's name. The young writer's lips, which looked very pale without lipstick, quivered slightly in response, but that was all.

Keiko took some antiseptic and cotton wool out of her pouch, and cleaned the wound. Then she turned to the other three.

"The wound itself is not very deep, but I fear she's suffered more than just a concussion. If she's bleeding internally, there's nothing I can do here for her."

"But there must be something we can do," said Samejima, whose face was very pale.

Keiko shook her head. "The only chance is to get her to a hospital at once."

"But…"

"I'll have another look at the entrance doors," Shimada proposed.

"But we know all the doors to the hall are locked," Utayama said.

"I might figure something out. I'll also check in on the house-keeper too just to be sure. It might be dangerous for her to be left on her own."

What did Shimada mean by dangerous? Was he worried about the housekeeper's safety, or was he afraid the old woman was the murderer? speculated Utayama.

"Could you also fetch another blanket, and a bowl filled with warm water?" Keiko asked.

"I'll go with you," said Samejima, and followed Shimada to the door. "You two will be all right, won't you?"

Utayama looked at his wife, and then nodded to Samejima. Shimada paused in the doorway and turned to Utayama:

"Oh, and you might want to have a look at the word processor. I was curious, so I switched it on while you were gone."

"You mean… the same thing has happened again?"

"No… it seems she hadn't started her story yet."

2nd April. 11:20 p.m.

I can feel myself calming down as I type on the word processor like this, even though I don't have the habit of keeping a diary.

Is it because I usually work like this too? Apparently, writing is like taking a sedative for me. How silly.

I did take a sleeping pill just now. I don't think I would be able to get to sleep without it. Even if it doesn't do the trick, I don't feel like working on my manuscript, but I might as well write down my thoughts here before I fall asleep.

Who is the murderer?

That is the one question that has been lingering in my mind ever since I returned alone to my room.

What Junichi said seemed to make sense at first, but if you think about it, the possibility that the murderer could be some-one besides Ino was never disproven. And even if Ino was the murderer and left the house afterwards, how can we be sure he won't return to commit more murders?

We are not safe. We are still in a very dangerous situation.

I think Junichi knows that very well, despite what he said.

Of course, I get where he's coming from. I don't want to give up on Mr Miyagaki's inheritance either. But…

188

But what bothers me the most is the way the scene of the murder was set up. Shimada mentioned this too. Why would the murderer make an allusion to Suzaki's story?

Did the murderer go to all that trouble because the allusion was more important than the actual act of killing Suzaki? I don't have any proof, but I can't help but feel that's the case...

If so, I absolutely shouldn't start my own story while I'm here...

Perhaps it's a kind of compulsion of the murderer's? If I don't write a single line of my story, the murderer won't be able to make an allusion to my work and therefore won't be able to kill me, no matter how obsessed they are with that idea. So what would happen then?

I haven't written a single line yet. All I could manage to come up with tonight was a broad outline anyway. Should I perhaps consider myself fortunate?

Will I regret not taking part in the competition?

... I don't know.

If I can get to sleep soon, perhaps tomorrow my feelings will have changed.

* * *

I thought of something just as I was going to bed. I am afraid I'll forget it, so I'll write it down now.

It's about the car...

No, I'm probably just imagining things. It might not have anything to do with all of this.

Anyway, I'd better get some sleep now. I can feel the pill starting to work. I will think about this tomorrow.

4

About thirty minutes later, Shimada and Samejima returned to Icarus, bringing Kadomatsu Fumie with them. They must have explained what was going on to her, because she looked terrified. The moment she saw Madoka lying in the bed, she retreated to a corner of the room, put her back to the wall and sank to the floor. Then she sat up, put her hands together and started to mutter Buddhist prayers.

"There's no way to get into the entrance hall. The lattice door's locked tight," Shimada said, putting a bowl of warm water on the small table at the back of the room. "How's she doing?"

Keiko slowly shook her head. Samejima handed her a blanket, which she draped over Madoka.

"No sign of her waking up any time soon..." Keiko said, with a worried glance at Madoka's unconscious form. Shimada let out a short sigh, crossed his arms and went over to the wall opposite the doorway.

"You'd better sit down. You shouldn't be on your feet for so long," Utayama told his wife, and he wheeled the swivel chair over to the bed.

"Thanks," said Keiko with a sigh and sat down. Utayama put his hand on her shoulder and looked at Shimada. He still had his arms crossed and was pacing back and forth along the back wall, like a caged animal.

"I had a look at the word processor," Utayama said.

Shimada stopped in front of the full-length mirror at the end of the bed.

"Quite an interesting 'diary', don't you think?" he said.

"Err, yes."

The text was indeed a kind of diary. Or at the very least, it was not a work of pure fiction. Utayama didn't think it seemed like Madoka had been writing a fictional story based on real events and using the diary as a literary device either.

"She wrote that the murderer wouldn't be able to do anything if she didn't start her own story," Shimada went on. "I can certainly see why she would have thought that."

Utayama looked at the word processor. "I agree, but there was something I didn't understand."

"You mean the comment about the car?"

"Yes."

"Is this what you're talking about?" Samejima asked, bending over the desk to examine the screen.

"Yes," said Utayama. "She wrote that just before going to bed it seems. She says so at the very end."

Just then, they were all surprised by the sound of a low, almost bestial groan. By the time they realized it had escaped from Madoka, she was already trying to lift her head.

Keiko immediately rose from her seat. "Oh, no, you mustn't get up."

They couldn't tell whether Madoka had understood. Her whole body seemed to convulse as she tried to sit upright and pushed away the blanket.

"How do you feel?"

Utayama looked at Madoka's twitching face. Her staring eyes were filled with fear. Her pale lips trembled.

She slowly lifted her right arm, and extended her shaking fingers. Her hand was pointing at a startled Shimada.

Keiko put a hand on Madoka's shoulder and gently tried to push her back down, but suddenly she gave an even louder cry. Her right arm was immediately clapped to her mouth, and she bent forward. Yellow vomit trickled through her fingers.

"Oh, no!" Keiko cried, rubbing Madoka's back. "Get a towel quickly!"

Even Utayama knew that vomiting after being hit on the head was an extremely worrying symptom. Shimada ran to the toilet for a towel. Samejima rushed over to the bed. Meanwhile, the old woman was still sitting in the corner of the room, praying…

*

Thirty minutes later, Funaoka Madoka passed away. As Keiko had feared, the blow to the back of her head had resulted in a fatal brain injury.

It was 5.35 a.m. Above ground, it was almost dawn.

CHAPTER NINE

DISCUSSION

1

"Let's go somewhere else. It might be better to be near the entrance hall. Just in case."

Following Shimada's suggestion, the five started towards the reception room. Keiko was clearly exhausted, so Shimada was thoughtful enough to refrain from asking her to examine Kiyomura's and Hayashi's corpses.

The dark ceiling, covering the underground labyrinth, slowly was taking on the colours of dawn. One by one, the glass panes set between the steel frames let in the light from outside.

The labyrinth seemed even longer and more complicated than usual as they trudged along. Utayama was the first to step into the reception room, his arm around Keiko's shoulders, followed by Samejima and the housekeeper.

Utayama was sluggishly making his way to the table when he noticed Shimada still hadn't entered. He jogged back to the door to see where he was, calling Shimada's name.

Utayama found him standing in front of the statue of Ariadne, to the right of the door. He was examining it with a deep frown on his face. He didn't even seem to have heard Utayama calling him. He reached out his hand to the bronze right arm.

"What's the matter?" Utayama asked.

Shimada felt Ariadne's right wrist and then examined her left hand, which she held against her chest. Then, finally he turned to face Utayama:

"Oh, excuse me…"

"What's the matter with that statue?"

"Oh, nothing. I don't know why, but there's just something about it that bothers me…"

Utayama remembered that it had attracted Shimada's attention on their first day in the house too. He finally left it and they came into the reception room.

The housekeeper had made straight for the sofa, where she curled her small body up and continued to mutter her prayers. Shimada, Utayama Keiko and Samejima all sat down around the table.

Utayama was next to Keiko, but got up again and went over to the sideboard for a bottle of whisky.

"How about a drink?"

"No, thank you," said Shimada with a wave of his hand. Samejima and Keiko both silently shook their heads. An awkward silence descended on the table, during which the old woman's coarse mumblings echoed eerily in the room.

Utayama returned to the table with a glass of straight whisky. It was top-shelf alcohol, but for some reason it didn't taste good at all.

"One a day," Shimada muttered silently. He was holding a small black case, barely larger than a pen. He put it to his mouth and out came a cigarette. Then he held the other end, which gave a metallic click, and out came a small flame. It appeared to be a custom-made combination case and lighter.

It didn't take long for the cigarette to turn to ashes. Shimada looked somewhat unsatisfied as he stubbed the butt out in the ashtray.

"The night is over, but I hope you'll agree that doesn't mean we should all return to our rooms. I fear we find ourselves in a situation where we must watch each other."

Samejima looked up:

"What do you mean?"

"At the moment, we can't be sure that one of us won't commit another murder."

"You mean Ino isn't the killer?"

"That's still possible, of course, but we can't be sure," Shimada said. "Especially since we have four victims now, and nobody would have trusted him after the first murder."

"That is true, but if Ino isn't the killer, does it mean one of us killed all four of them? What possible motive could any of us have?" Samejima asked.

"I would like to know that myself," the "great detective" said bluntly and rested his head on his hands. Samejima didn't say anything more. Keiko was staring into space. The housekeeper was still praying. Utayama sipped his whisky.

After a short silence, Samejima spoke up:

"At any rate, we can't just sit here glaring at each other, waiting for somebody to let us out of the house. We should go over the case again, from the start. That is all we can do for the moment."

Shimada straightened up again. "I agree with you. Actually, I have the feeling something is about to take shape in my mind. But it is still vague and impossible to make out clearly."

Utayama felt that way too, especially regarding the meaning of the dying message left on Hayashi's word processor. And what was the meaning behind Madoka's behaviour after she woke up? She had raised her arm and pointed at Shimada, who had been standing at the end of the bed.

An inevitable suspicion began to grow in Utayama's mind yet again. Had she been pointing at the person who had attacked her? Was Shimada the murderer? He couldn't believe it. For one thing, Shimada had been with Utayama in Hayashi's room when Madoka's personal alarm started ringing. But did that really prove he wasn't the killer?

The tense atmosphere in the room was broken by the clear bells of the gold mantel clock on the sideboard, announcing that it was six o'clock.

2

"Let us begin with the first murder," Shimada proposed, resting his long forearms on the table. "The victim was Suzaki Shōsuke. The crime scene: the drawing room, Minotaur. The killer first used a blunt instrument to hit Suzaki on the head and knock him out, after which some kind of cord was used to strangle him. Then the killer used the axe, which had been hanging on the wall, to cut off Suzaki's head partially. Finally, they positioned the stuffed bull's head, which had also been on another wall, in place of Suzaki's head. The best estimate we can make for the time of the murder is somewhere between the middle of the night and three in the morning. None of us had an alibi for all of that time.

"Furthermore, we found the beginning of a story, 'The Minotaur's Head', on the word processor in Suzaki's room, Talos. The crime scene as described there is more or less the same as the real one. In the story, the bull's head was placed in such a way as to cover the victim's face, as an allusion to the legend of the Minotaur. So, taking into account the reference to

Suzaki's story in the real crime scene, we have what is in fact a double allusion."

Shimada paused and then began again: "For the time being, let's try and establish the order of events based on what we know about the first night. That evening, everyone went back to their own rooms. The killer must have waited for us to go to bed before they went to Suzaki's room. They must have somehow tricked him into following them to the drawing room. Or perhaps they had already told Suzaki to go there at a specific time beforehand. The killer could have read the beginning of the story on an earlier visit to Suzaki's room, or perhaps they snuck into the room while he was waiting for them in the drawing room. Either is possible. And while the two were talking in the drawing room, the killer must have caught Suzaki off guard and hit him on the head.

"Now then, that brings us to at least two very obvious questions. The first: why did the murderer arrange the crime scene so as to allude to 'The Minotaur's Head'?

"And second: why did the murderer go so far as to try to decapitate the victim in setting up that allusion?"

Shimada paused for a second, as if considering his own rhetorical questions.

"We discussed this at length yesterday, of course. In particular, I gave my own interpretation regarding the second question: my theory on the reason for the decapitation. We then conducted a physical examination of all of us based on my theory, but you know how that turned out. None of the eight people fitted the profile I had drawn up. Nobody had any injuries on their faces or hands or feet, no nosebleeds…"

Shimada still seemed fixated on the matter of the reason for the decapitation. He still believed the killer had cut the head off to hide their own blood, which had stained the carpet.

The thought then occurred to Utayama: if that's what Shimada thinks, then doesn't logic dictate that Ino must have been the murderer?

"For the moment, let's set my ideas on this aside," said Shimada, looking around the table. "Do any of you have something to add?"

Samejima spoke up. "It's not anything important, but the first question you just posed… about why the murderer decided to mirror Suzaki's story in the first place? I don't know how to put this, but to me, the whole thing feels like a big egotistical display on the killer's part. There's something dramatic… theatrical about that murder."

"You mean the scene was intentionally staged like that, for our— the audience's sake?"

"Yes, it comes across like that to me. Of course, I suppose only a madman would do something like that…"

"Actually," said Utayama, "we found Kiyomura's and Hayashi's bodies arranged in ways that seemed to allude to the stories that they had been working on too."

Samejima's eyes widened upon hearing this.

"I can't take it any more…" Keiko muttered softly, her eyes fixed on the table. She looked up pleadingly at her husband. "Can't you stop? I don't want to hear anything else about those murders."

Up until now, Utayama had been amazed by his wife's bravery in the face of everything that had happened. But even a former doctor couldn't take all of this. And she was pregnant too. True, Keiko had shown no visible signs of distress when she examined Suzaki's gruesome corpse, or when she was by Madoka's side as she passed away in that terrible manner, but perhaps that lack of response had actually been a sign of how greatly disturbed she was. Utayama gently put his arm around her shoulders.

"It'll be all right. As long as we're all here together, nothing can happen to us. Do you want to rest on the sofa?"

Keiko finally got herself together again. "Hm… no, I'll be fine. I'm sorry. Please continue."

Shimada was stroking the tabletop with his fingers, then he looked up at Samejima. "All right then, I see what you mean. Whenever mystery fans come across a murder that seems to refer to something in a book, like a nursery rhyme for example, they immediately start trying to think of the reason for the reference. But, like you say, perhaps not all such allusions have a proper reason behind them. This might just be an expression of the murderer's own ego.

"But we can talk more about the allusions later. Let's move on to the next problem. I'd like to talk about the missing Ino."

"Actually, I've also been wondering about him since last night," Samejima said. "Yesterday, Kiyomura proposed that Ino had killed Suzaki and then fled the house. You and Mr Utayama checked his room, the library and the unoccupied room, but found no sign of him. At the time, I was quite convinced by Kiyomura's theory, which is why I agreed we should continue with the competition.

"But later, I thought about it some more. What if Ino was the murderer, but hadn't left the house? What if he was still lurking here somewhere?"

"Do you mean you think this house might have a hidden room or something like that?" Utayama couldn't resist asking. He remembered Shimada bringing up this possibility the previous day. Samejima seemed surprised by his question.

"What's that? A hidden room? Here in this house?"

"Well, I'm not saying there is one. It's just something Shimada was wondering about…"

Shimada gave the critic a serious look. "You are aware that Nakamura Seiji designed the Labyrinth House. Aren't you also aware of his famous love of including quirks and gimmicks in the construction of his buildings? Considering that his client in this case was the mystery writer Miyagaki Yōtarō, I think it's more than likely that there are some surprises hidden in this house."

Samejima didn't look quite convinced. "In any case, that wasn't what I was getting at. It would be possible for Ino to hide somewhere without there being a concealed room."

Utayama finally understood what was being suggested. There was indeed such a place, not beyond the locked door above, but here, in the underground house. A place where someone could easily hide, as long as they had the keys. A room that, for some reason, everyone had forgotten about…

"Mr Miyagaki's study…" Utayama said.

"Yes," Samejima confirmed. "For one thing, the killer must have been covered in blood after practically cutting off Suzaki's head. Of course, they would have needed to wash off the blood. Wouldn't the study be the perfect place for that, given that it has a connecting bathroom?"

Shimada stroked his angular chin, looking vexed at having missed such an important detail himself.

"I see… In that case, I suspect we might need to break down the door to the study sooner or later…"

3

At this point, they still couldn't say for sure whether Ino was the murderer or not, so they continued their discussion.

"You came across the second victim, Kiyomura Junichi, by chance, didn't you?" Shimada asked Utayama. "You found him in Medea, the room adjacent to his own room, Theseus. Could you tell us how that happened?"

"Of course," said Utayama. He explained why he had decided to look for Kiyomura and how he ended up finding his body, in as much detail as possible.

"… After I cried out, Shimada came running, and then we examined the room and the body together."

Utayama explained about the poisoned pins fixed around the light switch, and the note signed by Madoka they found in Kiyomura's pocket. He hesitated:

"… But we didn't learn whether she really wrote the note."

"Hmm. It doesn't seem inconceivable to me that she might try to meet with Kiyomura in secret to discuss the competition," said Samejima, eyes closed, and probably reliving the dreadful scene when Madoka had died before them.

"Even so, I think the note was fake," Shimada said. "Remember the diary she was writing on her word processor. You read it too, didn't you? Based on what she wrote, it doesn't seem she had any intention of working on her story for the competition."

"So you think the murderer wrote that note?"

"Yes, indeed," said Shimada confidently. "Of course, it's possible that Madoka was the murderer herself."

"The murderer? Madoka? But she was a victim!" cried Utayama.

"What does that matter?" Shimada said, grinning. "There are plenty of stories in which the murderer is one of the victims, like that famous one by Van Dine."

"But she's dead…"

"Perhaps that was unintentional."

"What do you mean?"

"Suppose she planned to fake an attack on herself, to become the final victim. She would kill Kiyomura and Hayashi, then injure herself and set off her personal alarm. It's an old trick—trying to evade suspicion by portraying yourself as a victim. However, when she hit herself on the head somehow, she inflicted a heavier blow than intended, and she ended up dead."

"Err, I don't think that's possible," said Keiko, timidly interrupting Shimada. "She couldn't have hit herself on the head in that spot…"

Shimada's fingers tapped on the table, like he was playing piano. "I suppose you're right. Shooting or stabbing yourself is one thing, but it's hard to imagine hitting yourself so hard on the back of your own head that you actually pass out. And we didn't find anything pointing to some kind of mechanical trick, like a weight being set up to drop on her head automatically. And if the idea was to make it seem she had been attacked by the killer, it wouldn't make sense to bolt the door.

"It's a bit embarrassing to say this since I was the one who proposed the idea in the first place, but for now I think we can safely rule out the possibility that Funaoka Madoka was the killer."

Shimada put his hand in the pocket of his tracksuit jacket, and got out a roughly folded piece of white paper. The other three watched as he unfolded it and placed it on the table. It was his copy of the floor plan. Shimada looked around at them.

"Let's get back to our main points. What I want to draw your attention to with regard to the second murder—that of Kiyomura Junichi—is the trick the murderer used in order to poison him.

"We don't know when the killer read the story Kiyomura wrote on his word processor. Whether the murderer was Ino or someone else, we should assume they are in possession of the spare keys. So they easily could have snuck into Kiyomura's room and read the story, then decided to poison Kiyomura in Medea, as an allusion to the opening of 'A Yearning for Poison'. However, it seems to me that this would be quite hard to pull off time-wise."

Shimada paused for a second, and a frown appeared on his face.

"Anyway, the killer somehow got hold of some concentrated nicotine liquid, putty and pins, and set the trap.

"It was created in Medea, the room in which Kiyomura's story began. There is of course also another possible logical explanation for the choice for this room, besides the allusion. You see, the booby trap had to be set in an unused room for it to be successful."

Utayama let out an impressed groan and leant back in his seat. They had discussed the crime scene four hours earlier, but apparently Shimada had already arrived at a new conclusion.

"First of all, note the layout of the room. As far as I have seen, the guest rooms are all more or less the same. The door opens inwards, towards the right. The light switch is on the wall immediately to the left of the entrance. So it's easy to imagine Kiyomura arriving to find the room in darkness, searching for the switch with his left hand and falling right into the trap of the poisoned pins.

"Suppose the murderer had chosen a different room, like this reception room, or the games room or the library. The reception room wouldn't have been suitable for a trap like that, because even in the middle of the night someone else might have come here. As for the games room, library and drawing room... haven't you already noticed? Their doors also open inwards, but to the left. Thus the light switch in those rooms is to the right of the door. Also, compared to the guest rooms, it is located slighter further away from the door. So if the trap had been set in any of those three, the 'prey', being in an unfamiliar situation, would likely have looked at the switch first before pushing it, and he might have noticed the trap."

"We talked about this earlier, but wouldn't Kiyomura have been on his guard the moment he was asked to come to Medea by the killer?" Utayama asked.

"Exactly. And the more on his guard he was, the greater the chances of the trap failing. That's why the killer used Madoka's name on the note and told him to go the games room."

Shimada pointed:

"Look at the map. Do you have your own copy with you?"

Utayama had his in his trouser pocket. He took it out, and spread it out on the table so he and Keiko could examine it together. Samejima moved next to Shimada to share his.

"I'm guessing the fake note signed by Madoka was slipped beneath the door of Kiyomura's room. He followed the instructions and went to the games room at one o'clock. He waited for a while, but she didn't show up. At this point, he could have gone to her room, but given his pride I don't think that was very likely. I think it's more likely he was annoyed at being made to wait for no reason, so decided to return to his own room.

"Now I want you to look at the floor plan. You see the long corridor with the sixteen passages branching off? Please compare the routes through the labyrinth that lead to Theseus and Medea."

These two side-passages were the thirteen and tenth respectively, counting from the south.

"... Ah!" Utayama exclaimed when finally saw what Shimada meant. Keiko and Samejima also grasped it simultaneously.

"You see? The paths are exactly the same."

It was indeed as Shimada had pointed out. Those two parts of the labyrinth were identical in terms of their layout.

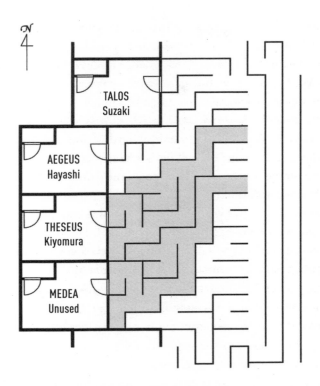

Fig. 2   Routes to Medea and Theseus

"And now I want to draw your attention to the fact that when Utayama visited Kiyomura's room, he found a copy of the floor plan on the desk. That means Kiyomura had left for the games room without his. As you can see, the games room is in an easy-to-find location and he would have gone back and forth between there and his own room several times since he arrived, so he had probably already memorized the route. And of course, the most convenient markers would be the plaster masks hanging from the wall."

"Ah!" Utayama exclaimed once more.

It was those plaster masks! That weird feeling he had had when he went to Kiyomura's room alone and then when he and Shimada were heading to Hayashi's room after discovering the body in Medea... Now he finally knew what had been bothering him.

It was those masks! The mask of the lion baring its teeth, and the beast with a horn growing from its forehead.

When he and Shimada went looking for Ino and checked in Medea, Utayama had noticed the lion's mask on the wall. But what about the next time he went to the room? He had seen the lion when he took the path to Kiyomura's room, Theseus, but it was the unicorn that had watched them on the route to Medea that time...

The two masks had been swapped!

"Which of the sixteen side-passages branching off that long corridor leads to their own room?" Shimada went on. "It might be easy to remember if it's just the first or second one, but imagine what a pain it would be if you had to count up to thirteen each time. It would be far easier, and foolproof, to simply navigate by the masks."

Utayama nodded. He remembered the route to his own room by using the masks as waypoints.

"So the killer waited until Kiyomura had left for the games room, then swapped the masks next to the passages leading to Theseus and Medea. Kiyomura would have come back down the long corridor from the south, and as usual he'd have been on the lookout for the mask next to his turning. But this time he came across it on the wall next to the tenth turning, not the thirteenth. The killer swapped the masks between those two side-passages— they are just close enough for Kiyomura unwittingly to make a mistake and not realize he was taking the wrong turning.

"And thus Kiyomura went to Medea, believing he was returning to his own room. That brings me to the doors. The nameplate on the door to Medea had been removed when we got there tonight, and that on the door to Theseus had been missing for a while. The murderer must have removed the plate on Medea in advance, so Kiyomura wouldn't know he had gone to the wrong room."

The fog of mystery surrounding Kiyomura's death was finally clearing. The crime now had a clear shape.

"Of course it would have been possible to set the trap in Kiyomura's own room, if the killer hadn't been bothered about making an allusion to his story. It would certainly have saved a lot of trouble. But the trap must have taken some time to set up—time the killer might not have had if they had only been able to prepare it after Kiyomura had left his room.

"Anyway, the prey had been led to the booby-trapped room, thanks to the trick with the swapped masks. The door was left unlocked. The lights were switched off. We can't know whether Kiyomura switched the lights off when he left his room, but it is unlikely he would have left the door unlocked, so of course, finding it unlocked on his 'return' would have aroused his suspicions. But even if he imagined that someone might be lurking inside, what would be more natural than to switch on the lights before entering? After all, he thought it was his own room."

"But when I went to Kiyomura's room, I did find the door unlocked," Utayama said.

"The killer probably unlocked the door to Theseus after the success of the murder," Shimada said. Then he looked over at Samejima.

"I think what you said earlier about the murders being theatrical must be close to the truth. The killer must have been trying to make it as easy as possible for us to discover Kiyomura's corpse."

"But why?" Samejima asked.

"I suspect the killer expected us to discover the body only after we got up in the morning. We'd meet in the reception room and realize Kiyomura, Hayashi and Madoka hadn't showed up, and it was only at that point that we would go to their rooms. The killer could not have foreseen that Utayama would decide to visit Kiyomura in the middle of the night.

"The killer must have left the door open so that we wouldn't need to break it down when we went to check on Kiyomura in the morning. It's as if they were eager for us to discover the bodies as quickly as possible. Doesn't that seem to correspond to your suggestion that the killings were driven by the murderer's own ego?"

Utayama listened intently, struggling to make up his mind. Was the murderer an egotist? If so, wasn't Shimada Kiyoshi himself, currently playing the role of the "great detective", the person most likely to fit the part? Or even Samejima, who made a living by criticizing writers. At any rate, it didn't seem to fit his impression of the missing Ino.

"Which of us five could have murdered Kiyomura like that?" Shimada asked, slowly looking around their faces: Samejima, Utayama, Keiko and finally Kadomatsu Fumie, who was still curled up on the sofa. "It could have been any one of us, as long as they had the spare keys. That's all I can say at the moment."

4

"Let's discuss the third murder now. After discovering Kiyomura's body, Utayama and I decided to alert everyone else, so we headed for the nearest room, Aegeus, occupied by Hayashi. On our arrival we found him dead, with a knife in his back.

"The first question is: could Hayashi's murder have occurred before Kiyomura's? After giving it some consideration, however, I do think we can safely assume that Hayashi's murder was the third to take place. His room is next to Kiyomura's, so considering the noise that must have been made during Hayashi's murder, it would have been safer for the killer to commit it after Kiyomura's, which was likely between one and half-past one. The killer first made sure Kiyomura had fallen victim to the booby trap, then headed to Hayashi's room with the murder weapon. That wouldn't have been later than, say, two o'clock? Let us consider the crime scene now."

Shimada explained the position in which they had found Hayashi's body, and how the small table and stools had been used to barricade the door.

"And of course, there was a word processor in this room too. We found Hayashi dead, with his hands on the edge of the desk. The word processor was still running. The story he had been working on before he was attacked was on the screen."

"And that story matched the crime scene too?" Samejima asked. Shimada nodded.

"Yes, but this story, 'The Ghost in the Glass', had a rather unique structure. Did the killer arrange the crime scene after the murder? Did it end up like that by coincidence? Or did the victim himself cause the scene to mirror the story? It was difficult to tell what really happened in that room."

Samejima exclaimed, "What? You mean Hayashi arranged his own body?"

"Possibly. You see…"

Shimada explained the story they had found on the word processor: the framing device, with the narrator writing a story in the room Aegeus; the narrator's explanation that the story-within-a-story would revolve around a message left by someone in his last moments; the description of the crime scene…

"… and after that, the story just ends abruptly. There are four blank lines, and then an incomprehensible message. The text cursor was blinking right after the last letter."

Samejima frowned at Shimada's explanation. "So you are suggesting Hayashi might have been lying like that because he was trying to type a dying message?"

"Yes, more or less. Or perhaps the killer read the story and then moved the body in order to make an allusion to it, but then after they left, Hayashi, who was still clinging on to life, used the last of his strength to type that message."

"What was the message?" Samejima asked.

"Just four letters. N-u-e-i."

"Nuei…"

Once more, Utayama started racking his mind for a possible interpretation.

Nuei. What if it wasn't one word? What if there was supposed to be a space in there? *Nue i*? And maybe Hayashi was meaning to write "Nue is…"

The word "nue" did ring a bell, actually. The Nue was a supernatural chimera-like being from Japanese folklore. In the classic *The Tale of Heike*, it was described as a beast with the head of a monkey, limbs of a tiger, body of a Japanese raccoon dog and tail of a snake. Like the Minotaur, it was therefore a creature made up of parts of others. But what did that tell them? How could the Nue, a Japanese supernatural being, be connected to a murder that occurred in a house designed after Greek mythology?

Utayama thought about the books each of the four writers had published, but none of them had written about the Nue or had used it in a title.

The Nue is said to have a horrifying, eerie bird-like cry, like that of the scaly thrush. This sorrowful call was considered an ill omen. Utayama suddenly thought back to the terrible sound of Madoka's personal alarm shrieking in the labyrinth. Would the Nue have sounded like that, striking fear in those who heard its cry?

The Nue also reminded Utayama of a certain book. *The Island of Evil Spirits* was the final mystery written by Seishi Yokomizo, starring his detective Kosuke Kindaichi. He is investigating the death of a man whose dying words were "Beware the night when the Nue cries." Hayashi would have been aware of this novel. Could his message be a reference to it?

Of course, this seemed very unlikely too. Utayama knew the book, but could not think of any obvious parallels with Hayashi's murder.

In any case, all his thinking always brought Utayama back to the same question: why would Hayashi not leave a dying message pointing clearly to the murderer?

"Do you have any idea what that message could mean?" Shimada asked Utayama, who shook his head.

"I have considered a few possibilities, but I can't think of anything that seems likely."

Shimada frowned. "I see. To be honest, I can't think of a good explanation either. Perhaps the others have some ideas?"

He looked at Samejima and Keiko. The former replied with a shake of the head, while the latter leant her head on her husband's arm.

"Let's move on for now, then," said Shimada, pouting his thick lips thoughtfully. "I want to focus on the barricaded door. It seems Hayashi was afraid of the murderer, so when he got back to his room, he locked himself in, bolted the latch and barricaded the door with the table and stools. However, when we arrived at the room, we found the door unlocked, the latch unbolted and the barricade moved aside.

"So, the mystery is: how did the murderer get inside? On the face of it, it appears that Hayashi himself let the murderer in. But would he really have welcomed a visitor in the middle of the night? Any thoughts?" Shimada asked Utayama.

"Either it was someone he trusted deeply, or the killer must have made up a really good excuse. Either way, I think it's unlikely Ino was the killer."

"Indeed. Under no circumstances would Hayashi have willingly let Ino in his room. But who *would* he have let inside?" Shimada looked at Samejima and Keiko.

"I can imagine him letting in either of you. You had no stake in the competition. The housekeeper seems an unlikely suspect, but we can't rule her out. And of course, Utayama, we cannot rule you out either."

"What?… Me?" Utayama's eyes opened wide in shock. "How could I have been the killer? I was with you when the alarm went off, right after we discovered Hayashi's body."

"Yes, that's a fair point, but I'm not sure your alibi is watertight."

"Why not?"

"Allow me to present a hypothesis. Yes, we were together when the personal alarm went off, but what if you had planned that in order to give yourself an alibi?"

"What do you mean?" Utayama asked, shooting a quizzical look at Shimada.

"You might have attacked Madoka before you 'discovered' Kiyomura's body and somehow rigged a timer mechanism on her personal alarm. Then you met me and we discovered Hayashi's body together, at which point your timer set the alarm off. We raced to the room, but couldn't open the door, so I had to go to the drawing room to fetch the axe. While I was gone, you could've used the spare key to get into the room and get rid of the timer."

"This is a sick joke!" Utayama barked. "If you think I'm the murderer, let's do a body search, right here, right now."

"I doubt you'd be so foolish as to walk around with the timer mechanism in your pocket all this time," said Shimada with a straight face.

Utayama didn't know how to answer that, but then snapped back:

"This hypothetical trick of yours could just as easily have been played by you, you know. You could have rigged a timer mechanism on the alarm, and after we broke down the door and entered the room, you could have secretly disposed of it while I was distracted by Madoka lying on the floor."

However, Shimada seemed unimpressed by Utayama's counter-attack.

"That seems rather unlikely. The whole point of the trick would be create an alibi for the killer, but if I were the killer, how could I have foreseen you'd discover Kiyomura's body, and at that time too?"

"Perhaps you were planning to visit someone's room right after setting the timer to create your alibi," Utayama countered stubbornly. "And remember what happened just now, in Icarus? Madoka regained consciousness briefly before she died. Why did she point at you?"

Shimada grinned. "Who knows? Oh, but please, you don't need to be cross with me. As always, I was simply talking possibilities. It can be proven that neither you nor I was the killer."

"Huh?"

"Why didn't the murderer finish off Madoka after their attack? The killer hit her once on the back of the head and then fled the scene, even though leaving a victim alive would put the culprit in grave danger of being caught. If either of us had attacked her much earlier on—before we met up and the alarm went off—we would have been in no rush. We could have made sure Madoka was dead before leaving her room."

"Aha," said Utayama, nodding and frowning pensively. Shimada rubbed the back of his head, smiling awkwardly.

"The dying message on the word processor and the question of why Hayashi carelessly let the murderer inside his room: these are two mysteries, but regarding the latter, there's another possible explanation I have not mentioned yet."

Samejima nodded, taking a cigarette out from the pack. "Really? But what could that be?"

"I ask you to be patient for a little longer. When we discuss the fourth incident, it will become quite obvious."

Shimada suddenly stood up and went towards the kitchen. "But first, allow me to get a glass of water. I'm thirsty."

5

After drinking half of the water, Shimada continued:

"Let's discuss the fourth incident, and for the time being, forget my hypothesis of the killer having set a timer mechanism to ring the personal alarm.

"Utayama and I were in Hayashi's room when the alarm went off. That was around half-past three. The murderer must have gone to Madoka's room straight after killing Hayashi. Their plan must have been to get it all over with in one night. Regardless of who the murderer is, it would obviously have become more difficult to commit further murders after the second and third bodies were discovered.

"However, when the killer attacked Madoka, she set off her personal alarm. The killer only managed to hit her on the head once, but then panicked and left the room in a hurry, without taking the time to make sure she was dead.

"Although it only took about three minutes for the two of us to reach the door to Icarus, the murderer had managed to lock the door and bolt the latch from inside. Not only that, but when we broke the door open, the murderer was not in the room, confronting us with what is commonly referred to in crime fiction as a 'locked room mystery'."

"So you stumbled upon a genuine locked room murder?" Samejima said, playing with the cigarette.

"The latch on the door has a very simple mechanism, so perhaps it could have been manipulated by poking something through the gap between the door and frame, for example by using some string and a needle. But of course, the killer's plan didn't count on the victim using her personal alarm. So it is difficult to imagine why the killer would've gone to all that trouble to bolt the latch during the three minutes it took us to get there. Why would they want to create a 'locked room' in the first place?

"And if you consider the question why the murderer created the locked room together with the question of why Hayashi let the murderer into his room… well, can't you think of the answer to both these questions?"

Utayama and Keiko gave each other puzzled looks. Kadomatsu Fumie wasn't even listening, but had stopped praying. She was still sitting curled up on the sofa.

"It was never the murderer's intention to leave the room locked," Samejima muttered. "The murderer never wanted Icarus to become a locked room. Just as with Kiyomura's and Hayashi's rooms, they wanted to leave the door unlocked. But the murderer was surprised by Madoka setting off her alarm and had to act quickly…"

A contented smile appeared on Shimada's face. "Exactly. The murderer was forced to flee the room, while the door was still

215

locked from the inside. And that was definitely quite unfortunate for them…"

"But… if the murderer fled the room in a hurry, how could the latch still be bolted?" Utayama asked, confused.

"You've got it the wrong way around," said Samejima. "He's saying the murderer didn't leave the room through the door. Isn't that right?"

"Yes, exactly," Shimada replied.

"But—" the bewildered Utayama began to protest, but Shimada answered his doubts with one short sentence:

"There is a secret passageway."

"What!"

"Perhaps, as an editor of mystery novels, you consider using secret passageways to be cheating?" Shimada said, grinning. "I am convinced that the rooms of the Labyrinth House, or at the very least Hayashi's Aegeus and Madoka's Icarus, have hidden doors built into them. While I was waiting for you and your wife in Icarus earlier, I tried looking for the door by knocking on the walls, but I couldn't find it. Still, I'm certain there is a secret entrance somewhere."

"But—"

"You still don't seem convinced. However, once you accept the existence of a secret door, it provides a logical explanation for the third and fourth murders.

"'Why did Hayashi barricade his door and yet let the murderer into his room?' we asked, but the premise is wrong because he didn't let murderer in. The murder entered via the secret door.

"And after the deed was done, what did the murderer have to do before leaving through the secret door again? They had to remove the barricade and unbolt the latch; otherwise the room would have been left locked from the inside, and that would have

216

led us to suspect that there might be a secret door. Perhaps the murderer expected this suspicion to arise in time anyway, but if so they still would have wanted to keep their hidden entrances a secret for as long as possible."

Utayama finally understood Shimada's reasoning. The murderer needed to hide the fact that Hayashi's murder had occurred in what was—or what would have initially seemed to be—a locked room, so they had to remove the barricade and unlock the door.

"And we can apply the same logic to explain why the attack on Madoka in Icarus ended up a 'locked room mystery'.

"Originally, the murderer planned to unlock the door once they had committed the crime, but something unexpected happened: the personal alarm being set off. And so the killer inadvertently presented us with a locked room mystery."

Shimada drained the rest of the water in his glass and sighed.

"The question is: where is the door to the secret passageway? I'm afraid we'll have to examine every nook and cranny of the room to see if we can find it."

Samejima finally lit the cigarette, and said:

"So doesn't this mean we must once again consider the possibility that Ino is the murderer? The idea that Hayashi would never have let Ino into his room is irrelevant now. And, as Mr Miyagaki's secretary, Ino could well have been aware of the existence of such a secret passageway."

Shimada nodded. "You're right, although we still can't be sure he is the killer. It could have been any one of a number of other people. Despite what I said earlier, we can't prove one hundred per cent that it wasn't Utayama, or even me. It could be you, or Keiko, even though it's her first time here. She could've stumbled upon the hidden passageway by sheer chance. It is impossible for us to rule it out absolutely."

6

"With that, I believe we've covered everything that has happened up to now. After considering it all, we are left with a few major questions."

Shimada rested his elbow on the table, and started to count on his fingers. "One," he began, bending down his thumb.

"Are my thoughts about the reason for the decapitation of the first murder victim correct or not?

"Two: what is the meaning of the message left on Hayashi's word processor?

"Three: where is the entrance to the secret passageway?"

"Here's one more," put in Samejima. "What was Madoka getting at with that stuff about the car in her diary? I can't help but feel that might be important."

Shimada nodded.

"Ah, yes, you're right. She wrote that she had thought of something about the car…"

But what car could she have meant? The only cars currently parked outside the house were Miyagaki's Mercedes and the car the Utayamas drove there. What was significant about either of them? He was pondering these questions, when Keiko suddenly let out a cry.

"What's the matter?" he asked.

"I just thought of something," she said, rather excited.

"About the car?"

"No, not about that. It's about Hayashi's dying message."

"Yes?"

"We met Kiyomura and Hayashi in the hallway on the first day. And then Hayashi started talking to us…"

"Err…"

"You don't remember? He complained how the 'R' key on his word processor sometimes got stuck; then he mentioned that he could touch-type, but would still occasionally make mistakes."

Utayama clapped his hands together. "Oh, yes, he told us that! Touch-typing!"

"That's it!" Shimada suddenly cried.

"Really? The touch-typing?" asked Utayama eagerly, but Shimada looked at him blankly.

"What's that?" he asked vaguely and got up from his chair without waiting for Utayama's reply. He quickly walked over to the telephone. Apparently, he hadn't been listening to the Utayamas.

"The car... that car..."

Shimada seemed as excited as Utayama now. He was muttering to himself as he sat down in front of the telephone stand. For some reason, he got the directory from the shelf beneath and started paging through it.

"What's the matter?" asked Utayama. "The phone's still out." But Shimada didn't look up, just carried on silently examining the telephone directory. After a while, Utayama started to fear the man had lost his mind...

"I knew it..." Shimada said just then, closing the thick book. "So that's it. But that means... Hmm..."

Samejima went over to Shimada's side and shook him by the shoulder. He looked up distractedly:

"Yes?"

"You should listen to what the Utayamas have to say. I think they've figured out what the dying message means."

"Oh! Really?"

Shimada had apparently been so lost in his own thoughts that he had not heard a word of what the Utayamas had recalled.

"Please explain," Shimada said, hurrying back to the table, and so Utayama started to explain it all from the beginning.

"Do you know what 'touch' or 'blind' typing is? It's when you type on a word processor without looking down at the keyboard to make sure you press the right keys. Because your fingers have memorized the layout of the keyboard, you can focus on the screen while your fingers do the work. People who work on word processors have to learn to touch-type; otherwise typing a lengthy text takes too long. But of course, sometimes they make mistakes…"

"Aha," said Shimada, nodding at Utayama. "I think I see what you mean. You think Hayashi might have blindly typed a message on the keyboard as he lay dying… but somehow, it went wrong?"

"Yes, that's right. He was typing blindly, but because he was gravely wounded and on the verge of death, he didn't notice that the starting position of his fingers was off, so he hit the wrong keys by mistake."

"Hmm. The message left on the screen was 'nuei'. What could he have intended to type?"

"I'm not sure. I'd have to look at the keyboard."

"Let's go to a room with a word processor then. We also need to look for the entrance to the secret passageway."

"Yes, that sounds like a good plan."

But what had Shimada been looking for in the phone directory? Utayama wondered. For the time being they should focus on deciphering the message first. If they could figure it out, it might tell them the name of the killer. Trying to calm his racing thoughts, Utayama took Keiko's hand and got to his feet.

CHAPTER TEN

THE DOOR OPENS

1

Kadomatsu Fumie was very reluctant to join them, but eventually they convinced her it would be dangerous for her to be left alone. And so, all five of them stepped into the labyrinth.

Any room with a word processor would have helped them decipher the message, but if they wanted to follow Shimada's suggestion and look for the secret passage, it would have to be either Hayashi's or Madoka's room. They naturally preferred to avoid Hayashi's room, since his body was still lying in front of his word processor with a knife in its back. They therefore decided to go to Icarus.

It was seven a.m. The sun was up and light shone in through the blue-tinted glass ceiling. However, the sunlight did nothing to dispel the gloomy atmosphere in the house, and the feeling something was lurking in the dark remained. Now that they knew what role the emotionless white masks on the walls had played in Kiyomura's murder, they seemed much grimmer than before, almost as if they were grinning demonically.

When the group arrived in the long corridor with the sixteen side-passages, they took a good look at the masks next to the tenth and thirteenth openings. The lion and unicorn had indeed been swapped. A simple trick had fooled Kiyomura into going to the deadly room.

When the five finally arrived at Icarus, they saw Funaoka with a white towel draped over her face. Her long black hair was spread out across the linen bedclothes. The smell of vomit lingered in the air.

Utayama went straight to the word processor. Shimada and Keiko joined him, standing on either side of him. Samejima peered at the screen over his shoulder. The housekeeper sat on the floor in a corner of the room.

The word processor was still on. Madoka's diary was still on the screen.

"Have a look at this keyboard," Utayama told Shimada. "Do you own a word processor yourself?"

"Yes. A small one."

"What brand?"

"Canon."

"It should be similar to this one then."

Due to his work as an editor, Utayama was quite used to working on a word processor.

"People who have only just started writing with a word processor often have to look down at the keyboard to search for the letters they want to type. This makes typing quite slow, as each time you type a letter, you have to look back up at the screen to check whether it's appeared correctly and then back down again before typing the next one. That's why some authors still prefer to write by hand. But once you learn to touch-type without looking at the keyboard, work goes much more smoothly.

"Usually people have a starting position where they rest their fingers, and from there their fingers reach out to the keys they want to type. Their fingers have memorized the position of the keys, so they never need to look down."

Utayama placed both his hands in front of the keyboard, and spread his fingers wide.

"But Hayashi was dying, using his last reserves of strength to type the message, so he wouldn't have been able to check his fingers were in the right place. If they were even slightly out of position when he started, his key inputs could have been off by one or two places."

Shimada nodded. "I see, yes. So what could his intended message have been?"

"Please wait a second."

Utayama looked at the keyboard.

"Let's see. Suppose his fingers were out of position by the space of one key to the right. So he was actually intending to push the keys one key to the left of those he did push. 'Nuei' would then have been 'bywu'."

Utayama looked at Keiko. "Do you agree?"

"Yes, I think you're right," his wife said. Shimada nodded too.

"Or suppose his fingers were positioned one key-space too low. Then he would have intended to write out 'j849', or perhaps 'h738', since the two rows don't line up exactly."

"Yes, interesting," said Shimada, carefully examining the keys.

"None of those messages seems any more meaningful than the original, though," said Utayama disappointedly. Then he tried shifting the message one key to the right.

"Miro…"

"That is it!" Shimada cried out. "Mirror!"

But Utayama seemed confused.

"Mirror? How?"

"Keiko mentioned it in the reception room. The 'R' key of Hayashi's keyboard would sometimes get stuck. So what he actually wanted to type wasn't 'miro', it was the word 'mirror'! Look over there! There's your mirror."

223

Shimada pointed his long, slender index finger at the full-length mirror on the wall.

Utayama cocked his head. His mirror-image looked back at him with a puzzled expression.

"But why would Hayashi type 'mirror'?"

"Oh, come on!" Shimada said exasperatedly and strode over to the mirror. "He wasn't writing down the name of the murderer. He was telling us where the entrance to the secret passageway is, where the murderer came from!"

2

Shimada stood in front of the mirror, which was slightly taller than him. He closely examined where it met the wall panels, then began tapping lightly on its surface. Finally, he tried pushing it with both hands.

"Is it really supposed to open?" Utayama asked doubtfully. Keiko and Samejima were looking on sceptically too.

"It *will* open," Shimada said confidently. "Earlier, you said that when Madoka was lying on the bed and woke up, she pointed at me. But she wasn't pointing at me. She was telling us how the murderer had got into the room. She was pointing at this mirror."

"I see…"

"I can't seem to find a switch or anything, though…" Shimada cocked his head, then gave the mirror a shove with his shoulder, but it would not budge.

"That's weird," he muttered and started to push even harder.

"If you're not careful it'll brea—" Utayama began, but left off as Shimada stumbled forward.

"It really opened!?" cried Utayama, running to Shimada's side.

A large gap had opened between the edge of the mirror and the wall. The mirror had swung inward, like a door.

Shimada carefully examined it.

"It's brilliant," he said admiringly. "Once I applied enough pressure, it suddenly opened smoothly. The mechanism must have been designed deliberately like that. Unlike a wall or door, you would naturally expect a mirror to break if you pushed it too hard, so you wouldn't dare give it such a strong shove. In a way, it's a psychological trick."

Utayama crossed his arms. This was a lot to take in at once.

"So do all of our rooms have secret doors like this?"

"I fear so. All the guest rooms, probably the reception room and drawing room too. There are full-length mirrors in all those rooms, aren't there?"

Utayama sighed loudly, then peered into the dark crack between the mirror door and the wall.

"Are we going inside?"

"Yes, of course— Oh, wait, hang on…" Shimada broke off and crouched down on the floor. He carefully pushed the mirror door wide open.

"There's something on the floor here."

His long arm reached out and picked up a floppy disk from the floor behind the door.

"A floppy," said Shimada, his eyes fixed on the disk in its light-blue sleeve. "Aha. I knew it…"

"What was that doing there?" Utayama asked. Shimada looked up at him with a triumphant smile, as if he had solved the whole case now.

"Someone dropped it there. That someone being the murderer."

"The murderer?"

"Yes. Who else could it be?"

Shimada removed the floppy disk from the sleeve and went over to the word processor.

"Let's have a look. The word processor can read floppy disks of course. And I already have an idea what's on this one…"

3

First they saved Madoka's diary on a different floppy disk, then examined the one they had just found. It contained a single text file. The document was dated the second of April. The title was "Killing Wings – 1".

KILLING WINGS – 1

His hand was wrapped around the handle of the black hammer. Hot sweat was seeping into the fabric of the white glove.

Starlight shone through the glass ceiling. The dim room was ruled by silence.

It was the middle of the night. Nobody was awake in the house. Nobody, but him.

He was standing motionless in the middle of the dark room. He tried to calm his heavy breathing as he looked down at the body lying at his feet.

She was dead. She would never move again. But only a few seconds earlier, this body had still held what could be called the gift of life.

It had been over before he knew it.

He had not killed her out of hatred. Nor for money. But…

He softly placed the hammer on the floor. It wasn't over yet. There was more to do.

The woman had been lying on her side, but he rolled her face down. He ripped the back of her light negligee open, exposing her fair skin in the darkness.

From his pocket, he took out a small glass bottle.

"Wings... Burnt wings," he whispered.

He removed the cap. Out came the pungent, penetrating smell of petrol.

He crouched down next to her and tilted the bottle above her bare back. The petrol made an almost eerily pleasant sound as the liquid was poured onto her pale skin.

It wouldn't take much. He only needed to draw two lines, from her shoulder blades to her sides.

When he was done, he carefully sealed the bottle again and put it back in his pocket. He then took out a lighter. He lit it, and slowly approached her back...

Flames rose up in the darkness.

He left the room with red flickering reflected in his almost-intoxicated eyes.

Burning wings...

A deranged look appeared in his eyes, as he watched the gruesome wings being burnt into her flesh by the heat of the sun...

1

On the morning of the third of April, the body of Funaoka Madoka was discovered in the room Icarus in the Labyrinth House...

"'Killing Wings'... It appears to be the first part of a story, like those we saw in the other rooms..." Shimada looked around at the other three. "What do you make of it?"

Utayama stared at the blackness beyond the mirror door as he spoke:

227

"The file for this story was on a floppy disk, dropped by the murderer near the secret entrance… It appears Madoka had in fact begun writing a story for the competition. The title is 'Killing Wings', and she herself is the victim. Her story seems to refer to the myth of Icarus. I assume this floppy disk was in the word processor and the murderer took it…"

Shimada loudly clicked his tongue, silencing Utayama.

"Please think again from the start."

"Huh?"

"We went over the circumstances of Madoka's death in the reception room just now. The murderer was surprised by her personal alarm and had to flee the room in a hurry, without making sure she was dead, and also leaving the door locked and bolted. How would they have had the time to take this floppy disk with them?"

"Oh, I suppose you're right."

"Also, in the diary Madoka wrote yesterday, she clearly stated that she hadn't written a single line of her story. Her diary was dated 11.20 p.m. on the night of the second of April. Yet this 'Killing Wings' is also dated the second.

"Please also consider the following: in Suzaki's, Kiyomura's and Hayashi's rooms, we only found three floppy disks on which they could save their documents, exactly as Ino outlined to us on the first day. But, counting this floppy disk I picked up, how many floppy disks do you see here?"

"… Four."

"Indeed. That's one too many."

"Ah!"

It was Samejima, rather than Utayama, who gasped this time: "I get it now. So that's why… Oh, I can't believe it…", now looking down at the floor.

"I see you finally understand," Shimada said.

Samejima's thin lips twisted. "Yes… I think I do now. We got it all the wrong way round."

"The wrong way round?" Utayama echoed, mystified.

Samejima frowned. How much of what Shimada was driving at did the critic truly understand?

"The order in which we assumed things happened… it's actually the wrong way round, isn't it?"

Samejima looked at Shimada for confirmation.

Shimada's sharp eyes were aimed at the mirror door.

"Yes, that is correct. The murderer killed the victims and arranged the crime scenes in order to allude to the stories the writers had begun. At least, that's what we've all assumed happened, until now. However, the truth is quite different. The stories were written by the murderer! The killer didn't carry out the murders in such a way as to refer to the stories written by the victims. The murderer had already written the stories, effectively as models for the murders!"

Utayama couldn't believe it. The killer had written the stories!

"And this floppy disk proves it," Shimada went on. "The murderer wasn't trying to take it away from the crime scene; they brought it here. This document is dated the second of April. The murderer had planned to open this document on the word processor and then arrange the crime scene so as to allude to this story. But because things didn't go to plan, they had to flee the room in a hurry. They must have dropped the floppy disk as they fled."

Utayama's mouth was gaping. Shimada went over to the mirror door, then turned to Samejima.

"Let's go. You'll come with me, I trust?"

"… Yes, of course."

"Wait, I'll come too" said Utayama and joined Shimada by the mirror. Shimada looked at Keiko.

"Could you then please take Ms Kadomatsu to the reception room? I think you'll be safe there."

"Yes, yes," replied Keiko, nodding vaguely. She also seemed quite confused by the sudden turn of events.

"Will they really be safe?" Utayama asked.

Shimada nodded determinedly.

"Yes. The murderer won't strike again."

Utayama still seemed worried.

Shimada explained: "We have four murders, which made allusions to four stories. The fourth murder did not go as planned, but in a way, the murderer did manage to complete their work. So you don't have to be afraid any more."

Utayama didn't know what to say.

"You still don't see it? Think back to the titles of the four stories the murderer left us," Shimada said.

"Ah!" Utayama suddenly looked up in utter shock.

"'The Minotaur's Head'. 'A Yearning for Poison'. 'The Ghost in the Glass'. 'Killing Wings'. This was the signature left to us by the murderer himself."

"His signature?"

"Yes. Take the first letters of each title—you can skip the article—and what do you get?"

Utayama did as he was told, and…

"What!?" he exclaimed loudly.

"Yes, that's the answer," Shimada said coldly. "MYGK. Miyagaki Yōtarō is the culprit behind this series of murders."

230

CHAPTER ELEVEN

ARIADNE'S THREAD

1

The cramped passageway was only about fifty centimetres wide and led to the left and the right. The secret corridor must encircle the whole Labyrinth House, allowing access to all of the rooms, Utayama guessed.

Its walls, floor and high ceiling were all just bare concrete. The rear of the mirror door was a black panel with a steel handle and, like the "proper" door to Icarus, bore a bronze nameplate.

There was a light switch immediately next to the door. Naked light bulbs hung from the ceiling, which were widely spaced and barely gave enough light to see.

Shimada led the way, followed by Samejima and Utayama. After going through the mirror door, they turned right. Shimada had not announced his plan, but Utayama assumed he intended to follow the passage around the house all the way to Minoss, the study and private quarters of Miyagaki Yōtarō.

The air was stale and smelled faintly of dust and mould. On their left, the outside wall of the house was cracked here and there, and marked with black smudges.

Utayama still couldn't believe the bombshell Shimada had just dropped. Was Miyagaki really the murderer? Frustratingly, Shimada had not provided any further explanation. After delivering the revelation, he had simply raised his hands at Utayama, as if to indicate that he had said all he was going to at that point, then stepped through the mirror door.

But how could Miyagaki be the killer? Hadn't he died two days ago? Hadn't he ended his own life in his bedroom, leaving his will for them to find?

Utayama had seen the old man lying peacefully on his bed, eyes closed. Had he not been looking at a dead man? Ino had told them Miyagaki had died. Actually, not only Ino. That Kuroe Tatsuo had also declared him dead. So how could he be the murderer?

They followed the passage around the outer wall of Icarus. First, they took a right turn, and after a while a left turn. After another right turn, Shimada stopped.

"This is the reverse of the mirror in the games room," he said, pointing at a door to his right. Indeed, there was a bronze nameplate etched with Daedalus.

"Have a look at this too."

Shimada was pointing at something about thirty centimetres from the door. It was a black plastic flap hanging on the wall at eye height, each side barely ten centimetres long.

"What is that?" Samejima asked. Shimada touched the flap with his right hand. There were hinges on the upper edge, which allowed him to flip it up.

"It's a peephole."

A hole had been cut in the concrete, allowing a view of the room. Light leaked through a chink between the wall panels of the room.

"It's a very small gap, so it'd be impossible to notice this peephole from inside the room when the plastic flap is covering it."

Shimada's low voice echoed through the passageway:

"He could spy on any room whenever he wanted using these."

Did Shimada mean Miyagaki Yōtarō? Had the master of this house had this passageway built in secret, so he could lurk in the darkness? This did not sound implausible. Perhaps Miyagaki had enjoyed himself sneaking from room to room whenever he had visitors, like a genuine Stroller in the Attic.

They went on past the games room, then the drawing room, Minotaur, the library, Eupalamus… Eventually, they were in front of a door bearing the nameplate "Minoss".

Shimada placed his hand on the steel handle.

"Here we are. As I recall, there was no mirror in the study, so, based on the route we just walked, I expect this leads into the bedroom."

He slowly opened the door. The room looked the same as when Ino had showed them into it two days earlier. The morning sun was shining in through the glass ceiling.

Against the wall to the left of the mirror door stood a large bed. On the bedside table stood a glass and a bottle of white tablets. Beneath the duvet on the bed, the contours of a human body could be seen.

The three stepped into the bedroom and looked at the figure whose face was covered by a white sheet.

Utayama asked Shimada:

"So how do you explain this? Mr Miyagaki is right here…"

However Shimada ignored him and made a beeline for the bed. Without any hesitation, he lifted the sheet up.

"Ah!"

"What!?"

Utayama and Samejima cried out simultaneously.

Shimada looked away from the horribly contorted face that had been concealed beneath the sheet.

"As you can see, we finally found him."

They were looking down at the face of Miyagaki's secretary: Ino Mitsuo.

2

Ino was dead.

Shimada removed the duvet and quickly examined the body. There were no external injuries, though there were signs that he had clawed at his throat, like Kiyomura. It seemed likely that Ino too had been poisoned with concentrated nicotine.

Shimada then opened the door to the study and urged his stunned companions to follow him.

"There's nobody here…"

Opposite the door were the same wooden racks packed with audio-visual equipment and Miyagaki's collection of records, CDs and video tapes. On the desk stood a word processor and telephone, and in front of it a leather chair. Shimada looked around the empty room.

"Where did he go?" he muttered and quickly crossed to look in the bathroom and toilet. "Nobody here either."

He turned to Utayama and Samejima.

"Perhaps he's left the house already. Hang on… What's that lying over there?"

Shimada was pointing at a small table in a corner of the room, under which some objects were lying on the floor. Utayama stayed in the doorway, while Samejima went over to the table:

"It's a dressing gown and gloves. I recognize the dressing gown—it's Mr Miyagaki's. Look, they're both covered in blood."

"And that black thing is a hammer, I believe," added Shimada. "He must have used that to attack Madoka."

"And here's the cord he used to strangle Suzaki," said Samejima. "And this bottle… I think there might be petrol inside, like in the story. The nameplate from Medea is here too, the one he removed."

Shimada stood in the middle of the room, his arms crossed. "Hmm. The weapon, and clothes all covered in blood. If he left all of this here, it means—"

At this point, Utayama couldn't restrain himself any more and cried out the question that had been troubling his mind ever since leaving Icarus. "But didn't Mr Miyagaki die before the murders? Please, you have to explain it all to us!"

"You saw the corpse in the bedroom. That was Ino."

"Yes. But two days ago, we all saw Mr Miyagaki's body…"

"… Yes, but it wasn't a *dead* body," Shimada said, sounding as if he were explaining things to a slow student. "He simply closed his eyes and pretended to be dead. All of us were completely fooled by him."

"But Ino? And the doctor?"

"They knew he was alive, of course. They were in on the game and helped Miyagaki deceive the eight of us. They were playing a trick on us on his birthday: April Fool's Day."

"What!?"

Shimada unfolded his arms and pulled out the chair from the desk. "Yes, all of this started as a joke. The day before yesterday, when Ino conveyed to us that Miyagaki had committed suicide, Kiyomura laughed, didn't he? How ironic in hindsight.

"The suicide of Miyagaki Yōtarō, the tape of his will that we listened to here, the competition to decide who'd inherit his immense fortune… It was all a lie. A big act, set up by Miyagaki, with the assistance of Ino and Kuroe."

Shimada leant forward, resting his elbows on his knees.

"I only realized this just now, in the reception room, when I reconsidered Madoka's diary. What car was she thinking about?

"Was it Miyagaki's Mercedes? Or your car, Utayama? But neither of those cars would have seemed suspicious to her. In fact, she arrived here before we did, so she might not have known about your car at all. So there remained only one option."

"The doctor's car?" Utayama remembered there had been a white Corolla parked next to the Mercedes.

"Indeed. It must have been the Corolla that was bothering her. It looked like an older model, didn't it?"

"Yes, but what does that have to do with anything?"

"Don't you think it's odd? You assumed that car was owned by Kuroe Tatsuo, a man in his late fifties. Ino introduced him to us as the head of the Department of Internal Medicine of Miyazu's N— Hospital. Could you imagine someone in such a position driving a Corolla like that?"

"Oh, you have a point…"

"That was what was bothering Madoka, I am sure. So that got me thinking some more. Was this Kuroe really the head of Internal Medicine at that hospital?"

"Aha…"

Samejima clapped loudly. "So that's why you checked the phone directory!"

"Yes. I was looking for someone called Kuroe Tatsuo. I found one person with that exact name living in Miyazu. I checked other towns in the local area too, but found nobody with precisely the same name. And as I expected, the profession specified in the directory wasn't 'doctor'. He was a teacher.

"I suspect, therefore, that Kuroe Tatsuo was a childhood friend of Miyagaki's. He was asked to play the 'doctor' who would announce Miyagaki Yōtarō's death."

Utayama gasped. Samejima could only nod. They looked at each other.

Shimada went on:

"Now, some of what I'm about to say might be nothing but my imagination, so please keep that in mind.

"First, I do think that Miyagaki is gravely ill. When he learnt that he didn't have long to live, it drove him to map out this unprecedented crime.

"He planned to kill his four disciples in the Labyrinth House. I can't say for sure what his motive exactly is, but…" Shimada stole a glance at Samejima. "But as you pointed out earlier, these murders feel like a display of ego. I suspect Miyagaki considered this whole business to be his final creative work. However, only he could tell us whether that is true.

"Anyway, the next thing Miyagaki did was to convince his secretary Ino and his friend Kuroe to put on an act for us on the first of April. I don't know whether he told them about his real illness or not, but he must have come up with some story to talk them into participating.

"For example, he might have told them that he didn't believe any of the four young writers had yet fully made use of their talents, so he was planning to fake his death and have them compete for his inheritance: surely this would push them to go beyond their previous limitations. Miyagaki would play dead for the duration of the competition, and, when the time came for the stories to be judged, he would reappear and reveal that it was all a hoax.

"Miyagaki would have stressed that he wasn't just playing a trick on us for no good reason. He was trying to force his budding disciples into writing the best story they could.

"And so, we arrived at the Labyrinth House, with absolutely no idea of Miyagaki's plan of course. Ino and Kuroe acted their parts well. We all fell for the announcement that Miyagaki Yōtarō had committed suicide. Then we listened to the tape of the fake last will, which had been recorded in advance."

Utayama glanced over at the desk. The cassette tape was still lying on the desktop.

"But that evening Miyagaki began to put into action his *true* plan, one not even Ino and Kuroe knew about.

"The first murder was committed in accordance with the first story, which he had written on the word processor in this room. He probably went to Suzaki's room via the secret passageway. You can imagine how startled Suzaki would have been to see the deceased Miyagaki suddenly appear in his room. Miyagaki must have made up some plausible reason to lure him to the drawing room. Once there, he caught Suzaki off guard and struck him on the head, after which he strangled him to death. Then he arranged the murder the scene to allude to the story and returned to Suzaki's room, where he opened 'The Minotaur's Head' on the word processor, so it would be on the screen when we arrived to investigate."

"But why did he try to decapitate Suzaki? What was the meaning of that?" Utayama asked.

Shimada hesitated for a second, as if he couldn't quite find the right words. "I think… I don't want to sound stubborn, but I still believe the logic I presented earlier was correct."

"You mean he did it to hide his own blood?"

"Yes. It might not have been blood from a wound to his body or face, or even from a nosebleed, despite what I proposed then. I also have the feeling Miyagaki isn't actually trying to evade justice, so it wouldn't matter to him if a police forensics team were able to find traces of his blood. What he wanted to avoid was the possibility of us beginning to suspect him earlier than he'd planned.

"So that got me thinking. What if the reason for him leaving blood at the crime scene… was because he coughed it up?"

"Coughed it up?"

"Yes. I'm no expert, but suppose Miyagaki is suffering from lung cancer, and suppose that as a result he coughed up some blood while killing Suzaki. Perhaps we would have been able to tell that the resulting stain hadn't come from an external injury. Imagine a particularly violent attack. If for example your wife, a doctor, had pointed out that the blood looked as if it had been coughed up, or that it was mixed with saliva, and we realized that none of us would have been likely to do that, then our thoughts might have turned to Miyagaki."

Samejima nodded. "I see. They say such blood foams, I believe?"

"Yes, I think so. In any case, after Miyagaki had finished with Suzaki, he called Ino, who was in the room next door to his, to his study. On second thoughts, perhaps he did that before he killed Suzaki. He had to kill Ino, who knew he was alive and had a key to the entrance doors, before we discovered Suzaki's body the following morning. Anyway, Ino, unaware of his master's intentions, would have been easy to poison with the nicotine.

"The subsequent three murders must have occurred essentially as we discussed earlier. However, what we were completely mistaken about was the reason the crime scenes were arranged to allude to the stories.

"'A Yearning for Poison', which we found on Kiyomura's word processor, and 'The Ghost in the Glass', which we found on Hayashi's… were not written by those two authors. Miyagaki himself brought those documents on floppy disks and opened them on the word processors after each murder. The fact that

Kiyomura was poisoned in Medea and Hayashi stabbed in front of his word processor: that was all part of the murderer's plans, to make allusions to his own work.

"Miyagaki also planned to do the same after murdering Madoka of course, but, because she unexpectedly set off her personal alarm, he was not able to complete the allusion to 'Killing Wings'. Instead he had to flee in a hurry, and accidentally dropped the floppy disk in the secret passageway."

"And what about the message left by Hayashi: 'nuei'? Are you suggesting that was planted by Mr Miyagaki too?" Utayama asked.

Shimada suddenly sprang up from the leather chair. "I think that is very likely. I also think the blood on the keyboard was smeared there by him. He moved Hayashi's body to the desk and arranged him in that posture. He then opened the file from the floppy disk and left the room by the passageway. It would be a bit far-fetched if, after he had done all of that, Hayashi just happened to still be alive, and used his last reserves of strength to leave us that message."

"But why would Mr Miyagaki go the trouble of leaving us a clue pointing to the mirror door?" Utayama asked.

Shimada placed his hands on his narrow hips. "It is curious, isn't it? It would seem contradictory to do that after going to all the trouble of removing the barricade to hide the fact that there was a secret passageway.

"But if you consider this series of murders as being one of Miyagaki Yōtarō's creative works, one he decided to dedicate the remainder of his life to, you could say perhaps he left that message for us precisely because there needed to be a clue to help us solve his puzzle."

"But—"

240

"It seems to me that this case is littered with such messages from Miyagaki. As we discussed earlier, all the murders feel very dramatic and theatrical. Almost as if this whole affair were deliberately arranged to resemble... a detective story. We have a competition to win an immense fortune, an underground house sealed off from the outside world. The first murder features an allusion to the Minotaur. The second murder features a trick that uses the layout of the labyrinth. The fourth murder was supposed to feature the motif of the burnt wings of Icarus. So why not a dying message in the third murder, which functions as a hint to the solution? Well, what do you think?"

Utayama was speechless.

"And what makes this all too clear is the signature hidden in the titles of the four stories: MYGK. Miyagaki. It's exactly the kind of childish game he would revel in. He has thrown down the gauntlet to us, challenging us to solve the mystery he has created."

Shimada then turned around to look at the desk, as if something had just occurred to him, gave a cry and ran over to the word processor.

"Look at this!" he exclaimed, staring at the screen and beckoning Utayama and Samejima over.

"Did he write something?" Samejima asked in a strained voice. Shimada moved his head away from the screen and showed the other two.

"I think Miyagaki returned to the study, and wrote this message, expecting us to come here sooner or later."

Follow the thread from Ariadne's right hand to open the door of the labyrinth. The final act awaits in the chamber of King Minos.

3

It was nine o'clock in the morning. They left the study and headed to the reception room, where the two women were waiting.

Kadomatsu Fumie seemed to have calmed down slightly, having to some degree accepted Shimada's earlier announcement that Miyagaki Yōtarō was the murderer. In fact, when the three returned there, she was sitting completely motionless. Upon their arrival she silently got to her feet, went to the kitchen and returned carrying tea for everyone on a tray.

"Oh, thank you," said Shimada gratefully. He held his cup in both hands and sipped. Then he looked up at the door leading out into the labyrinth and frowned. "So it all comes down to the statue of Ariadne..." he muttered.

This remark puzzled Keiko, so Utayama briefly explained what they had discovered in the study.

Shimada then turned to Samejima. "Do you happen to know where I could find something like a ball in this house?"

"A ball? Like something round?"

Shimada nodded. "Something like Ariadne's ball of thread. Something round, something that rolls."

"And what then?"

"Then the door will open," said Shimada, as if it were self-explanatory. "I am ninety-nine per cent sure that there is another secret passageway, one that will lead us to the chamber of King Minos, as stated in the message on the word processor."

"But the study is named after King Minos, isn't it?" Samejima put in.

"Yes, but I suspect there is another room, the real Minos. Surely, you must have noticed that the nameplate on the study door reads 'Minoss'. There's one 's' too many."

"Yes, I was wondering about that."

"It's another clue, indicating that the study is not the true Minos room. The real Minos is elsewhere, a room nobody else knows about. And I bet Miyagaki is waiting there—"

"In the games room," a rasping voice said, interrupting him. Shimada, Samejima, Utayama and Keiko all looked up in surprise.

"Pool balls are round," Kadomatsu Fumie continued. She was standing right behind Shimada.

Shimada slapped his forehead and got up from his seat. "Oh, of course. Thank you, dear lady."

And with that, he bowed to the long-haired woman, whose head barely came up to his chest, and ran off into the labyrinth.

*

"Right. I think this should do it…"

Shimada stood in front of the statue of Ariadne, holding a white cue ball.

"The message told us to follow the thread from Ariadne's right hand. This will function as the ball of thread."

He placed it on Ariadne's extended right hand. And then…

"Move out of the way. Don't touch it," Shimada ordered. The palm was tilting forward slightly, so the ball slowly rolled off it and fell.

It made a hard sound as it hit the floor, then kept on rolling straight forward.

All five watched as the ball rolled west down the corridor. It struck the wall that formed a protruding corner in front of the bathroom and toilet, but then began to roll towards the north wall of the corridor. When the ball came up against the north wall, it stopped for a moment, but then began to roll east, back along the corridor towards them, until it went north again, through an opening in the wall, and then continued rolling east once more on the smooth tiled floor.

Shimada followed the ball. "I knew it. The floor of the labyrinth is built on a slight slant, with the statue of Ariadne as the starting point. Now we must follow Ariadne's thread… I think the ball will stop at a secret door in the labyrinth."

The ball hit the wall again and began to roll north. Utayama still couldn't quite believe it, but took Keiko by the hand, and they followed Shimada.

Eventually the ball came to rest in a cul-de-sac. Shimada waited to be sure the ball had really stopped, then he turned to the others.

"I think this is it."

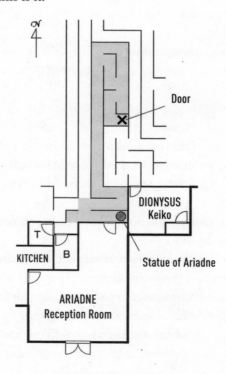

Fig. 3   Route of Ball

On the wall at the end of the cul-de-sac hung a plaster mask moulded to resemble the face of a beautiful woman. Shimada approached it, removed it from the wall with both hands and gently placed it on the floor.

"There it is."

Protruding from the wall was a small black lever, which had been hidden by the mask. Shimada pulled it down.

There was a metallic clank, and almost simultaneously part of the floor started to move. Four tiles, covering a surface of about sixty centimetres square, suddenly dropped away.

Shimada looked down at the dark hole that had opened up in the floor.

"A fantastic job by Nakamura Seiji once again," he said with admiration.

And thus the door leading out of the labyrinth was found.

4

A steel ladder led down into the dark. Shimada was the first to carefully lower himself into the hole. After a while, the rest of them saw a yellow light appear in the blackness below. He had apparently found a light switch.

"This is amazing," said Shimada's echoing voice from below. "Please come down too."

Keiko and the housekeeper remained in the corridor while the other two went down the steps.

Utayama's head was about to disappear through the hole when he looked up at his anxious wife.

"Wait here. There are three of us, so we'll be fine."

"Be careful."

Utayama gave her a wave and continued down. The ladder went down further than he was expecting, several metres at least. After a while he emerged from the narrow tube and reached the bottom. He looked around him at the dimly lit space and gasped in shock.

"But this is… It's like a cave."

Everywhere he looked there were bare rock walls. Up above, the ladder disappeared into a square hole in the ceiling.

"I think this is a natural cave," said Shimada said, walking into the interior, following a slight curve in the rock wall, which was dimly lit by a series of flickering electric lights set in the walls. The air was chilly, and Shimada's voice echoed eerily:

"It doesn't look like a limestone cave. It could be a wind cave, or perhaps it started out as a sea cave originally."

"So he had the house built on top of this cave?"

"I doubt it was intentional. They probably stumbled on the cave while digging to build the underground house. It happens sometimes. Supposedly there is a government building somewhere built right on top of a gigantic natural cavern… Anyway, let's see what's up ahead."

Utayama was glad of the lights. He would probably have been too scared to explore the cave with just a torch.

"This might even take us up to the surface. If so, Ariadne's thread will indeed have guided us out of the labyrinth."

The ground wasn't too difficult to walk on. A kind of path had been cut into the rock.

The cave slowly widened, and openings began to appear in the walls on both sides, but they stuck to the main path with its lights. If Miyagaki was hiding in any of those side-tunnels, it would be impossible to find him.

Finding himself in a place so far removed from his normal life, Utayama felt overcome by an indescribable sense of anxiety.

"Hey, this chamber of King Minos… Do you really think it's down here?" he asked timidly, but the answer followed sooner than he had expected.

"Yes. Here we are."

Shimada pointed at the left wall, where a dark brown patch stood out on the rock.

"I think that's a door."

He jogged over to take a closer look.

"It's a door all right. Quick, come and see for yourselves."

The small wooden door bore a bronze nameplate with a name: Minos.

Shimada reached for the handle. Utayama held his breath, waiting for him to open the door. He heard Samejima take a deep breath too, in anticipation of what they would find in the room.

The door swung open to reveal a small room with bare rock walls, lit by a single light bulb dangling from the high ceiling. The floor was covered by a crimson carpet.

There wasn't much in the way of furniture. It must have been tricky to bring anything bulky down here. In the middle of the room sat a small writing desk, with a folding chair in front of it. On the desktop lay a few pens, a bunch of keys, a single white envelope and Miyagaki's beloved gold-rimmed glasses. On the floor near the desk was an electric heater. A bookcase and a set of display shelves stood against the wall.

And at the back of the room was a steel pipe bed. When Utayama saw what was lying on it, he let out a loud gasp.

"Ah! It's… it's Mr Miyagaki…"

His arms were sticking out from beneath a rumpled duvet. An expression of excruciating pain was frozen on his face. This was how the aged writer had finally met his end.

"Would you like to know the desire I've harboured ever since I was young?"

Utayama recalled the lines Miyagaki had spoken to him when they met three months ago.

"I have always wanted to kill someone with my own hands...
Writing stories about murder for all these decades: that was little
more than a surrogate for this wish."

Utayama stumbled past Shimada into the room. He slowly walked over to the bed and softly touched the bony hand lying on the duvet.

He thought it still felt a bit warm. But that was probably just a figment of his imagination. After that single moment, the cold, hard touch of the skin let him know that Miyagaki was no longer among the living.

Something caught his eye on the carpet near his feet. Utayama slowly stooped down and reached out to pick the object up, but suddenly stopped.

It was a small syringe, and on the sharp, shining tip of the needle, a drop of dark red liquid gleamed.

EPILOGUE

In the white envelope found on the desk in the room Minos on the second underground floor of the Labyrinth House, were several sheets of paper with the following text printed on them.

EPILOGUE

These last words I will ever write can be considered my will. Let's call it my epilogue. The final chapter to the final story penned by the writer Miyagaki Yōtarō.

Who will be the one to solve all the mysteries I have spun, find their way to this room and read these words?

Suzaki Shōsuke. Kiyomura Junichi. Hayashi Hiroya. Funaoka Madoka. Assuming I have succeeded in killing all four of these writers, will the "great detective" Shimada, who helped solve the case at the Mill House last year, crack this one too? Or will it be Samejima, or perhaps even Utayama?

Whoever it may be, by the time you (singular or plural) are reading this, I will already be on the other side of death's door — for real this time.

When I made the decision to commit this series of murders, I also decided that the climax would be my taking of my own life. I'm not one to try to cling on as long as possible, knowing that my body is being ravaged by an illness from which I shall not recover, and now that my creative talents have waned too. I shall instead leave this world with pride, putting all my remaining strength into one final work.

I truly feel sorry for my four soon-to-be-victims — five including Ino. I imagine you will be outraged by my behaviour. You will wonder why I helped them make their debuts as writers and looked after them all this time. I have no personal grudge against them. If you wish me to apologize to them, I shall devote my next life to doing so.

However, I do not regret my decision. You see, when it comes down to it, I must admit: this is who I truly am.

My whole life has been devoted to my work, to creating detective stories that I myself can admire. If I were a narcissist, I might even say my passion has been the art of crime. That is why I decided that, to bring my life to an end, I, Miyagaki Yōtarō, would create one last murder mystery—a mystery set in the Labyrinth House, written with the blood of those four victims.

I am not completely devoid of remorse. But an emotion like that is not enough to stop this deep conviction (or is it a madness?) that resides within me.

Anyway, that's enough of that kind of talk. It'll sound like I'm trying to make excuses for myself.

A cold-hearted murderer with no equal. I'm sure that's what society will brand me, but I have no intention whatsoever of attempting to justify myself.

Before I lay down my pen (since the advent of the word processor, this phrase seems to be losing its meaning), I need to clarify the matter of my inheritance.

Of course, I will not be setting up a prize bearing the name of a criminal. I have given up on that idea. So allow me to confess here that I have an heir bearing my blood. Legally, I foresee no troubles regarding this matter. I shall bequeath my whole fortune to my heir.

THE END

1 April 1987, 2:00 a.m.

Moments before a magnificent downfall.

Miyagaki Yōtarō

THE END

AFTERWORD

These words should really have come at the beginning of the book, but because so few readers are disciplined enough to actually read an "Afterword" after the main story anyway, I thought I might as well put it at the end instead. Please consider the following as a kind of introduction for people who have yet to read the book.

Even now, I still feel somewhat uneasy about publishing this story as a novel. As I assume many of you will have gathered when you saw the title, *The Labyrinth House Murders* is directly based on a real-life murder case.

It occurred in April 1987, over the same days as in the book. The media made a sensation out of the incident at the time, since it was such a baffling case, and because it occurred at the curious residence of a well-known mystery writer.

However, it is safe to say the press have not managed to provide a proper analysis of the whole affair.

That is only to be expected, of course. The incident occurred under highly singular circumstances and all those who knew the truth declined to speak to the press. Even the police were perplexed by this extraordinary case, and while they ostensibly accepted the "truth" that had been revealed, they did not make any definitive announcement about it. The press were therefore restricted to writing vague articles based on non-committal police statements.

If the truth about the case was never made public, what gives me the right to write about it, you might wonder. Perhaps it seems arrogant, or presumptuous of me to do so.

Allow me to make a confession, therefore. I was present when it all happened. I, Shishiya Kadomi, was one of the people in the Labyrinth House in April 1987, when that series of murders occurred there.

I have decided to publish an account of my experience in this format for two main reasons.

The first is that a certain editor very strongly urged me to do so. As for the other reason, perhaps I could say this is my memorial to those who passed away during the tragedy.

That might sound somewhat tasteless, but I know at least some of the victims were great lovers of the unique genre that is the murder mystery. That is why I truly believe that a reconstruction of what happened in the form of a book is the best way to honour those who perished.

However, I doubt many readers will care much about these personal circumstances.

No matter what inspired me to write it, after all, this is nothing more than a murder mystery, a piece of entertainment that allows the reader to escape the boredom of daily life. Of course, that is perfectly fine. No, in fact, that is precisely what this book should be.

Finally, I want to make clear that after careful consideration, I have changed the names of most of the people and places in this novel. I appear in the story myself, but not under my pen-name of Shishiya Kadomi.

So which of the characters is Shishiya Kadomi?

Some readers might be interested in that mystery. But some things are best left a secret.

Summer of 1988
Shishiya Kadomi

THE LABYRINTH HOUSE MURDERS
First printing: 5th September 1988
KITANSHA NOVELS

RRP: 680 yen

EPILOGUE

1

Upon finishing Shishiya's *The Labyrinth House Murders*, Shimada mused on its contents. He was still feeling a bit feverish.

It consisted of a reconstruction in the form of a murder mystery novel of the events that occurred in real life in April last year. The story of an ageing writer who had murdered five people before taking his own life.

As mentioned in the Afterword, the author had changed the names of the characters, excluding Shimada Kiyoshi, but the story itself was a very faithful reconstruction of the actual ordeal, and the conclusion presented in the book did not differ from Shimada's own.

The surviving group had used the keys they found in the chamber of King Minos to escape the Labyrinth House and alert the police. The authorities were baffled by the bizarre case, but accepted that the author, the owner of the house, had committed a series of gruesome murders. They wrapped the case up quickly, despite the best efforts of the media to turn it into a big circus.

Shimada closed the book and looked wearily at the light purple cover.

He couldn't help but feel that something was off. Why had this book been written? he wondered.

The author, Shishiya Kadomi, had written in the Afterword that the book was intended as a memorial to those who had died.

However, Shimada still couldn't shake a funny feeling about the book. He was convinced there had to be another reason for writing it. Otherwise, he couldn't understand why the author had been so particular on a certain point.

Shimada forced his exhausted body to get up. He picked up his address book lying on the desk and went over to the telephone.

2

Three days later it was Monday, the 5th of September 1988.

Shimada was having dinner with Shishiya Kadomi in a hotel restaurant in Fukuoka.

Shishiya was currently living in Tokyo, but fortunately had plans to go to the island of Kyūshū that day, in order to do some research for a new book. When Shimada had learnt about the trip when he phoned, he had suggested they meet for the first time in a long while.

After some casual chit-chat over the meal, when their coffee had been served, Shimada finally decided to bring up what had been bothering him. Shishiya seemed to have been expecting it, and perked up, grinning.

"And now, if you agree, maestro, let us turn to the main topic of this evening's conversation," said Shimada in an ironically formal tone. He nodded at the copy of *The Labyrinth House Murders* on the table. "Your book.

"I read the copy you sent me as soon as it arrived," he went on. "It might be based on real events, but I have to admit, it was pretty enjoyable as a murder mystery too."

"You can keep the compliments," said Shishiya with a smile. "They don't suit you. And besides, I seem to recall you had plenty of nit-picking criticisms on the phone the other day."

"Yes, I suppose I did," admitted Shimada, a smile on his face too. He reached for the cigarette pack on top of the book.

"Anyway, after I had finished it, there was one thing that kept bothering me. It wasn't the sort of thing to mention over the phone, so I didn't bring it up then, but now feels like the right time. You okay with that, maestro?"

"Could you stop calling me that?" The author's trembling hands were wrapped around the full coffee cup as Shishiya looked uneasily at Shimada. "You're just making fun of me."

"Oh, you'll get used to it, maestro," said Shimada, now with a broad grin.

"I doubt it."

Shimada lit his cigarette, enjoying Shishiya's awkwardness.

"I'll just ask you straight."

"Pray do."

"Why is *The Labyrinth House Murders* written in a way to deliberately mislead readers regarding one of the characters?"

"Aha, so you noticed?"

"I could tell something was off right away. Your descriptive passages were awkward, and as you are well aware, I am not completely ignorant of the facts of the case."

"Well, of course, that is true."

"I'm not saying that you outright lied to the reader, of course. No, you simply wrote the story so that it would be interpreted in the wrong way. You were writing a story based on real events, so, naturally, you could not distort the facts."

"Indeed, I could not. The rules of fair-play mystery novels are so strongly ingrained in my mind that perhaps I was even more careful on that point than was necessary."

Shimada nodded. "I see. Well, there are still some points in the story where you sailed close to the wind, but I have to admit, you did your best to play a fair game. This isn't exactly what I wanted to discuss with you, but take the end of the prologue for example."

"You mean where it says: '*Of course, Utayama could not have known then that this was the last time he would ever speak with Miyagaki Yōtarō in this life*'?"

"Yep. Indeed, that was the last time Utayama actually spoke with Miyagaki. He did see Miyagaki alive, when he was playing dead later on, but they did not actually exchange words with each other. That was quite crafty of you.

"And then there's the bit in chapter two, when the guests are brought in to see Miyagaki in his bedroom. The narrator never refers to Miyagaki, who is pretending to be dead, as a 'corpse,' or 'body'. Only the characters themselves refer to his death or suicide, never the narrator, who also avoids referring to Kuroe Tatsuo as a doctor."

"Yes, you'll find more of those slight tricks in the book," Shishiya agreed. "As the author, I must admit I am glad an attentive reader has noticed my hard work. But let's get back to the main matter at hand. You say the book was written to deceive the readers regarding a certain person. Tell me—what do you think was the reason for that? Surely, you must have an idea?"

Shimada looked into Shishiya's mirthful eyes.

"Well, yes."

"Please, tell me."

Shimada placed his cigarette in the ashtray and began to explain.

"I suspect the publicly known truth of this case—the truth as presented in your novel—is actually false. The person who killed five people in the Labyrinth House in April last year was not Miyagaki Yōtarō."

Shishiya did not seem surprised. "I see. Why do you think so? And who do you think did kill them?"

"I'm afraid I don't think I can definitively disprove the publicly accepted version of events. I don't have access to physical evidence, nor do I have an absolutely watertight line of reasoning. But if I had to focus on something, it would be the idea that the killer coughed up blood during Suzaki's murder. Would the elderly Miyagaki, his lungs supposedly so ravaged by cancer that he coughs up blood, still have had the physical strength to commit all those murders? I suppose he might have only just begun to cough up blood, but still…"

"Very well. What else do you have?"

"This was also mentioned in the book, but the killer's behaviour during the third murder seems contradictory: supposedly Miyagaki left a fake dying message on the word processor, as a clue pointing towards the mirror door, and yet also removed the barricade from the door into the room, so as to lead us away from thinking that the killer might have got in another way. And then there were the dressing gown and syringe he left in the study just waiting to be discovered…"

"But there was a logical explanation for him leaving those clues, was there not? The mystery was Miyagaki's final great work, and he wanted it to be solved eventually."

"Yes, and that is convincing enough up to a point. But it seemed a bit too neat somehow. All the clues pointed too obviously to Miyagaki. He was just the kind of person who *would* do a thing like that."

Shishiya didn't say a word.

"And once you start reading between the lines, it becomes possible to arrive at a completely different conclusion: Miyagaki Yōtarō was not the murderer. The true killer was someone else, and they framed Miyagaki. You just need to focus on one particular question."

"And what is that question?"

"It's this: why did the murderer need to cut off Suzaki Shōsuke's head?"

The writer let out a chuckle of admiration. "Well, well. You really are sharp. So what's your answer?"

"The book already gave the answer. The murderer needed to hide their own blood."

"But it seemed that none of those alive in the house, besides Miyagaki, could have left a trace of blood."

"Precisely, because nobody was injured or showed signs of a recent nosebleed. Right, maestro?" Shimada took out another cigarette. "And yet the murderer did leave a bloodstain. So, if it didn't come from a wound, or a nosebleed, and if Miyagaki couldn't have coughed the blood up either…"

"Yes…"

"There remains only one possibility: a woman's menstrual bleeding."

A bright smile appeared on Shishiya's face. "Exactly. I'm ashamed to confess that I only realized that possibility myself long after the case had been wrapped up."

"The murderer was a woman. She would have been in shock after murdering Suzaki and committing such a horrible deed for the first time in her life. She collapsed on the floor and landed on her bum. The mental strain she must have been under before the act could also have led her period to start early.

"She was probably wearing a skirt, not prepared for her period coming on that day, so the blood stained her underwear and the carpet when she fell. Imagine her blind panic when she saw it. If the forensic investigators examined it, not only would they learn the blood wasn't Miyagaki's—the scapegoat—they might also match it to her."

"Bravo!" said Shishiya.

"Of the women who made it out of the house alive, Utayama Keiko was already six months into her pregnancy and had suffered no complications, so we can discount her. In addition, according to the *List of Characters*, Kadomatsu Fumie was sixty-three and would have been past the menopause. Which means—"

Here, Shishiya cut in: "It's a simple process of elimination. Apart from those two, there was only one other surviving woman. Samejima Tomoo. Yes, I too think she is the murderer."

3

"I started to have doubts after I heard the results of Miyagaki's autopsy," Shishiya said gravely. "He had been poisoned with nicotine. The time of death was estimated at around four o'clock on the morning of the third of April, though it could have been a couple of hours earlier or later. That would have allowed him time to kill Funaoka Madoka, return to the study, go down to the chamber of King Minos and commit suicide there.

"The autopsy also revealed that his lung cancer was not as serious as we all thought. It would likely not have caused him to cough up blood, and certainly not a large amount of it.

"However, the police were never very interested in the reason for the decapitation anyway, so they just dealt with the case according to the apparent 'facts'. Of course, I can understand why, but I wasn't too happy about it. And then there was the matter of Miyagaki's will, where he revealed he had a successor bearing his blood."

"And that successor was the nine-year-old Samejima Yōji, I believe, if we go by his name in the book. Am I right?"

"You are indeed."

"Perhaps Samejima being assigned the room Pasiphaë was also a hint of some sorts. She was the consort of King Minos, mother of the Minotaur…"

Shimada went on to elaborate his theory.

Who was the character the book deliberately tried to mislead readers about? The critic Samejima Tomoo. The author did not once state that Samejima Tomoo was a woman. (As she was, and is, in real life.) In fact, the novel often implies that she is a man, but never states it.

Tomoo is a name that can be given to a man or a woman. There was one tricky descriptive passage early on that reads: "*Some years ago, the critic might have been taken for a very handsome young man indeed, if only Samejima had made a little more effort to dress fancier,*" but all the descriptions of Samejima were written in a manner that was ambiguous as to her sex.

Shimada slowly blew out some smoke and explained what he had been thinking over the past few days.

"Miyagaki Yōtarō and Samejima Tomoo must have been lovers at some point in their lives. The book even hints at it, with the passage that said they '*once spent a whole summer together here in the Labyrinth House, having heated discussions about the murder mystery genre that lasted through the night*'."

"Her child was nine, so that would have made her twenty-seven or -eight when he was born. Miyagaki would have been fifty. He was known as a ladies' man. That summer they began an affair, and she fell pregnant with his child.

"However, not only did Miyagaki wish to remain single, he hated children. And unfortunately, the child was born with a severe intellectual disability. Miyagaki would not recognize him as his own son."

What must have gone through Samejima's mind then, and over the following decade? It was impossible to imagine. She could not tell anyone who the father was and had to raise Yōji alone, while still remaining friendly with Miyagaki, who completely ignored the child's existence. Shimada couldn't help but shudder at this thought.

Would she have hated Miyagaki for his cold-heartedness, both as a lover and a father? Of course she would.

Would she have wanted to make sure Miyagaki's immense fortune went to her poor child? Of course she would.

Samejima must have kept her feelings hidden for almost a decade while she maintained her friendship with Miyagaki. She eventually convinced him to acknowledge Yōji as his child, but Miyagaki would not give up on the idea of using his fortune to set up the Miyagaki Prize. Since he had acknowledged the child, Yōji would be legally entitled to some of his money, but in a just world Yōji would have got all of it…

And then last spring, Miyagaki, suffering from terminal cancer, was prompted to play a grand game on his sixtieth birthday. He would push his four disciples to their limits and draw out their full potential. Perhaps he was even planning to write his own "Labyrinth House Murders" story, to be published along with those of his four disciples in a special anniversary anthology.

He had mentioned that he was "playing around with an idea" to Utayama when the latter visited the writer for New Year. Perhaps he meant the anthology.

Samejima had probably been told about the plans in advance and ordered to act as a "plant" among the deceived guests. Of those who were in on Miyagaki's game, it is likely that Kuroe Tatsuo at least was unaware of her role. Samejima decided to use Miyagaki's plans as a starting point for her own plot.

Her plan would allow her to finally act upon the resentment that had been building up inside of her for a decade. At the same time, she would secure Miyagaki's fortune for her child and avoid justice. True, Yōji would be branded as the son of a deranged murderous father, but because of his disability, he would not understand fully how society viewed him anyway. Thus, Samejima decided to put her plot in motion.

She would need to kill five people before, finally, killing Miyagaki himself. It would have to be just the kind of spectacular sequence of crimes you would expect him to dream up.

She had written the openings of all four stories, with titles that spelled out Miyagaki's name, in advance, on the same model word processor that would be used in the competition. Miyagaki must have already told her about the secret passageway and the cave.

Suzaki Shōsuke. Ino Mitsuo. Kiyomura Junichi. Hayashi Hiroya. Funaoka Madoka. She would need to kill these five as sacrifices for Miyagaki Yōtarō's final work, and he would finally be found in the secret chamber of King Minos, having committed suicide there. He would leave a will where he confessed to all the crimes and revealed that he had a child who would be his heir. The signature at the end of the will was probably traced over Miyagaki's actual signature. A last will completely written on a word processor save for the signature might be contested legally, but at the very least it would inform those who needed to know that Miyagaki had a child, Yōji, and that alone would be very important.

"She had to be careful," Shimada went on, "not to get blood spatters on herself when she carried out the crimes, especially when she cut off Suzaki's head and stabbed Hayashi in the back, so I suspect she wore Miyagaki's dressing gown over her clothes during those murders. She left the dressing gown in the study deliberately, along with the gloves she wore to avoid leaving fingerprints. The floppy disk we later found in the word processor in the study, with the Epilogue saved on it, was of course also planted there by her.

"The most perilous of her crimes was the murder of Funaoka Madoka. Utayama stumbled upon Kiyomura's body much earlier than expected, and then Madoka set off her personal alarm, neither of which events Samejima could have anticipated. She had to quickly flee the scene and then hurriedly tie up the loose ends."

First, Shimada explained, she had returned to the study to leave the weapon and dressing gown there. She also left a message on the word processor hinting at Miyagaki's whereabouts, before hurrying to the secret cave, carrying with her the fake last will, the keys and a syringe of nicotine. The personal alarm might have woken people up, so in order to avoid them, it was likely she had used the secret passageway to get to the reception room and hurried to the cave entrance from there.

Once down in the cavern, she found her way to the chamber of King Minos, snuck inside and injected the sleeping Miyagaki with nicotine to make it seem like he had committed suicide. That done, she planted the fake will and keys on the desk, before hurrying back up the ladder to the labyrinth once more. That was when she ran into the Utayamas and pretended to have been to the reception room.

After that, she only had to wait for the others to arrive at the wrong conclusion: that Miyagaki Yōtarō was the murderer. If they hadn't got there on their own, she probably would have played the role of detective herself.

"But she wasn't out of danger yet, because she hadn't finished Madoka off, and there was a chance her victim might survive."

When she attacked Madoka, the nightlight in the room was on, so Samejima must have known Madoka had probably recognized her. That was why, when she regained consciousness, Madoka pointed towards the mirror, in front of which a certain Shimada Kiyoshi happened to be standing.

"In the book, this was interpreted as an indication of where the killer had come from, but was that really the case?"

Shimada paused for a second. He picked up *The Labyrinth House Murders* from the table, and paged through the book.

"Let's see where everyone was in the room when Madoka regained consciousness. The Utayamas were next to the bed. Kadomatsu Fumie was sitting in a corner of the room. And Samejima was in front of the word processor. That means she was standing opposite the mirror on the other side of the bed.

"In other words, Madoka wasn't pointing at Shimada, or at the mirror door. She was pointing at Samejima's reflection in the mirror."

"A wonderful deduction. I applaud you," said Shishiya, actually clapping as Shimada finished his explanation.

"I have to say it feels a bit strange to hear you praising me like that," Shimada said, pouting his lips. He folded his arms and continued:

"And now, there is one more last thing I want to ask. Tell me the real reason why Shishiya Kadomi wrote *The Labyrinth House Murders*."

4

Shishiya looked thoughtfully back at Shimada.

"The book is a message from me. The official investigators would not believe me, even if I told them what you just explained to me. And even if they did believe me, there would be no evidence. It's also not like me to tell tales, like some Goody Two-Shoes. But I like to think of myself as a conscientious member of society, and I do feel a bit guilty about staying quiet even though I have arrived at a solution that is very likely the truth.

"A certain editor, who appeared in this book as Utayama Hideyuki, also happened to have been asking me to write something, so I decided to use the book for this purpose.

"In short, people who don't know the details of the case can read this book as a straightforward murder mystery. People who know some of the details, will recognize the events as described in this book to be a proper reconstruction of the facts. Some might be puzzled by the fact that the descriptions of Samejima Tomoo seem to suggest she's a man, but extremely few will manage to reach the conclusion you did. However, one specific person—the murderer, Samejima Tomoo—will without a doubt recognize my book as a direct accusation. And that's what this book is.

"She will of course be taken aback at first. Why does the book suggest she is a man? she'll wonder. But there's no actual line that describes her as such, and depending on how you read the text, it is compatible with her being a woman too. This will no doubt make her suspicious of the author's motives for writing the book this way. The most important clue to identifying the murderer is her sex and she, of all people, is most aware of that. Eventually, she will understand: the author of this book has concluded that the answer to the question of the reason for the decapitation means that the killer is a woman.

"Of course, I have not the faintest idea how she will react to this message. She might turn herself in to the police, or perhaps not."

Shimada groaned, his arms still crossed. "I see, so that's the idea…"

"Oh, come on," Shishiya scoffed. "Surely you could have figured out what I was trying to do without me telling you."

Shimada shrugged. "You think too highly of me, although I admit I do like to think I have a fairly flexible mind, unlike the second son in our family, that inspector with the Ōita police…"

Shishiya grinned.

"By the way, I had one more question actually, maestro."

"Oh, you just won't quit, will you! I cringe every time you call me that."

"But you're a proper mystery writer now."

"I've hardly even made my debut."

"I'm sure you'll become a big name soon."

"Well, I hope so," said Shishiya. "So, what did you want to ask me about? Let me guess: about my pen-name, Shishiya Kadomi."

"Oh, that I figured out in a second."

Shimada crushed the empty cigarette pack in his hands. "It's an anagram of your name, right?"

"Full marks."

"What I wanted to ask you about is the one outright lie in your book. About halfway through the first chapter, Shimada Kiyoshi is talking with Kiyomura Junichi. The 'great detective' Shimada intentionally deceives the reader there."

Shishiya grinned. "Oh, that part! Did it bother you?"

"Not really."

268

"I think the line was… '*I guess I'm revealing a family secret here, but my oldest brother is missing. His name is Tsutomu and he went abroad fifteen years ago, but never returned.*' Haha, perhaps I was a bit mean about my big brother, painting him as an irresponsible runaway when in fact he is the pride of the family, a professor teaching criminal psychology at a national university."

"You bet you were," said Shimada Tsutomu, the oldest son of the Shimada family, frowning at the writer.

"Don't be angry, big brother. I never could stand that look on your face. I just lied a little bit to make the story more interesting," Shishiya Kadomi—Shimada Kiyoshi—said with a childish grin on his face. "You see, I wanted to tell one little lie on April Fool's Day too."

AVAILABLE AND COMING SOON
FROM PUSHKIN VERTIGO

Yukito Ayatsuji
The Decagon House Murders
The Mill House Murders

Boileau-Narcejac
Vertigo
She Who Was No More

María Angélica Bosco
Death Going Down

Piero Chiara
The Disappearance of
Signora Giulia

Frédéric Dard
Bird in a Cage
The Wicked Go to Hell
Crush
The Executioner Weeps
The King of Fools
The Gravediggers' Bread

Friedrich Dürrenmatt
The Pledge
The Execution of Justice
Suspicion
The Judge and His Hangman

Margaret Millar
Vanish in an Instant
A Stranger in My Grave
The Listening Walls

Baroness Orczy
The Old Man in the Corner
The Case of Miss Elliott
Unravelled Knots

Edgar Allan Poe
The Paris Mysteries

Soji Shimada
The Tokyo Zodiac Murders
Murder in the Crooked House

Akimitsu Takagi
The Tattoo Murder

Josephine Tey
The Daughter of Time
The Man in the Queue

Masako Togawa
The Master Key
The Lady Killer

S. S. Van Dine
The Bishop Murder Case

Futaro Yamada
The Meiji Guillotine Murders

Seishi Yokomizo
Death on Gokumon Island
The Honjin Murders
The Inugami Curse
The Village of Eight Graves
The Devil's Flute Murders